"You look like you're having doubts about me kissing you."

Jake smiled and lifted one hand from the roof of the truck. Just the tip of his index finger touched Kylie's cheek, and the incredible urge to rub against him shot through her. Slowly he drew that fingertip to her chin. He tilted her head back so she couldn't look anywhere but at him, his gaze dark and intense with hunger. He wanted to kiss her, needed to. He leaned closer, and she tried to close her eyes but couldn't break his gaze.

"Aren't you?"

His smile was faint and rueful. "I could fall for you real easily."

"But you're not sticking around."

"And we're adversaries."

"Partners," she corrected.

"Maybe we should leave it at that. No complications. No broken hearts," he murmured.

And then he kissed her anyway.

This Valentine's Day, add a little thrill to
your life with four new romances from

Silhouette Romantic Suspense!

This is our first month of new covers to go with
our new name—but we still deliver adrenaline-packed
love stories from your favorite authors.

This month's highlights:

- A doctor and a detective clash when *USA TODAY*
  bestselling author Marie Ferrarella kicks off
  her new series, THE DOCTORS PULASKI, with
  Her Lawman on Call (#1451).

- Meet two captivating characters with a shared past
  in *Dark Reunion* (#1452), the latest in Justine Davis's
  popular REDSTONE, INCORPORATED miniseries.

- Veteran storyteller Marilyn Pappano brings you a
  bad-boy hero to die for in *More Than a Hero* (#1453).

- Voodoo, ghosts and pirates? You'll find them
  all in *The Forbidden Enchantment* (#1454),
  the long-awaited sequel to Nina Bruhns's
  Ghost of a Chance.

Silhouette Romantic Suspense
(formerly known as Silhouette Intimate Moments)
features the best in breathtaking romantic suspense
with four new novels each and every month.

Don't miss a single one!

Marilyn Pappano

MORE THAN A HERO

Silhouette®

Romantic
SUSPENSE

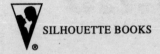 SILHOUETTE BOOKS

ISBN-13: 978-0-373-27523-6
ISBN-10:   0-373-27523-4

MORE THAN A HERO

Copyright © 2007 by Marilyn Pappano

All rights reserved. Except for use in any review, the reproduction or utilization of this work in whole or in part in any form by any electronic, mechanical or other means, now known or hereafter invented, including xerography, photocopying and recording, or in any information storage or retrieval system, is forbidden without the written permission of the editorial office, Silhouette Books, 233 Broadway, New York, NY 10279 U.S.A.

All characters in this book have no existence outside the imagination of the author and have no relation whatsoever to anyone bearing the same name or names. They are not even distantly inspired by any individual known or unknown to the author, and all incidents are pure invention.

This edition published by arrangement with Harlequin Books S.A.

® and TM are trademarks of Harlequin Books S.A., used under license. Trademarks indicated with ® are registered in the United States Patent and Trademark Office, the Canadian Trade Marks Office and in other countries.

Visit Silhouette Books at www.eHarlequin.com

Printed in U.S.A.

MARILYN PAPPANO

brings impeccable credentials to her career—a lifelong habit of gazing out windows, not paying attention in class, daydreaming and spinning tales for her own entertainment. The sale of her first book brought great relief to her family, proving that she wasn't crazy but was, instead, creative. Since then, she's sold more than forty books to various publishers and even a film production company.

She writes in an office nestled among the oaks that surround her home. In winter she stays inside with her husband and their four dogs, and in summer she spends her free time mowing the yard that never stops growing and daydreams about grass that never gets taller than two inches. You can write to her at P.O. Box 643, Sapulpa, OK 74067-0643.

Dear Reader,

Love at first sight—I'm not sure I believe in it precisely, but I'm living proof that you can know pretty darn quickly when you've met "the one." That was exactly how I felt soon after meeting my husband, Bob. Within a few weeks we were engaged, and in less than five months we were married. Now we're closing in on thirty years together, and never once did I doubt that he was "the one."

The senator's daughter and the writer start out as adversaries, but it takes them mere days to realize that they're meant to be. Fate, destiny—in the beginning, Jake's not sure what to call it, but by the end, he and Kylie both realize that it's not how long you've known each other that matters, it's how well. And that, in their case, fate and destiny are just other words for the real thing: love.

Hope you enjoy their journey!

Marilyn Pappano

Chapter 1

If Jake Norris had ever had a shy bone in his body, six years of interviewing people about traumatic events in their lives had chased it away. He was never at a loss for words and didn't mind asking tough questions with tough answers. He was skilled at getting people who didn't want to talk to do just that and he hadn't yet met the person he couldn't persuade to tell him *something*.

Until now. Who would have guessed that person would be a teenage girl whose chin barely topped his belly button?

"Look, I just want to talk to Senator Riordan for a couple minutes—five, tops." That was probably about how long it would take Riordan to figure out who he was and throw him out of his office.

"You don't have an appointment," the girl said for the third time.

"I know. I didn't know what time I'd be getting into

town today." First lie. He'd spent last night in a motel on the northeast side of Oklahoma City, slept in late and made the final hour's drive into Riverview that afternoon. "But if the senator's not busy—"

"The senator only sees people who have appointments."

"Oh, come on. He's a *senator*. If his constituents drop by to have a little chat, don't tell me he turns them away."

She fixed her gaze, enormous behind a pair of thick-lensed glasses, on him. "You're not one of his constituents."

"No," he agreed. "I'm not. But pretend I am. Does the senator have a few minutes to see me?"

"No. Not without an appointment."

Was that Riordan's usual policy? Or had it been instituted sometime in the past week—on Wednesday, maybe, right after Jake had tried to make an appointment with Harold Markham, retired judge and Riordan's good friend? "Can I make an appointment?"

The girl pulled a business card from the holder on the desk and offered it to him. "Call that number anytime between eight and four."

He glanced at the card. "This is the office number. It rings right here at your desk."

She looked at the phone as if it might ring at any moment and prove him right. "I don't do appointments. I'd better get…" Her voice trailed off as she scurried away from the desk. When she disappeared behind a door at the end of the hall, he sighed and turned away.

He'd driven from his home in Albuquerque to Riverview to conduct interviews, do research and take photos for his next book. He wrote true-crime books, and the subject he'd chosen for his sixth book was one of the town's few claims to fame, along with Senator Riordan and the aforementioned Judge Markham. It was, no doubt, something most of the town would rather leave forgotten in the past— but they weren't still paying for it every day of their lives.

Charley Baker, who woke up every morning behind the walls of the Oklahoma State Penitentiary in McAlester, was. He said he was innocent. Every inmate Jake had ever met said the same thing. But there was a difference: he believed Charley.

Charley didn't have an affair with Jillian Franklin. Didn't kill her. Didn't kill her husband. Didn't leave their three-year-old daughter alone in the house overnight with her parents' bodies. Didn't send his ten-year-old son in the next morning to "discover" them. Didn't deserve to have spent twenty-two years in prison.

Despite his own bias, Jake's plan for this project was to write an accurate account of the Franklin murders. He just wanted the facts. He wanted to study the details, to know that the authorities had done their jobs fairly, without any agendas of their own. Whatever the evidence told him, that was the story he would write.

If the evidence told him Charley hadn't been wrongly convicted...

His fingers knotted into a fist.

"Can I help you?"

He turned to find himself facing the munchkin again. Standing beside her was a woman—*make that a goddess*— in blue. She was tall, slender, with blond hair pulled up and back in a kind of sensual mess, with pale golden skin, pink lips and brown eyes. He'd always had a weakness for blondes with brown eyes. Her dress was simple and elegant, her heels low and sensible, and her legs were damn fine.

And she had spoken to him.

"I was trying to get past your guard dog here—" he gestured toward the girl, and for an instant he would have sworn she'd bared her teeth "—to get a few minutes of the senator's time."

"We pay her to not let anyone past." She sounded as good as she looked—a bit of an Oklahoma twang, feminine, firm. He wondered what her relationship with Riordan was. Purely business? Not likely.

"You're getting your money's worth."

The blonde smiled coolly. "We always do. Lissa, you can get back to work."

The girl returned to her desk, all of ten feet away, but made no secret of the fact that she was watching them.

"I'd like to see the senator."

"He's out."

"When will he be back?"

"Next week." Seeing his skepticism, the blonde went on. "He's on a well-deserved vacation."

"Let's see…it's too early for his annual ski trip to Aspen and not time yet for his annual hunting trip to Montana. Maybe his annual fishing trip to the Florida Keys?" Just how hard could the man work that he deserved three expensive vacations a year?

A muscle twitched in the blonde's jaw, and steel underlay her voice. "That's private. Can I ask what your business with him is?"

Rocking back on his heels, he grinned. "That's private."

"Well, Mr.…"

"Norris. Jake Norris." He extended his hand, and she shook it without so much as a hint that she'd rather not. Her skin was soft, her palm warm, her fingers quick to squeeze, then relax.

She didn't recognize his name, which told him two things: she wasn't a reader of true-crime books, and Riordan hadn't mentioned him to her. Because he didn't take Jake seriously? More likely because he thought he could handle Jake. Jim Riordan was accustomed to things going his way. Personally and professionally, he'd always gotten what he wanted. And he probably saw this situation as more of the same. He was in for a surprise.

"Well, Mr. Norris, if you won't tell me what this is about, then I suggest you schedule an appointment with the senator after his return."

"Yeah, right, like that's going to work," he muttered. He would get the same treatment Markham had given him— *I'm not interested. Leave it alone. There's nothing to discuss.* He considered it a moment, then decided he had nothing to lose by telling her. Riverview was a small town. Everyone would know why he was there by noon the next day. "All right. I want to talk to him about Charley Baker."

She glanced at Lissa, seated in front of the computer. With a flurry of keystrokes, the girl leaned closer to the screen, then began culling facts from the text there. "Charley Baker…tried and convicted in the murders of Bert and Jillian Franklin…the senator prosecuted the case…trial lasted two and a half days…jury deliberated twenty minutes…sentence was life in prison."

"Lissa's working on the senator's biography." The blonde smiled affectionately at her. "She knows everything."

"Everything? How did Riverview get its name? No river, no view…"

Lissa pushed her glasses back into place. "The original town was called Ethelton, after the founder's wife. But no one liked it, so after Ethel died they settled on Riverview. They thought it would attract people to at least visit and that some of them would stay even after finding out there wasn't a river."

She sounded so serious that Jake resisted the urge to grin. He simply nodded as the blonde turned back to him. "It sounds fairly cut-and-dried. What is your interest in Mr. Baker?"

"I'm working on *his* biography," he retorted, then relented. "I'm researching a book about the Baker/Franklin case."

"I can't imagine there's enough of an interest there to fill a book."

"Then you should read more."

The steeliness returned. "I can't imagine anyone outside Riverview would be interested."

"People are always interested in other people's suffering."

"And you exploit that." This time she made no effort to hide what she thought.

"Oh, come on. You can't look too far down on me. You work for Senator James Riordan, who buys, sells and trades influence just like the guy down the street does cars. He'd do anything for a vote. He had his fifteen-year-old daughter out on the campaign trail with him only a week after her mother died, parading this grief-stricken kid with puffy red eyes in front of the world so he could get the sympathy vote."

It was too late when he became aware of the change in the air. He could actually feel the anger coming off her in waves. That muscle in her jaw twitched again, and her eyes chilled. She glared at him, her breathing shallow but even. Then, after a moment, utterly controlled, she turned away and walked to the desk. "Would you prefer a morning or afternoon appointment?"

"Afternoon. Late. I'm not a morning person."

She made a note in the appointment book, then on the back of a business card, and handed the card to him. Thursday, 8:00 a.m.

"A little passive-aggressive, aren't we?" he murmured as he slid the card into his hip pocket.

"Be on time, Mr. Norris. The senator doesn't rearrange his schedule for people who can't keep theirs." Turning on her heel, she walked back down the hall and into her office and quietly closed the door.

Moving to the desk, he scanned the appointment book, still open to the next week. "What schedule?" His name was the only one on the calendar pages.

Lissa snatched the book away and closed it.

With a curt nod to the girl, he left the office and walked the half block to his truck. He'd been in town less than thirty minutes and he'd already pissed off Riordan's receptionist and whoever the hell the blonde was. He was breaking his own record for bringing hostility in his subjects out into the open.

But he wasn't writing this book to make friends. All he wanted was the truth—for Charley's sake. For his.

Because *he* was Charley's son. And he'd discovered the Franklins' bodies.

Jake Norris was an arrogant, obnoxious, exploitive, bottom-feeding vulture.

He was also, according to the Internet, an acclaimed author in the true-crime genre. *Heir to Ann Rule's throne...nonfiction in his capable hands is every bit as captivating as the best thrillers...his page-turners set a high standard....*

Kylie Riordan sat back in her chair and studied the photograph on the screen. Dark hair short enough to require a trim every few weeks. Eyes much darker than her own. Straight nose. Strong jaw. Nice mouth. His dark coloring hinted at Indian or Latino heritage, and his smile hinted at the arrogance she'd already experienced for herself.

The only bio she could find was short and told little: *Jake Norris got his start in the newspaper business. The author of five books, he makes his home in New Mexico.* A private man, apparently…who considered everyone else's lives fair game for his books. Vulture.

Albeit a handsome one.

She signed off and picked up the notes she'd been working on earlier. Before she'd gotten her pen poised to continue, though, she set it and the pad down again and turned her chair to gaze out the window. At her father's insistence, she had the best office in the building, because she spent more time there than he did. Dark wood and hunter-green walls, a sitting area with a fireplace and large windows that looked out on the courthouse square across the street—it was a pleasant place to work.

She could sit there all day watching people come and go and never see a face she didn't recognize. As the senator's daughter, it was her job to know everyone in his hometown; as his aide, it was her job to know everything about them.

She already knew more than enough about Jake Norris. He wanted to write a book about her father, whom he obviously didn't hold in the highest regard. He profited from others' suffering. He was smug. And handsome.

Not that she held looks against a man. She appreciated a handsome man, especially one whose black T-shirt tucked into his snug-fitting jeans to display impressive muscles.

Who didn't look as if he spent too much time at a desk. Who didn't look as if he was always *on* in case someone happened to recognize him.

No, she was as susceptible to a handsome face as any woman, though she wasn't always free to take advantage. From the time she was in the first grade her mother had repeatedly reminded her who she was—a representative of not only her father and her mother but also of the Riordan and Colby families. She'd lived her entire twenty-seven years thinking of reputations, considering consequences. As a result, Kylie Riordan had led a very dull life.

A man like Jake Norris could change that.

If he wiped that smug smile off his face.

There was a rap at the door, then Lissa came in. "I'm going home unless you need me to stay."

Kylie glanced at her watch. Officially the office closed at four. Realistically it closed when Lissa left, usually sometime after five. Depending on the senator's schedule— whether there was a dinner to attend, a speech to give, an interview to tape—Kylie called it a day around six. When he was out of town, her evenings were her own. Dinner alone. Television alone. Bed alone.

A *very* dull life.

"No, Lissa, go on. Have some fun."

Lissa smiled as if she didn't quite grasp the meaning of Kylie's words, took a step back, then stopped. "That guy who was here today…what do you think about him writing a book about the senator?"

"I think he's wasting his time."

"He seems to sell a lot of books. His numbers on Amazon.com are really good, even for his older books. And in one of them—it came out last year—he found new evidence that got a convicted felon a new trial after fifteen years in prison, and he was acquitted."

Kylie refused to admit she was impressed. "Was there ever any question of Charley Baker's guilt?"

Lissa shook her head. "He was having an affair with Mrs. Franklin. He wanted her to leave her husband and daughter and run away with him. When she refused, he killed her, and when her husband walked in, he killed him, too. Thank God he let Therese live."

Kylie blinked. She hadn't made the connection earlier between the case and Therese Franklin, the shy young woman who lived down the street from her. Therese had been taken in by her grandparents after her parents' deaths, and after they'd raised her into her teens, she'd begun caring for them in their declining years. Her grandfather had died just a few months ago, and Kylie had heard talk about her grandmother being placed in a nursing home.

"Perhaps after Mr. Norris learns about the story he'll see it's not worth his time."

"But what if he doesn't?" Lissa persisted. "The senator's campaign for the governor's office is just getting started. This could have a very negative impact."

Rising from her chair, Kylie circled the desk and slid her arm around Lissa's shoulders. "My father didn't prosecute the wrong man," she assured her as she eased her through the door and down the hall. "He didn't send an innocent man to prison. We've got nothing to worry about."

She wasn't the only one who'd been ever conscious of reputation and consequences. Her father had known from the time he was ten years old that he wanted a career in politics. He'd never had more than one drink in public and never got behind the wheel of a car after that one drink.

He'd never fudged a dime on his tax returns, never accepted money from special interest groups, never looked twice at another woman while his wife had still been alive. He'd lived above reproach as a father, a husband, a man and—despite Norris's accusation to the contrary—a politician.

There was nothing Jake Norris could do to threaten her father's career.

"Okay," Lissa said when they reached the reception area. "I won't worry…yet. See you tomorrow."

Kylie waited for her to step outside, then turned the key in the lock. With a wave, she returned to her office, settled behind her desk and picked up her notes again. The senator was giving a speech to a veterans' group in Oklahoma City two weeks after his vacation ended, and she had a rough outline sketched out. He'd done a tour in the Army after high school—because he was patriotic, because he'd needed the college tuition assistance and because he'd known it would come in handy down the road when he was seeking votes. No doubt Norris would see that as calculating, but Kylie defined it as smart. Without voters, no one would ever get the chance to make a difference in office—and the senator *had* made a difference.

But when forty-five minutes had passed while her thoughts roamed everywhere except the speech, Kylie put the pages in her bag, shut off the lights and left the office. For a moment she simply stood on the sidewalk out front, letting the evening's warmth seep into her bones. It was the third week of October, and the weather was warm with just a hint of the chills to come. The leaves had started changing colors, and the occasional whiff of wood smoke in the air made her think of weenie roasts and campfires and burning piles of leaves.

She loved Riverview. "'No river, no view,'" she mimicked as she started down the street. The rolling hills, pastures and cultivated fields provided plenty of great views. It was a lovely little town in a lovely part of the state, and if Norris didn't like it, he was more than welcome to leave.

She doubted she would be that lucky. But handling nuisances was nothing new. That, too, was part of her job.

When she reached her car halfway down the block, she took a deep breath. The Tuesday dinner special at the Riverfront Grill was baby back ribs, rich, smoky and sticky with secret sauce. If she went home, she would have a salad or a frozen dinner in front of the television—probably better for her hips but not for her mental state. Turning away from the car, she covered the few remaining yards to the restaurant, greeted everyone by name and was shown to a booth at the front window.

No sooner had the waitress left after taking her order, a shadow fell across the table—no doubt one of her very popular father's friends or acquaintances. She glanced up, first seeing a pair of jeans so faded that they were practically white, hugging a pair of narrow hips so snugly she couldn't help but think for one instant about exactly what they cradled.

Heat seeping into her cheeks, she forced her gaze upward, across a simple belt—leather, brown, no tooling—and a T-shirt that could be had for six bucks at the local Wal-Mart. Half the men in town wore similar shirts every day. None of them looked half as good.

Jake Norris's expression was a mix of chagrin and suspicion. "You should have told me you were his daughter."

She unrolled the napkin in front of her, left the silverware on the table and spread the white linen across her lap. "When I asked your name, you should have shown a little interest in mine. Besides, you learn such interesting things when people are being honest rather than tactful."

He took a drink from the frosted mug he held, the muscles in his arm flexing as he lifted, his throat working as he swallowed. Something about the action struck her as sensual, though she rejected the thought as soon as it popped into her head. He was drinking beer. Period. It was nothing to raise a woman's temperature.

"I apologize if I offended you."

"If?" she repeated mildly.

"But, in fairness, you accused me of exploiting other people's suffering."

"Isn't that what you do? Dig into traumatic events, lay them out bare for everyone to see, then pocket their money?"

Without waiting for an invitation, he slid onto the opposite bench. "How many of my books have you read, Ms. Riordan?"

"None."

"Then doesn't it seem wise to withhold judgment until you know what you're talking about?"

She smiled faintly at the waitress as she returned with a tall glass of iced tea. "Fine. I apologize for calling you a vulture."

The insult brought a grin to the mouth she had inadequately described as "nice." It was a great mouth—a really sexy mouth, especially with that bold, brash, amused grin. "You didn't call me a vulture," he pointed out. "At least not to my face. Were you and Lissa talking about me after I left?"

"No, of course not." It wasn't a total lie. Those few minutes of calming Lissa's worries didn't count.

"So you were talking to yourself when you called me a

vulture. Some people consider that worrisome. Not me, though. I talk to myself a lot when I'm working." He set the beer on the table and laced long, strong fingers around the stein. "What did you think of the reviews?"

"What reviews?"

He grinned again, and she had to admit that, arrogance aside, there was a certain charm to it. "Aw, come on. Don't tell me that you or the munchkin didn't go online as soon as I was gone to find out what you could about me."

Rather than admit the truth, she frowned. "Don't call Lissa that."

"So…what did you think?" Norris prompted.

Kylie summoned a cool smile. "I think you're smug and conceited, but I didn't have to go to the Internet to learn that."

"I'm not conceited. I'm confident. There's a difference."

"But you admit to being smug?"

He shrugged. "No one's perfect."

She liked his easy manner. Liked his grin. Was even starting to kind of like his smugness…until he went on.

"Including your father."

Her spine stiffened. "You think the senator mishandled the Baker case."

Another easy shrug rippled the fabric of his shirt. "I think Charley is innocent."

"Why? Because he told you so?"

The easiness disappeared in a flash—no doubt chased away by her snide tone. "I'm not naive, Ms. Riordan. I've spent a lot of time with more convicted murderers than you can even name. They write me letters, call me, send me e-mails. They tell me things they've never told anyone else. Yes, Charley told me he's innocent. My gut tells me he's innocent. More importantly, the evidence raises reasonable doubt."

Kylie leaned back, crossed her legs and folded her arms across her chest. A body-language expert would say her posture meant she was closed off, not open to hearing what Norris had to say, and he would be right. She knew her father—knew his morals, ethics and beliefs. He *didn't* send the wrong man to prison. "Such as?"

"The whole basis for Charley's arrest and conviction was his affair with Jillian Franklin, and yet there was no evidence that it ever happened. No one ever saw them together. His wife swears his time was pretty much accounted for—if he wasn't at work, he was with her or their son. Jillian never mentioned him to any of her friends. His fingerprints weren't found anywhere in the house. *Nothing* connects them."

"Illicit affairs are generally conducted in secret."

"This affair appears to have been fabricated to serve as a motive for Charley to kill Jillian."

Anger swept through Kylie with a force that made her tremble. "My father *never* fabricated evidence."

"I didn't say he did. It could have been the sheriff's department."

"All you have is Charley Baker's side of the story, and he's in prison. He obviously can't be trusted. You know *nothing* of the facts."

He remained as calm as she wasn't. "That's what I'm here for. The facts—or an approximation thereof."

"So you can include them in your book—or an approximation thereof," she said sarcastically.

He merely smiled. "My books are as accurate as they can be under the circumstances. I rely on trial transcripts, newspaper accounts, public record, interviews, letters—whatever sources I can find. The most recent crime I've written about took place eleven years ago. Time affects people's memories. They want to make themselves look better—or, on occasion, worse—than they really were. I present what I find and I let the readers draw their own conclusions."

"And hope for a new trial to boost the sales of your book."

His grin was unexpected and all the more powerful for it. "So you *did* look me up."

She stared stonily at him. "You won't get a new trial out of this one. If my father believed Charley Baker was guilty, he was guilty."

They were sitting there staring at each other when the waitress approached with a platter of ribs, baked beans and coleslaw. "You planning to eat here or go back to your table?"

Norris held Kylie's gaze a moment longer before turning to the waitress. "I'm going back to my table." As she walked away, he slid to the edge of the bench, stood up, then grimly said, "No one's father is infallible. Not mine, and sure as hell not yours. Enjoy your meal, Ms. Riordan. I'm sure I'll be seeing you around."

She knew it was petty, but as he walked away she muttered, "Not if I see you first."

Jake's motel was about a mile from downtown, a small place that had started life as a motor court back in the heyday of getting your kicks on Route 66. Tiny stone buildings, each consisting of a bedroom and a bath, formed a semicircle around the office, disguised as a giant concrete tepee. It was tacky, but his room had a high-speed Internet connection and plenty of space to spread out. That—and running water—was all he needed.

He parked in the narrow space that separated his room from the next and climbed out of his truck as a white car slowed to a stop behind it. The seal of the Riverview Police Department decorated the door.

He took his duffel bag, an attaché and the backpack that held his computer from the passenger side, slung the straps over his shoulders, then stood a moment in the fading light, trading looks with the young officer behind the wheel. Jake didn't speak, and neither did the cop, though he did make a show of calling in Jake's tag number to the dispatcher.

Resisting a grin, Jake climbed the steps and let himself in, flipping on lights as he went. The chief criminal investigator for the Davis County Sheriff's Department twenty-two years ago was Coy Roberts, currently Riverview police chief. If he thought Jake could be intimidated by a cop barely old enough to shave, he was mistaken.

He'd expected a lack of cooperation from the primary subjects in the case. He suspected they'd arrested, prosecuted and condemned the wrong man. If it was merely a mistake, they, like most people in authority, wouldn't want to admit it. If it was deliberate, naturally they would want to hide it. After all, they had reputations, careers and freedom to protect.

Reputations and careers made off Charley's case. Coy Roberts had been elected sheriff six weeks after Charley's conviction. Jim Riordan had been elected to the district attorney's office soon after. The case had been a boost to Judge Markham's bid for a seat on the state supreme court, and Charley's court-appointed lawyer, Tim Jenkins, had parlayed the media attention into a big-bucks criminal defense career.

Everyone had come out of Charley's case better off than before. Except Charley.

Jake booted up the computer on the square table that served as a desk, then signed online. He checked his e-mail, then Googled Kylie Riordan.

He got a lot of hits, most of them having to do with her father. She worked for him and had since graduating from Oklahoma University and according to an article on old oil families, she still lived in the family mansion. That aside, he found only one entry of any real interest.

Senator's Daughter to Wed, the headline read. There'd been no mention of a Riordan son-in-law in the search he'd done. She still used her maiden name and she'd worn no ring on her left hand. So what had happened to the wedding?.

The article was from the Riverview paper, three years old, and focused as much on the senator as on Kylie. The prospective groom was, at the time, a lawyer as well as a newly elected representative to the statehouse, one of the up-and-coming power players.

The photo that accompanied the article was… It seemed wrong for a writer to find himself at a loss for words, but Jake was. There was Kylie, in all her goddess beauty, wearing a smile that could make a man weak, looking beautiful. Sexy. Unattainable.

It was arresting. It would have caught his attention even if he hadn't had two run-ins with her in the space of a few hours, even if he'd never had the good luck to see her in the delectable flesh.

What she didn't look like, he thought, was a woman in love. Had she hidden it well? Or had her father arranged the match as some kind of political alliance? Who had called it off—the bride, the groom or the senator? Had she been relieved at her narrow escape or heartbroken by her loss?

He preferred to think relieved.

Without considering his reason, he saved the picture to a folder, then shut down the computer. It wasn't even eight o'clock—far too early for bed—but he was too restless to work. Taking the computer and the attaché with him, he went back out to the truck, backed out of the parking space and pulled onto Main Street. In the rearview mirror he caught a glimpse of a white car pulling onto the street a hundred yards back. Chief Roberts's flunky?

There was a lot about Riverview that Jake didn't remember. He'd lived more places by the time he was ten than most people saw in a lifetime. His father had wanderlust, his mother had liked to say. For a time it had charmed her, but then she'd gotten tired of the moves, the new jobs, trying to make a place a home for a few weeks or a few months but never more than a year. Since the divorce, she'd lived in the same small town. She'd put down roots and nurtured them carefully.

Jake drove the length of Main Street, then Markham Avenue, the other primary thoroughfare. The school he'd attended for six or eight months was located two blocks off both streets, its red brick more familiar than any other place he'd seen. Sacred Heart Church was on the same corner as before, but the old building was gone, a newer, blander version in its place.

He located the courthouse and jail where Charley Baker had spent his last weeks in Riverview. Chief Roberts's house, in the neighborhood where all of the town's old money had settled. Tim Jenkins's showplace where the new money lived. Judge Markham's place, stately and impressive, and Senator Riordan's home, even statelier and more impressive.

Riordan had lived in the house for more than thirty

years, but everyone still called it the Colby mansion. He'd had dreams and determination but not much else when he'd married Phyllis Colby and her family fortune. Given her money and his ambition, the only surprise was that he hadn't already moved into the governor's office and used it as a springboard to get into politics on the national level.

Built of sandstone blocks, the house reached three stories and was surrounded by grounds that spread over an entire block. A wrought-iron fence kept the lush plantings in and the common folk out. Somewhere inside there Kylie Riordan was…doing what? Watching television? Working? Maybe thinking about Jake?

It would only be fair.

He drove past one other house, where Therese Franklin had lived with her grandparents since her parents' deaths. It was in the old-money neighborhood, too, though nowhere near as fancy as the Riordan place. But then, nothing in Riverview was.

When he turned back onto Main Street, the same white car followed. It must be a slow night in town if Roberts could assign an officer to watch him.

Or was it a sign of how much Roberts and the others were worried about what Jake might find? If they didn't have anything to hide, there would be nothing for him to find.

But Jake suspected—hoped?—that was a mighty big *if*.

Chapter 2

Kylie's college roommate had described her energy level before sunrise as obscene, and nothing had changed since then. By the time she parked outside the office downtown on Wednesday morning, she'd already run three miles, finished the senator's veterans' group speech, made a half dozen phone calls back east and sorted through all his e-mails as well as her own. She'd accomplished enough that she could have taken time for a leisurely breakfast at the tearoom two doors from the office, but instead she was going to have her usual—a protein drink and an orange at her desk.

She'd hardly settled in when the private line rang. Balancing the phone between her ear and shoulder while she peeled thick skin from the orange, she answered with, "Hello, sir."

The senator chuckled. "How'd you know it was me? It could have been Vaughan."

She rolled her eyes at the mention of the Speaker of the House, one of a half dozen friends who'd accompanied her father to the Keys. David Vaughan was handsome, charming and ambitious—a younger version of her father, except that while her father aspired only to the governor's mansion, David's eye was on the U.S. Senate and beyond. Neither of them made a secret of the fact that they thought she'd make a damn fine senator's wife or even First Lady.

Not in this lifetime.

"Listen, honey, I wanted to tell you there's this writer who's supposed to come to town—"

"Jake Norris."

Silence for a moment, then her father's grim voice. "So he's there. Have you met him?"

"He came by yesterday to see you. He has an appointment for a week from Thursday."

"Damn. Maybe he'll give up before then."

She closed her eyes and an image of Norris appeared, dark and handsome, that whiskey-smooth voice of his saying, *I'm not conceited. I'm confident. There's a difference.* He wasn't going to give up and go away just because everyone wanted him to.

"He's writing a book about Charley Baker," she said, refocusing on the orange to get the image out of her mind. "Do you remember the case?"

"It was a double homicide—a death-penalty case. Of course I remember it."

"Was there any doubt as to Baker's guilt?"

"None." The word was bitten off, the tone certain.

"Then why not go over the facts of the case with Norris and be done with it?"

The senator snorted. "The *facts* are the last thing he's

interested in. Have you read any of his books? He's an opportunist. He takes things out of context, twists facts, sensationalizes everything. Hell, who'd pay good money to read about an open-and-shut case like Baker's? There aren't any unanswered questions. There isn't any doubt about his guilt. The only one who says Charley Baker is innocent is Charley Baker. His own wife believed he did it. She didn't even stick around for the trial. She took the kid and disappeared."

Norris had mentioned a son at the restaurant the night before. Kylie wondered how old he'd been, if she'd seen him around town, spoken to him or played with him. Probably not. She'd been only five at the time of the murders, and her world had pretty much been limited to the few blocks surrounding her house. She hadn't socialized with kids from the wrong part of town—defined by her mother as any part outside their small neighborhood.

"But, sir, if you talk to Norris, at least you'll know you've given him the truth. What he does with it after that is on him."

He exhaled loudly, a habit to show impatience with her. "We don't need all this dragged out again, Kylie. It was an ugly time in our town's history. It just casts Riverview in a bad light. And think of that poor Franklin girl…Pete died just a few months ago, and Miriam's got to go into the nursing home. Therese is going to be all on her own. She lost her parents once. It's not fair to make her go through it again just so Jake Norris can make some money."

His first arguments didn't carry much weight. Every town had its crime; no one was going to hold a twenty-year-old murder against Riverview. But Therese Franklin…she was such a fragile creature. Horrified by what had happened to her parents, her grandparents had cosseted and protected her to the point of suffocation. She'd had few friends, little freedom and not much of a life. With the current upheavals, how difficult would it be for her to have that old tragedy opened up again?

"She pleaded with me, Kylie," her father went on. "She begged me to not let Norris do this, and I told her I would do my best to dissuade him. You know I'm a man of my word."

"What do you want me to do, sir?"

"Stay away from Norris. Don't talk to him. Discourage anyone else from talking to him."

She could do that, could put out the word that her father didn't want anyone cooperating with Norris, and most people in town would close the door in his face. The fact bothered her more than a little. The man wanted information about a case that was public knowledge—a case that was, according to the senator, open-and-shut. No questions, no doubt, no mystery. So why dissuade him from gathering information?

The town's reputation and Therese's state of mind aside, her father's biggest motivation, she suspected, was his planned run for the governor's mansion. He'd laid out a timetable for himself twenty-odd years ago, and the only deviation had been her mother's unexpected death. It was his time to be governor, and no one was going to interfere, least of all a convicted murderer and the writer who thought he was innocent.

How much damage could they do? If her father was accurate in describing Norris's style, a lot, especially when the Senator would face a popular incumbent. Even an unsubstantiated rumor of wrongdoing could upset a sure-to-be-close race.

"Listen, honey, I've got to go," the senator said. "Just promise me you'll do as I instructed. I'll call you again later."

He didn't wait for her promise before he hung up. He just assumed, as he always did, that of course she would do as he instructed. After all, she always had, hadn't she?

Slowly she replaced the receiver in its cradle, ate a segment of orange, then went online and ordered one copy of each of Norris's books. It wasn't that she didn't trust her father; she did implicitly. She just wanted to see for herself how Norris approached his stories.

That done, she forced her attention to work and succeeded for a time, until she raised her gaze to the window to give them a break from the dull text she was studying. A dusty red pickup had just pulled into the parking space directly in front of the window and Jake Norris climbed out.

His jeans weren't so faded, his T-shirt was still tight and his boots were beyond scuffed. Dark glasses hid his eyes, though her interest was lower, on the muscles bunching as he swung an apparently heavy backpack over one shoulder. He slammed the door and locked it, then started across the street without so much as a glance in the direction of the office.

Had she *wanted* him to look? Wanted him to wonder about her? If she was working, if she was watching him, if she was thinking about him?

She would like to say of course not, but honesty wouldn't let her. He was the sexiest guy she'd run across in ages, as well as the most annoying. Under different circumstances, she would certainly be interested in a discreet short-term fling with him. Under the current circumstances, that wasn't an option, but even so, it would be nice to know that the interest wasn't one-sided.

As Norris stepped onto the far curb, Derek West got out

of his patrol car and, after waiting for a car to pass, trotted across the street. He went into the courthouse about twenty feet behind Norris. Coincidence? Or was this part of the *dissuasion* her father had promised Therese? Since he was out of town, he would have called one of his close friends—probably Coy Roberts—to make sure Norris kept his distance from Therese. A little police harassment seemed right up Roberts's alley.

She sat there a moment, tapping one nail against her desk, before abruptly rising. "Lissa, I'm going to the courthouse," she called as she passed through the reception area. The girl popped her head out of the file room in time to watch her leave.

She crossed the street and entered through the same side door Norris had gone through. There were any number of offices he could have gone to…but she wasn't looking for him. She just wanted to see if Derek West was.

The officer was leaning against the wall outside the court clerk's open door, a broad grin stretching across his face. Voices filtered through the door—Norris's lower rumble, Martha Gordon's nasal tones. He sounded angry. She sounded bored. She always did.

Giving Derek a stern look, Kylie entered the office, then closed the door behind her. Norris, leaning on the counter, glanced over his shoulder. For just a moment something flashed in his gaze. Appreciation? Pleasure? Then he turned back to Martha. "You didn't even check."

Martha quivered from the top of her gray bun all the way down to the sensible support shoes she always wore. "I don't need to check."

"Is there a problem?" Kylie asked, moving to stand a few feet down the counter from Norris.

"This—" Martha's gaze traveled over what she could see of Norris, and her entire face tightened "—this *person* wants to see the trial transcript from the Charley Baker murder case. I *told* him it's been checked out, but he doesn't believe me."

"I asked for the file, and she said it's not here without even checking," Norris said, his jaw clenched.

Martha's face tightened more. If she got any sourer, she would look like a prune. "Why would I waste my time checking when there's no need? How many requests do you think I get in this office for twenty-some-year-old cases? I can tell you—two. In all the years I've been working here."

"Who checked it out?" Kylie asked.

Martha's shoulders went back. "That's private information."

"Martha," Kylie chided gently.

Her mouth pursed, Martha went to the card file on her desk, then returned with an index card, handing it to Kylie. Written there in the woman's imperious hand was Judge Markham's name, the date he took the file and the date it was due back—several days past. What was his sudden interest in the file?

"Have you called to remind him that it's past due?" Kylie asked as she returned the card to the clerk.

Martha sniffed haughtily. "I will now that there's been another request for it."

"When you have an answer, will you please let me know?" With a polite smile, Kylie caught Norris's arm and started toward the door.

He dug in his feet, pulling her to a stop. "These files are a matter of public record. You people can't hide them just because you don't want anyone else to see them."

Instead of tugging harder, she squeezed his arm tighter,

all too aware of the muscle beneath her fingers that didn't yield to pressure. "She can't give you what she doesn't have," she said quietly, warningly. "It's best if you leave now."

Throwing a dark look at Martha, who returned it balefully, he let Kylie lead him into the corridor. The instant she pushed the door open, Derek West jumped back a few feet, then tried for a show of nonchalance.

Norris let her pull him a few feet before jerking his arm free. She missed the contact immediately and at the same time was grateful for its cessation. She didn't need to be thinking about the silky-coarse texture of his hair-roughened skin or how he radiated heat or how long it had been since she'd experienced the pure tactile pleasure of touching a man even in so casual a way. If she wanted to touch a man, she could find plenty of volunteers—men who didn't care who her father was, who didn't have an agenda, who weren't her adversary. Who weren't so complicated. So handsome. So sexy.

"Who has the damn file?" he demanded.

She glanced at Derek, pretending disinterest. "We'll talk outside."

He glanced that way, too, then grudgingly nodded. They'd reached the door before Derek pushed away from the wall, and had gone down the half dozen steps before he opened the door. Kylie turned to face him. "Don't follow me."

"I'm not following you."

"Don't follow *him* while he's with me."

"But—" Derek's gaze shifted from her to Norris, then back again. Comprehension dawned, though he tried to hide it. "Oh. Okay. Not a problem." With a nod, he returned inside the building.

Kylie exhaled as she glanced around. They could go to

her office or take a seat on a bench in the square. Instead she gestured toward the street. "Let's walk."

They'd made it to the corner before Norris asked, "Are you going to report back to Chief Roberts on everything I say?"

"Apparently Derek thinks so."

"That doesn't answer my question."

They crossed the street and started down the next block. "I don't report to Chief Roberts."

"No, you report to the senator, who shares information with the chief, the judge and the lawyer."

She kept her gaze on the storefronts they passed, each smaller and shabbier the farther they got from the square. "I don't tell the senator everything," she said at last.

"But you told him about me."

"He called this morning to warn me that you were in town. I told him we'd met."

"And he told you…to stay away from me? Or to stay close enough to be able to track my activities?"

She tilted her head to one side to look up at him, and Jake forgot his question. She was so damn pretty—delicate in a strong sort of way. Her brown eyes were flecked with bits of gold, and she smelled of spices with just a hint of sweetness. If he'd met her at any other time in any other place…

She would still be Senator Riordan's daughter. He would still be the enemy.

Sunlight glinted off the diamond studs in her lobes as she returned her gaze to the sidewalk ahead. She wore heels again today, but there was nothing low or sensible about them. They brought the top of her head close to his, close enough that if they stopped walking and he turned her to face him, it would take only an inch or two for his mouth to reach hers.

Prove it, one part of him challenged.

Don't be a fool, another advised.

"The trial transcript was checked out by Judge Markham," she said.

Jake knew it must have been one of the four. "He's retired. Why is he still allowed to check out files?" *He* would have been allowed to look at it there in the court clerk's office or to have a copy made, but he wouldn't have been able to take it from the room. Lawyers could take them out, Martha had explained to him before she'd known which file in particular he wanted, but only for a few days.

"As long as his law license is active, he still has that privilege. As the senator's assistant, I occasionally check out records for him. We can take them for forty-eight hours."

"And Judge Markham's had this file for...?"

She sighed. "It was due back last Friday."

Jake's smile was thin. He'd tried to set up an interview with the judge the previous Wednesday. The old goat had turned him down, then gotten possession of the transcript. And it was the only copy the court had. Martha had told him that, too.

"Maybe he wanted to refresh his memory before he talked to you. Surely you want to interview him as well as the senator."

"Maybe. Except that he turned me down when I called him last week. Said he had nothing to say on the matter and hung up on me."

"So that's why you just showed up at the senator's office," Kylie murmured.

Jake kicked an acorn and sent it tumbling into the yellowing grass alongside the sidewalk. "Do you ever call him Dad?"

Kylie blinked.

"Most people call their fathers Dad or Pop or Father or even by their first names. What do you call yours besides 'the senator'?"

"Sir," she answered.

He would have laughed if she hadn't been serious. That was some kind of warm, loving relationship they shared. What inspired her loyalty to him? It had to be more than just a paycheck.

"So...if I want to see the transcript, I've got to get it from Markham."

She cleared her throat delicately. "It might be best if you let me get it."

"Why would you do that?"

"Because it's a matter of public record. He doesn't have the right to—to hide it." She swallowed hard, obviously aware that she was implying wrongdoing on the judge's behalf and not liking it.

And what if Markham was hiding the transcript on her father's say-so? Riordan might be out of town, but he was obviously in touch. Someone was keeping him informed...and, possibly, taking orders from him.

"I'll stop by Judge Markham's house later today," she went on. "I'll—I'll let you know if I get it."

They came to a stop at an intersection. They'd left the businesses behind and were in a neighborhood of moderately priced houses. Most of them were old, a few with their original wood siding, the rest updated to aluminum. The yards were roomy, the trees mature, their leaves turning shades of yellow, red and purple. The best friend he'd had in his months there had lived in the middle of the block. Back then, Jake had envied his house, his bike, his roots...but now he couldn't even remember his name.

"Does it bother you that everyone says this is an open-and-shut case," he began conversationally, "and yet no one wants to talk about it?"

"A lot people believe the past belongs in the past." Kylie started across the street to their left, and he followed. On the other side, she turned back in the direction they'd just come.

"Especially people running for governor."

She gave him a sharp look but didn't comment. "Just because you're interested in what happened to Charley Baker doesn't mean anyone else is."

"My agent is. My editor. My publisher. I'm already under contract. I'm going to write the book regardless of what your father and his cronies want."

"What about Therese Franklin? Doesn't what she wants count?"

He called to mind Therese's image as she'd been that September—three years old, a girlie girl, looking like an angel with silky brown curls, huge blue eyes, a Cupid's-bow mouth. She'd been left alone with her parents' lifeless bodies for at least twelve hours. When they were discovered the next morning, she was sitting next to her mother, blood staining her white nightgown, eyes red from crying.

Did she remember anything from that night? Probably not. Three was mercifully young. But it had changed her life forever. He knew her grandfather had died, knew the grandmother—the last family she had left in the world—had Alzheimer's and was also dying. This wasn't the best time to bring her parents' murders back into the limelight…but there was no best time to relive something like that.

"I haven't spoken to Therese yet," he replied. "I don't know what she wants."

"The senator has. She doesn't want you dredging all this up again. She pleaded with him to stop you."

Guilt niggled down his spine. "I may not need to interview her. She was so young."

"She's still so young."

"She's twenty-five."

"The youngest twenty-five you'll ever meet. The best thing you could do for her is forget this and go away."

Forget it. As if it could ever be that simple. From the time he'd started his first book, he'd wanted to write about Charley's case, though he'd found reasons to put it off. He was already contracted for a different book. He was too close to the story. He needed more experience to do it justice. And the worst reason: he hadn't been sure he could handle what he found out. But then the last book had come out, and the guy had gotten a new trial. Charley had pleaded with him, and he'd known it was time.

He shoved his hands into his pockets. "I can't do that. I told you—I'm already under contract. Besides, I made a promise to Charley."

"And you'd put a convicted murderer ahead of his only surviving victim?"

"You're very good at thinking the worst of me, you know."

A flush tinged her cheeks, but she said nothing.

"What if Charley's telling the truth? What if he's spent twenty-two years in prison for a crime he didn't commit? If the real killer is walking around free, still living here in Riverview, still pretending to be an upstanding citizen?"

She shook her head, her diamond stud creating small sun flashes. "There was no other suspect."

"Because they didn't look for one."

"They had no reason to."

"They had no reason to suspect Charley except that he was convenient. He lived next door. Didn't have any ties to the town. Didn't have money for a lawyer. Didn't have anyone who cared whether he was railroaded into prison."

"What about his wife? The senator said she believed he was guilty."

Jake scuffed his boots along the pavement. It was hard to say whether Angela Baker had really believed Charley was guilty. She'd been unhappy for a time before the killings. She'd wanted a different life, a better life, for herself and their son. She'd seen his arrest as the perfect opportunity to move away, change her name and start building that life.

But at one time she'd loved Charley. They'd been married fourteen years—had shared a lot. Today, on the rare occasion she talked about him, all she would say was, *I don't know*. Mostly she liked to forget that he existed. Who she was at this moment in time—that was her only reality.

"Back then, she just wanted out," Jake said. "Now she has doubts. For what it's worth, his son never doubted him."

"Children generally don't doubt their parents." Her voice was soft, her expression distant. Was she wondering if she was safe in blind loyalty to her father? Did she have even the slightest fear that Jake might uncover evidence that Riordan wasn't the man she believed him to be?

Would she hate Jake if he did find such proof?

"I'd better get back to work."

He glanced around and realized they were back where they'd started. The courthouse, tall and imposing, was across the street, the senator's office a few doors down. The cop she'd called Derek was sitting in the shade near his patrol car, authoritatively watching everyone's comings and goings. He perked up when he saw them.

"Will you have lunch with me?" Jake asked, turning his back on the cop.

"No. I can't."

"Come on. I don't like eating alone, and you're the only person I've met who doesn't look at me like I have two heads."

That earned him a hint of a smile. "Your book places us in an adversarial position, Mr. Norris. I think it's best if we act as such."

"The senator's orders?" he asked while imagining a few other positions he'd rather be in with her.

"I prefer to think of it as advice—good advice."

"You know I'm attracted to you."

His candor surprised her. Given that she worked in politics, she probably wasn't used to blunt honesty. On the heels of the surprise came a rosy flush that tinted her cheeks. "I—I—" She backed away a few steps. "I really need to get back to work."

He chuckled as she closed the few yards to the office door. As she reached for the handle, he called, "See you around."

This time, instead of a muttered *Not if I see you first*, her only response was a slight wave before she disappeared inside the building.

He went to his truck, tossed his backpack inside, then called, "Hey, Derek. You ready to go?"

Harold Markham was in his midseventies, round about the middle and white-haired. Through his religious pursuit of such activities as golf and fishing he maintained a year-round tan that made his eyes a more startling blue in comparison. Startling and suspicious as they fixed on Kylie's face. "What do you mean you're here for the transcript?"

Odd. She thought the request was self-explanatory.

She'd debated how to approach Judge Markham—whether to be up front and tell him she was returning the file to the court clerk's office so Norris could check it out, or to blur the truth a little. *I told Martha I'd pick up the file and save you both a trip.* Or even outright lie: *The senator asked me to get the file from you for safekeeping.* She'd settled on simply asking for it.

"You do have it, don't you? Martha told me you checked it out last week. She said you should have brought it back last Friday." She forced a friendly smile. "You know how she is with her records."

The judge didn't smile in return. He simply watched her stonily.

She sighed. Though it was only four o'clock, she'd had a long day filled with distractions. Correction: filled with one big distraction. If she wasn't catching glimpses of Jake Norris as he drove by the square, she was thinking about him. About his book. The threat the senator presumed him to be. The questions he'd raised. That last comment he'd made.

You know I'm attracted to you. She'd heard a few clever lines and a lot that weren't, but none had had the power of that simple statement. It had sent an icy shiver down her spine at the same time heat had curled through her belly. She'd wanted to admit that she felt the same, had wanted to agree to lunch, dinner, breakfast and anything—every-thing—in between. She'd wanted to be wild and wicked and wanton…. But in the end she'd simply been herself.

Kylie Riordan, living a very dull life.

It was for the best. He was a very determined man, and so was her father. Between them was no place to be stuck.

"Missy?"

She refocused on Judge Markham. When she was little,

he'd called her Miss Kylie and treated her like a princess. Somewhere along the way he'd dropped the Kylie and switched to Missy, and what had begun as affection had come to feel like condescension. She used the annoyance it stirred to shield her from the guilt as she prepared to lie. "I'm sorry, Judge. The senator called this morning and mentioned the transcript. His message was, naturally, a little vague."

Judge Markham nodded as if the senator being vague in a private phone call with his daughter made perfect sense.

"He mentioned you and the transcript. I thought he wanted me to take it for safekeeping."

"What time this morning?"

"Shortly after I arrived at the office."

He nodded as if that meant something. "Well, he called me this afternoon and told me to destroy it, and that's what I did. Clearly he recognized the wisdom of *my* method of safekeeping." Rising from his chair, he patted her shoulder on his way to the door. He didn't seem to notice that, despite his clear invitation to leave, she was frozen in her seat.

Destroying court records—that was a felony. Her father couldn't possibly have suggested…Judge Markham surely must have misunderstood…the senator never would have condoned…

Acid bubbled in her stomach, and her limbs were rigidly locked in place. When her brain finally gave the command to rise, she had to push to her feet, forcibly straightening her knees, mechanically lifting one foot, then the other, to walk across the judge's library and into the marbled foyer.

"You forgot your bag, Missy."

It took a moment for the words to clear the buzzing in her ears, for her mind to make sense of them. "My…bag?"

The judge disappeared into the library, then returned

holding her purse at arm's length as if carrying it properly might bring his manhood into question. He offered it to her, then, when she made no effort to take it, impatiently slid the strap over her limp arm to her shoulder. "Are you okay?"

She gave herself a mental shake. "Y-yes. Just a…a headache."

"Nothing a shot of good whiskey wouldn't cure, I bet." In his world, there was *nothing* a shot of good whiskey couldn't cure.

She smiled, hoping it looked halfway genuine. "I believe I'll settle for aspirin. I'm sorry to have disturbed you, Judge." She opened the door, gazed out at her car parked in the circular drive out front, then turned back. "I would appreciate it, sir, if you didn't tell the senator about this. I would hate for him to think that I misunderstood his instructions."

"Tell him about what?" Judge Markham grinned and winked as he lifted his own glass of whiskey in a salute. "Don't you worry, Missy. It's our secret."

Our secret. She'd never kept secrets from her father, and wasn't sure why she'd decided to start now. Because if he knew *she* knew the transcript had been destroyed, he might confess that he'd given the order?

No. She didn't believe that—couldn't believe it. Her father had devoted his entire life to public service. He was an honest, upright, moral person. He hadn't told Judge Markham to destroy those records. He would be horrified when he found out what the judge had done.

But Judge Markham had devoted his entire life to public service, as well, a small voice that sounded a lot like Jake Norris whispered slyly. He was also an honest, upright, moral person…who hadn't hesitated a moment before breaking the law.

You know nothing *of the facts*, she'd told Norris the evening before. She was beginning to fear that she was the one who needed an education.

She stopped at the street. If she turned right, she could be home in a matter of seconds…to do what? Fret? If she turned left, she could return to the office, where she could at least fret in an environment more conducive to work.

She chose left, driving the short distance downtown. She parked near the office but didn't go inside. Instead, impulsively, she crossed the square to the redbrick building on the far side that housed the Joshua Colby Memorial Library. After climbing the broad granite steps, she went through the double doors and headed to the reference section.

The *Riverview Journal* had been online for five years. Any article from that time could be found in their online archives, along with anything from their first twenty years in business. The rest was being added slowly but was accessible in the meantime on microfilm.

Usually.

The microfilm inside the box labeled September from the year of the trial was blank. So were the films for August and October. Kylie took the boxes to the desk. After exchanging pleasantries with the librarian, she said, "There's a problem with these films, MaryAnne. They're blank."

MaryAnne's gaze flickered to the worn storage boxes before returning to the books she was sorting. "Really? Isn't that odd?"

"Have they always been blank?"

"I wouldn't know, Kylie."

"Has anyone else looked at them lately?"

"I can't say. They're on the shelves. Anyone can use them. We don't keep track."

Kylie wanted to grab her, to make her stop what she was doing and look at her, but kept her hands at her sides. "Do you have a copy?"

"No. Afraid not. Sorry." With an apologetic smile aimed in Kylie's general direction the woman walked away from the counter, taking refuge in the small office behind her.

Puzzled, Kylie left the library. She'd known MaryAnne since first grade and she'd never seen her act quite so cavalierly. MaryAnne was generally as protective of her library materials as Martha was of her court records. Neither woman's behavior that day had been typical. Nor had Judge Markham's or the Senator's.

And the one common denominator was the Baker case.

Grimly Kylie walked the block and a half to the *Journal*'s office. *Does it bother you,* Norris had asked, *that everyone says this is an open-and-shut case, and yet no one wants to talk about it?*

More and more every minute.

The newspaper office was small and dusty, but the staff put out a good paper given their resources. Words were usually spelled correctly, sentences usually punctuated properly. Dale Bayouth, the owner, publisher and Web master, was sitting at his desk, tinkering with the Web site, when she walked in. He greeted her with an easy smile. "Kylie. What can I do for you?"

She explained about the microfilm at the library, then asked, "Can I see your copies from that time period?"

He began shaking his head before she finished. "Sorry. They're not available. I sent everything to my son down in Houston. He's working on the website archives."

How convenient. Frustration made her teeth grind, but she forced a smile. "It was worth a try. Thanks anyway."

She left before she could find the courage to ask when he had sent the archives to his son and at whose suggestion. She doubted he would tell her, and if he would, she wasn't sure she really wanted to know.

The answer might be more than she could bear.

Chapter 3

After striking out at the courthouse, the library and the newspaper—and with Kylie—Jake wasn't in the best of moods. The only thing he could think of doing at the moment was the one he really didn't *want* to do: visiting the scene of the crime.

The Bakers and the Franklins had lived three miles outside Riverview, at the end of a dirt road that forked to lead to each house. They'd been fairly close neighbors for the country, with no more than a third of a mile between their houses, but in every other way they'd been miles apart.

Bert Franklin had been president of the First National Bank of Riverview. Charley Baker had worked at the glass plant north of town. The Franklin home had looked like something out of *Gone with the Wind*, with columns and verandas and a vast expanse of lush green lawn, while the Bakers' rental had been small, dark and one good wind away from collapse. Jillian Franklin had spent her days lunching, shopping and planning events, and Angela Baker had waited tables at the truck stop outside town. The Franklins had been among the town's social elite. Riverview hadn't known the Bakers existed.

In the end, though, the Bakers and the Franklins had shared one thing in common: their lives had been destroyed that September night.

Wishing for any excuse not to go, Jake headed west out of town. With each tenth of a mile the odometer ticked off his fingers tightened around the steering wheel. When the sign for Woodlawn Memorial Gardens appeared ahead, he grabbed at the chance to delay the trip out of town at least a little longer.

He drove through a stone arch, then turned onto the first narrow road. There was an office to the right, but it was locked up tight. In an alcove near the door, though, he found a grave locator. He looked up the Franklins, then returned to the truck and drove slowly along the lane. Section six was at the far end of the second row of plots. It was also where the only other vehicle on the grounds was parked. A slender figure, a young woman, knelt in front of a double marker, tending the flowers planted there.

He considered driving on and returning after she was gone, but then she looked straight at him and smiled— really smiled. No one had directed a smile like that at him since he'd arrived in town.

She got to her feet and lifted one hand to stop him. He braked, then rolled down his window as she took a few steps toward him.

"You're Jake Norris," she said. "I was hoping to meet you. I'm—"

The angel. Silky brown curls, huge blue eyes, Cupid's-bow mouth. "Therese Franklin." All those years ago, he'd thought she was of no consequence—too young, too girlie, too spoiled. He would have been much happier if the Franklins had had a son or even a dog.

Except that one morning when he'd found her sitting next to her dead mother. When he'd grabbed her up, held her tightly and run from the house with her, yelling for his father at the top of his lungs.

She looked pleased that he'd recognized her. According to Kylie, she'd pleaded with the senator to stop Jake from researching this case. Kylie's lie? Or Riordan's?

He preferred to think Riordan's.

He parked in front of her car, then got out and joined her in the drab green grass. She was of average height and so slender that a stiff breeze could blow her away—quite possibly the most delicate creature he'd ever seen. Even her voice, light and airy, sounded as if it belonged in another world.

"I assumed I would be getting a visit from you sooner or later," she remarked in that ethereal voice as they walked back to her parents' graves. On the other side, another double marker bore her grandparents' names, along with the dates of their births and his death.

Jake thought it ghoulish to have your name on a grave marker while you were still alive.

"Actually, I hadn't decided whether I would try to interview you," he admitted. "You were very young at the time, and I'd been warned this is a bad time for you."

Her gaze shifted to her grandfather's grave, and sadness dimmed her eyes. But when she looked back at him, she was smiling again, albeit faintly. "I doubt I'd be able to contribute much, if anything. But there's a lot I'd like to know. My grandparents didn't talk about my parents. It was too painful for them. I thought they had died in an accident until I was in high school, when I found out they'd been murdered."

"That must have been tough."

She shrugged.

"So you don't object to my writing a book about this."

Bending, she tugged a stubborn weed from the base of the monument, then straightened again. "Truthfully…you're right. I was very young. I don't remember my parents. I don't feel a connection to them. They're symbols rather than people to me. Maybe through your book I can get to know them."

Abruptly she smiled and looked more like fifteen than twenty-five. "I'm reading your last book. I feel I know those people. That's what I'm hoping for with this one."

"What if you don't like what you see?" It was always a possibility. She could find out that her mother or father had done something to cause their murders…just as he could find out that his father really had committed the murders. "They say ignorance is bliss."

She smiled again. "Whoever says that isn't the one being kept in the dark. I don't think it's too much to ask that I know about the people who brought me into this world, good or bad."

"So you're willing to sit down and talk with me?"

She brushed a strand of fine hair from her face. "I'd like that. My number's—"

The squeal of tires on the highway interrupted her, and they both looked in that direction. A white police car was angled across both lanes as the driver made a clumsy U-turn.

"Derek," Jake and Therese both said at the same time. She went on. "You know him?"

"He's been following me, probably on the chief's orders. I didn't realize I'd lost him for this long."

"He's my boyfriend," she said with a shy shrug. "Maybe you should leave. My number's in the phone book. Call me?"

"I will." Jake returned to his truck as Derek sped through the gate, then skidded into the first turn. The kid was probably enough of a hothead to confront him, unless Therese persuaded him not to.

Apparently she did. A glance back that way as Jake approached the gate showed the police car stopped in the middle of the road and Therese standing beside it, gesturing as she talked.

Jake turned west again on 66. A half mile from the cemetery, he turned north onto another paved road, followed it for a time, then reached the dirt road. He turned and stopped.

Neither house was visible from there. The road climbed straight up a hill with heavy woods on either side. At the *Y,* a road to the left led to the Baker house, a road to the right to the Franklins'.

Were the houses still standing? Had anyone ever lived in them again?

He would find out...but not today.

Backing onto the road, he headed back to town.

This case was becoming more difficult every time he turned around. No trial transcript, no newspaper articles, no cooperation from any of the principals besides Charley and, now, Therese, who frankly wouldn't be much help. If her grandparents had refused to talk about her parents, then it was doubtful they'd saved anything that had to do with their deaths or the trial.

But after leaving the newspaper office empty-handed,

he'd gone back to the courthouse and copied the case file before it could disappear, as well. It contained information on the warrants, a summary of each court appearance and other such data, including the name of the court reporter. He intended to track her down and see if, by chance, she still had the original of the transcript. He could find out who'd written the newspaper stories for the *Journal* and whether he'd kept copies. He could try to locate people who'd known Charley or the Franklins. And he could keep agitating Riordan and his cronies.

Agitated people tended to make mistakes.

It was five-thirty when he circled the courthouse. The parking spaces on the block where Riordan's office was located were all empty but one. It held a silver Jaguar with the license tag designated for state senators. Since it had been parked there most of the day, he figured Kylie was driving Daddy's car. He eased into the space next to it, pulled out his cell phone and punched in the office number.

He saw movement through the partially open blinds at the window in front of him an instant before she answered. "Riordan Law Office. This is Kylie."

Shifting his gaze to the door, he saw the same name lettered in gold there. "And here I thought being a part-time senator was your father's only job. Does he actually have any law clients?"

She was silent a moment before replying, "A few. People who have been with him from the beginning."

"Judge Markham, Chief Roberts, Tim Jenkins…"

Somehow her silence took on an offended quality.

He rubbed his temple with one hand. "Sorry. Do you know that someone went into the library, took the mi-

crofilm containing all the newspaper stories about the
Franklins' murders and Charley's trial and replaced it with
blank film?"

"As a matter of fact, I do."

"And that the newspaper owner just happened to send
all his archives to his son in Houston just a few days ago?"

"I didn't know when."

"Does it bother you—"

"Yes," she interrupted. "I admit it. Something's wrong
here. Someone's trying to stonewall you, to dissuade you."
She gave the word *dissuade* a twist, as if it disgusted her.
"I just can't figure out why."

"Because they've got something to hide," he said quietly. "Because they're covering up something that happened twenty-two years ago."

He waited for her to argue with him, but she didn't. She
merely sighed.

"Did you go see Judge Markham?"

"Where are you?" she asked.

"Sitting next to Senator Riordan's Jag."

Again he saw movement inside, then the blinds moved
about eye level. He could vaguely make out her silhouette,
but all the enticing details—the curves, the colors, the
scent, the goddessness—were hidden. It didn't matter. He
had enough details about her stored in his memory to entice
him for a good long while.

The blinds moved again, then became still. "I'll be out
in a minute."

It was closer to ten minutes when she finally stepped
through the door, locked up, then started his way. She wore
the same green dress, the same sexy heels and the same
diamond studs, though there was no direct sunlight to make

them twinkle. The only difference from that morning was her hair—pulled back in a sleek braid—and her expression. She looked weary. Disappointed.

He hoped he wasn't the cause, though of course he had *something* to do with it.

She walked to the driver's side and waited motionlessly as he rolled the window down. Even then, she didn't say anything.

Finally he did. "Want to have a drink before dinner?"

"How about a few drinks instead of dinner?" she wryly suggested. Without waiting for an invitation, she walked to the other side of the truck and climbed in—and managed to do so without showing more than an inch or two of thigh, he was disappointed to notice.

He had to move his backpack to make room for her and her attaché. "My research," he remarked as he hefted it into the narrow space behind the seat. "The way things are disappearing around here, I'm afraid to let it out of my sight."

She didn't respond.

He didn't ask where she wanted to go but backed out of the space. When he reached Main Street, he turned east and drove past his motel, past the businesses that gave way to houses that gave way to countryside. There were plenty of restaurants with bars in Tulsa, if they didn't find someplace sooner, though he couldn't imagine the daughter of Senator Jim Riordan letting loose and tying one on. She was too image-conscious for that.

The sun was low on the western horizon when she finally spoke. "He destroyed it."

"Who destroyed what?"

"Judge Markham. The trial transcript. He destroyed it."

"He told you that?"

"No, I read it in his palm," she snapped. "Of course he told me."

"Why would he tell you? Destroying court records is a crime."

She opened her mouth, then closed it tightly and stared out the side window.

Jake's muscles tightened, then eased. He wasn't too surprised by the destruction. The admission, though…obviously Markham trusted Kylie enough to confide his own lawbreaking to her. He didn't expect her to do anything with the information, to turn him in or make a complaint.

And if Markham could trust her that much…Jake shouldn't trust her at all.

"Are you always this unpopular when you're researching a book?" she asked after a time.

He managed a grin. "No. Riverview is setting a new low in my career."

"But people aren't always happy when they hear what you plan to do."

"Not always. But this is the first time people have hidden or destroyed records. It's the first time a cop has dogged my every step." He saw her gaze flit to the outside mirror, checking the road behind them. He grinned again. "He turned around at the city limits. He probably recognized you and figured you'd fill in Chief Roberts."

"I avoid speaking to Chief Roberts when I can."

"You don't like him?"

She lifted one shoulder in a shrug. "He's a friend of my father's. Not mine." Shifting in the seat, she faced him. "The senator says your books are inaccurate, that you twist the facts and sensationalize the acts to maximize sales."

A muscle twitched in Jake's cheek, the annoying kind of jerk that he could damn near see. "He's wrong," he said stiffly. His work was important to him. It was all he really had besides his mother, whose past went back only so far as her current marriage, and his father, wasting away in prison. He was proud of every aspect of every book that had his name on the cover. "The senator also said—"

"Turn left up ahead," she directed, gesturing to where a flashing red light marked a four-way stop sign.

He obeyed, then followed her next direction into the parking lot that fronted a middle-of-nowhere bar. The smell of grease hung heavy on the air, suggesting the place also served food. He looked from the cinder-block building to the elegant woman unbuckling her seat belt. "Not quite your kind of place."

"Good hamburgers, good fries, good music—and no one gives a damn about the senator or his daughter." Leaving her attaché, she slid to the ground and slammed the door.

He grabbed his backpack and followed her inside, admiring the way the green dress clung to her hips and molded to her backside. She moved as if she'd gone through years of dance or gymnastics. Probably both had been deemed essential for the senator's sake. After all, what would people think if his daughter was a less-than-perfect klutz?

The bar was dimly lit, as all bars should be, with pool tables on the left, a jukebox to the right, a small dance floor in the middle and tables and booths all around. It was too early in the evening for much of a crowd, though a half dozen young men were gathered around the pool tables and twice that number occupied a few tables.

Kylie chose the corner booth, as far from the door as they

could get, and sat with her back to the room. He didn't mind. He'd rather face trouble than let it sneak up behind him.

When the waitress came, she ordered a burger, fries and a Coke. He asked for the same, except with beer, then settled comfortably on the bench to watch her. She didn't seem to mind.

"The senator also said what?"

He didn't understand her question without thinking back. He'd been about to tell her about Therese when she'd interrupted to give him directions. Now he half wished he hadn't said anything. She wasn't going to like it and she looked as if she'd had enough disappointments—disillusionments?—for one day. But she was waiting and she was going to find out anyway. "He told you that Therese Franklin didn't want me looking into her parents' murders. That she pleaded with him to stop me."

Kylie nodded once. Even in the near darkness her hair trapped light from somewhere, giving it a golden gleam.

"I ran into Therese today. She was enthusiastic about the book. She wants to talk to me, wants me to call her."

For a long moment Kylie simply stared at him, looking…*unsettled* was the best word he could come up with. There was a little surprise, a lot of dismay and a lot of…well, unsettledness. "You're saying the senator lied to me."

Yes. "I'm saying Therese doesn't appear to have any interest in stopping this book. That seems to be the senator's agenda. And the judge's. And the chief's."

Abruptly she covered her face with both hands, pressing her fingertips hard against her temples. He couldn't blame her if she had a headache. Learning ugly things about the person you've given unconditional loyalty to could be enough to make anyone sick.

"Hey." Leaning across the table, he caught hold of her left hand and pulled it away. "Let's forget about this for a while, okay? Let's just enjoy our dinner and each other's company and deal with the rest of it later. Okay?"

Kylie kept her eyes closed a moment, focusing her attention on his hand. His palm was callused, his fingers strong, his touch gentle and warm. Just that little contact, and her breathing was easing, her tension lessening. If he really touched her—pulled her close, slid his arms around her, stroked her body—she just might melt…or shatter.

Finally she opened her eyes, carefully withdrew her hand from his and called up a practiced smile. "How did you get into the newspaper business?"

His grin was crooked and charming. "You did check me out."

She'd been checking him out since the moment she'd first seen him.

"My mother married a man who owned three small-town papers, along with a ranch. I had a choice between castrating cattle and shoveling manure or working at the paper. Like many males, I get a little squeamish about castration, so I opted for the paper."

"Where you still had to deal with plenty of manure."

He nodded.

"Why did you start writing this kind of book? Why not fiction?"

The waitress approached before he could answer. After she left their food, he salted his fries, squirted ketchup onto his plate, then took a bite of his hamburger before facing her again. "Someone I was very close to was the victim of a crime. Writing about other victims seemed a reasonable way to deal with it."

He was choosing his words carefully. Because losing that person still hurt? Because he didn't like discussing his grief? And yet he expected other people to discuss theirs.

Not fair, Kylie admitted, at least in this case. The people who'd grieved in this case were Therese Franklin, Charley Baker and his family. They were willing to talk with Jake. It was the ones who'd made their careers off the case who wanted it kept buried.

It was her father.

Swallowing hard, she pushed all thought of the senator to the back of her mind. "Are you married?"

Jake looked offended. "Would I have said what I did today if I was married?"

You know I'm attracted to you. Desire feathered through her belly. Pure lust. She hadn't felt it in such a long time.

"Some men don't take their wedding vows seriously. I don't know you well enough to say." Just enough to know that she wanted to fall into bed with him. She probably wouldn't, but the wanting was there.

"I'm not married—have never come close. I do date, but there's no one serious and hasn't been for a long time. I'm thirty-two. I live in Albuquerque, though one of these days I plan to move out of the city and up into the mountains. I went to college for a couple years but quit when I realized it wasn't going to help me do what I wanted to do—write. This is my sixth book, and I'm under contract for one more. I've considered writing fiction and will probably give it a shot before too long—mysteries, probably, or thrillers. And I would *never* come on to one woman while I was involved with another." He took a breath, then fixed his dark gaze on her. "Your turn."

She delayed by taking a bite of her hamburger, then following it with a couple of fries. Finally she shrugged. "I'm not married either, though I did come close. He would have made a great son-in-law for the senator but not such a great husband for me. I'm twenty-seven, I live in Riverview and Oklahoma City and I don't plan to move anywhere. I began working for my father when I was fifteen, and after I graduated from Oklahoma State I continued to work for him. The pay is good, the hours are flexible and I like my boss. For a time I wanted to go into politics myself, but not anymore. I was raised to be a good politician's daughter and, someday, a good politician's wife. So far, I've succeeded at one and have no interest in the other. And I would *never* get involved with a man who was with another woman."

"So will you get *involved* with me?"

His whiskey-smooth voice made the word sound intimate and naughty and conjured up all sorts of images in her mind. Naked, hot, needy, wicked. Her clothing suddenly seemed too tight, too warm. She couldn't breathe. Couldn't think. Couldn't…*couldn't.*

"You know you're attracted to me," he pointed out.

Her hand trembled as she reached for her glass, then took a cooling drink. "I do?"

His grin this time was pure charm—no brashness, no arrogance. "You know how you're looking at me…it's the same way I look at you. There's something between us. Something…"

That sizzled. She knew it. She felt it. Still, she didn't admit it. "We're on opposite sides of this book."

"I don't think so. I want the truth. Isn't that what you want?"

Pulling her gaze from him so she could think clearly, she considered it. She did want the truth…didn't she? Or did she simply want it to go away so she could continue to believe—naively, perhaps—that her father would do no wrong? Did she want the truth or the pre-Jake Norris status quo?

"You think my father committed a crime," she said, her gaze fixed on a spot above Jake's head. If Judge Markham had been truthful, at the very least the senator had conspired with him in destroying court records.

"I thought we weren't going to talk about this."

She let her gaze slide down to his face. "I can't compartmentalize my life. Everything affects everything else. I can't just forget that you're investigating my father and go off and have wild sex with you."

"But you'd like to."

If not for his crooked and oh-so-confident smile, she couldn't have answered. As it was, she merely shrugged, then repeated her comment. "You think my father committed a crime."

"I think the people who sent Charley Baker to jail have something to hide. A mistake, misconduct, malfeasance…I don't know. But I want to know, and Charley needs to." He paused before quietly asking, "Don't you need to know, too?"

She did. These…she wouldn't call them doubts; she believed in her father, believed there was a logical explanation for everything. But these *questions*, as long as they remained unanswered, would drive a wedge between them. She would always wonder what he and his friends were hiding. She would always wonder whether he'd prosecuted an innocent man.

She would always wonder whether she knew him at all.

The only answer she could allow herself without feeling disloyal to the senator was a nod. She did need to know.

"We don't have to be adversaries," Jake said.

Her smile was mirthless. "You want to prove my father guilty. I want to prove him innocent. I can't think of much that would be more adversarial than that."

"I'm not trying to prove anything, Kylie. I want the truth, plain and simple. Work with me. Help me get it. And if it proves your father's innocence, great."

Work with him. Spend more time with him. Almost certainly have sex with him. And, along the way, prove that the senator did nothing wrong…or that he did. Could she handle that? Could she bear knowing that the man she'd loved and admired and respected all her life wasn't the hero she believed him to be?

Maybe. But she knew one thing for sure: she couldn't bear *not* knowing.

"All right." Her voice sounded hollow. She didn't want to do this. She really did want to go back to the pre-Jake status quo, when she'd been blissfully ignorant of the Charley Baker case. But there was no going back. She'd learned that when her mother died.

They finished eating. She'd expected her appetite to vanish, but the opposite happened. Must be all those butterflies in her stomach that needed nourishment, too.

"Want that drink now?" Jake asked as he signaled the waitress.

"No, thanks. I never had the chance to become much of a drinker…or a smoker or a rebel or anything else."

"Always had that reputation to consider. Did you ever wish your father had stayed just a lawyer or just a district attorney?"

"It would have been easier for me," she admitted. "But politics is his passion. My mother understood that and she made sure I understood it before I started kindergarten."

"No misbehaving in school, no wild parties, no experimenting with drugs and alcohol, no grand affairs, no making a spectacle of yourself."

She smiled at the very notion. "I wouldn't have done any of those things if my father *hadn't* been in politics. I live a very dull life."

He didn't smile back. "You would have had time to grieve for your mother in private."

Kylie watched as the waitress delivered the check, Jake's words from their first meeting—God, had it been only yesterday?—echoing in her head. *He had his fifteen-year-old daughter out on the campaign trail with him only a week after her mother died...*

"That was my choice," she said as he pulled a twenty from his wallet. "I asked to travel with him."

"Bullshit."

"No, really—"

"Why did you ask?" He waited, but when she didn't answer, he went on. "Because he wasn't going to let a little thing like his wife dying interfere with his reelection. Because he didn't cancel one damn appearance. Because if you wanted to spend any time with him rather than being left home alone with your grief and your housekeeper, you had to go with him."

"It's not as if it was a great deal of travel," she protested. "He's just a state senator, after all. He was just doing speeches, interviews, town-hall meetings, shaking hands." And pulling her onstage and in front of the TV cameras with him. All she'd wanted was a bit of his attention, to hang around backstage with his aides until he had time for her. She hadn't wanted him to—to take advantage of her.

Jake was shaking his head in disgust. "His wife had died. His only child had lost her mother, and he couldn't spare a little time out of the limelight to help her deal with it. You deserved better than that, Kylie."

What *she* deserved, what was best for *her,* had never been a consideration in the Riordan household. It was all about the senator. Always had been, always would be. She'd never known any other way. It touched her that someone saw it differently.

Be honest, she admonished herself. It touched her that *Jake* saw it differently.

The waitress returned to pick up the tab. "Keep the change," Jake said, then drained the last of his beer. "Ready?"

Not really. She would have liked to sit a while, to listen to the music and maybe even dance a dance or two. But she slid her purse strap over her shoulder and stood up.

No one paid them any attention as they crossed the bar to the door. Outside, the sun had settled below the horizon, and the sky was an inky expanse brightened by pinpoints of stars. There was a bit of a chill in the breeze, carrying the autumn scents she loved so well.

"This is my favorite time of the year," she remarked as she made her way carefully across the gravel lot. "The start of the holidays—Halloween, Thanksgiving, Christmas. The beginning of the end of the campaigns. The smells, the leaves, the cooler weather that brings out comfortable clothes and comfort foods."

With a laugh, Jake opened the pickup door for her. "I don't believe I know anyone over the age of ten who puts

Halloween in the same category as Thanksgiving and Christmas."

"It's a pretty cool holiday when you think about it. A time to put on a mask and for a few hours be someone else."

"I think you put on a mask and play someone else year-round. The senator's daughter, the senator's aide, maybe the governor's daughter soon."

She turned to face him. With the truck at her back, the door to one side and Jake in front of her, she was trapped…but she didn't mind. Like the winter clothes and the comfort foods she'd just mentioned, there was something warm and satisfying about this. "You're wrong. This isn't a mask. The senator's daughter is who I am."

"You're Kylie Riordan, whose father happens to be a senator. There's a hell of a lot more to you than that. When you were a little girl, did you say, 'I want to grow up and work for my father'? 'I want to devote my life to the things that interest him'? 'I don't want to fall in love and get married and have a family of my own unless it falls in with his plans'?"

"This is the life my parents planned for me from the time I was born."

"They don't get to make those plans. They can offer guidance and advice, but it's *your* life. *You're* the one who has to live it, who has to be happy with it, who has to make the decisions and take the blame for the failures and the credit for the successes. It's *your* life, Kylie. Not his."

She felt compelled to argue on her father's behalf. "The senator would be happy for me to fall in love, get married and have children."

"As long as the man you fall in love with is a younger version of him. As long as the children are perfect little robots willing to give up who they are to be nothing more than their father's children and the senator's grandchildren."

He was dead on-target with the first part. Her ex-fiancé *had* been a younger version of the senator. The man he was pushing now was a younger, more ambitious version.

Jake was probably right about the children, as well. Though she and her father had never discussed it, he would likely expect her children to be younger versions of *her.* While she wasn't really dissatisfied with her upbringing, she wanted more for any children she might bring into the world. She wanted them to run and laugh and play wildly, to climb trees and splash in the mud, to never worry that behaving like normal children might somehow disgrace the family name. She wanted them to live a normal life, to have dreams of their own, to pursue what made them happy.

While her parents had wanted her to pursue what made *them* happy. No—what made her *father* happy.

There was only one thing she could argue in Jake's statement. "I'm not a robot."

He smiled and lifted one hand from the roof of the truck. Just the tip of his index finger touched her cheek, and heat and need and the incredible urge to rub against him shot through her. Slowly he drew that fingertip to her jaw, then along her jaw to her chin. He tilted her head back so she couldn't look anywhere but at him, his gaze dark and intense with hunger. His breathing was as shallow as her own, and his amazingly sexy lips were parted. He wanted to kiss her, needed to, almost as much as she needed him to. He leaned closer, and she tried to close her eyes but couldn't—couldn't break his gaze.

He cradled his palm to her cheek, his fingertips moving

in a tiny, soothing caress. "You look like you're having doubts about me kissing you."

"Aren't you?" she whispered, unable to take in enough air to strengthen her voice.

His smile was faint and rueful. "I could fall for you real easily."

"But you're not sticking around."

"And we're adversaries."

"Partners," she corrected.

"Maybe we should leave it at that. No complications."

"No expectations."

"No broken hearts," he murmured and then he kissed her anyway.

It was incredible—everything a kiss should be and more. Passionate. Sweet. Demanding. Greedy. Hungry. Tender. Taking. Giving. She would have sworn that for just one instant she heard trumpets in the distance, saw starbursts brighten the dark sky. That she stopped breathing. That time stopped. That everything stopped except this one amazing, everything-and-nothing kiss.

But then the kiss ended, and she realized that the trumpets were music blaring from a nearby car, that the starbursts had merely been the car's headlights slicing through the darkness. That she was breathing, after all, and that nothing had changed. Or everything had.

For a long, quiet moment Jake just looked at her, then he shook his head. "We're in for it now," he murmured, then released his hold on her and started around the truck to the driver's side.

If by *in for it* he meant they'd taken a step they couldn't turn back from, she agreed. That kiss had been too much. Her knees were wobbly as she climbed into the truck. Her fingers fumbled over the seat belt as if she'd never fastened one before. Her heart was racing, and anticipation was quivering through her. She wanted more—and she could have it…as long as she was willing to pay the price.

She smiled at her reflection in the side window as Jake pulled away from the bar. Few people knew it, but she was a wealthy woman. Everyone assumed that her mother had left the Colby fortune to her father, along with a smallish trust fund for Kylie, but in fact the opposite was true. Her father had gotten a settlement that would support him and his political ambitions all the way to the grave, and everything else had gone to Kylie. The Colby riches had stayed within the Colby family. Financially she could afford to pay anyone's price for anything.

Emotionally…she wasn't nearly as well prepared there.

Several miles had passed before Jake glanced her way. "What would you have done with your life if your father had been Joe Blow, insurance salesman?"

"I don't know."

"What is your degree in?"

"Political Science and Marketing."

"You never really had a choice, did you?" he asked, shaking his head. "What are your interests besides politics?"

At the moment, you. Exploring this desire between them. Finding out if she could survive it.

Finding out what the senator and his friends were hiding and hoping she could survive that, too.

"I liked to draw, so when I was in college I took some art classes," she said, thinking back to those days of stained clothes, always smelling of paint and solvents, always striving and never quite succeeding but finding satisfaction in the effort. "Not art history, though I took that, too. My father approved of that—he couldn't have a daughter who didn't recognize the difference between a Gauguin and a Renoir. But art classes. Sketching, painting, getting messy, opening myself up to acceptance or rejection. My instructor said I had talent."

"But drawing nice pictures wasn't going to help the senator's career," Jake said drily.

She glanced at him in the dim illumination of the dashboard. His gaze was on the road, his jaw set. "'Pretty pictures aren't going to get us into the governor's mansion,' he said. When I took the second class, he made me pay the tuition myself."

"Call me crazy, but I think there's a place in the world for pretty pictures. And getting messy. And having fun. And teenage rebellion, even if you are a few years past being a teenager."

The image amused her…and enticed her. "Me? Rebel? I wouldn't know where to start."

"You've already started, darlin'." He locked gazes with her again for a moment. "You're with me."

Chapter 4

"Where are you staying?" Kylie asked as one of Riverview's three motels came into sight ahead on the left.

"At the Tepee Motor Court," Jake replied.

"I loved that tepee when I was a kid." Even without looking, he could hear the pleasure in her voice. "My father got a kick out of it, but my mother thought it was tacky and should be torn down."

"Your mother was a product of her upbringing."

She tilted her head to look at him. The streetlights they were passing lit her face briefly, then shadow again, then light. "You mean she was a snob. She was. She was spoiled and pampered from the day she was born until the day she died. She lived a privileged life. But all that privilege couldn't stop the cancer from slowly killing her."

"I'm sorry." Inadequate words, Jake knew from experience, but it was all he had to offer.

She nodded, then gestured ahead. "There it is. At Christmas, they outline the tepee with red and green lights. It really is tacky then."

He hesitated, then asked, "Do you want to go there?"

Her face was turned to the side window when she answered with a, "Yes," so soft that he could have imagined it. Then she glanced at him. "I can't."

Of course not. It was too soon. They didn't know each other well enough. This was a small town, and he was being watched by the cops. There was her father's reputation to consider.

And knowing all that, he was still disappointed. He wanted…

Swallowing hard, he drove past the motel and covered the remaining distance to her car in a few minutes. He parked beside the Jag and turned to face her. "Thanks for dinner."

Her smile was unsteady. "That's supposed to be my line. After all, you paid for it."

"And it would have been a bargain at twice the price." Words his father used to say whenever he'd spent a little money to make him or his mother happy. "I'd kiss you again except we have an audience."

She turned to gaze at the police car idling at the intersection. "They're not even making an effort to hide their surveillance."

"No. They want me to know they're watching. They're hoping to rattle me."

"Looks like most of the rattling so far has been done *by* you, not *to* you." She picked up her purse but seemed reluctant to open the door and leave.

Fair enough. He was reluctant to let her go.

"What do you have planned for tomorrow?" she asked.

He had plans, starting with tracking down the court reporter, but truth was, he wasn't comfortable with telling her. Yeah, he'd invited her to work with him, but that didn't change the fact that she'd never answered him that morning when he'd asked if she would report their conversation to Riordan. That no matter how much he wanted her, no matter whether they worked together, they were really still on opposite sides. That her loyalty was to her father.

"That depends on what I get done this evening," he hedged.

"This evening? It's almost bedtime."

He thought of her lying across a bed somewhere in that big old mansion, her hair down, her conservative dress gone…but maybe with the heels on. That image alone had the power to make him hard, and he hadn't even gotten to what she was wearing under the dress. Sensible undergarments in white or beige? Or silk and satin and lace lingerie, creamy colors, barely there, sexy and sinful and as painful to strip off as pleasurable?

He shifted in the seat, seeking a position that offered some comfort without drawing attention to his erection. What had they been talking about? Oh, yeah, bedtime. "Only for babies. I usually don't make it to bed before two or three in the morning. At home I do most of my writing at night."

"So you really aren't a morning person. Hmm. I'm at my best early in the morning."

I can change. But he wisely kept the words in. "Well, early for me is ten o'clock."

"Then why don't you come by the office when you're ready to get started?"

"Yeah. Sure."

She opened the door and the cab light came on, illuminating them clearly for the cop down the street. "Thanks for dinner."

"You're welcome." As she gracefully stepped down from the truck, he added, "Thanks for the kiss."

She looked back with a womanly smile. "You're welcome. Good night, Jake."

He waited until she'd backed out of the space and driven away before he did the same. He wanted to follow her home, just to make sure she got there safely, but when he reached Main Street, he turned left toward the motel. She was a grown woman; Riverview was her kingdom. She didn't need his protection on her own turf.

He was maybe fifty feet through the intersection of Main and Markham when red-and-blue lights flashed in his rearview mirror. The cop who'd pulled night-shift surveillance was on his bumper, light bar on. Grimacing, Jake pulled to the side of the street and shifted into park.

This wasn't young Derek but an older man with a pot belly and a swagger. He approached the pickup with one hand on his gun, as if Jake was stupid enough to start trouble.

He wasn't. But Chief Roberts's goons might be.

The cop shined his flashlight into Jake's face, then swept it around the truck cab before demanding, "License and proof of insurance."

Jake pulled his driver's license from his wallet and handed it over, then dug through the center console for proof of insurance. He didn't bother asking why he'd been stopped. He hadn't been speeding. He hadn't run a red light. He hadn't turned without signaling. But he *had* ticked off the chief of police.

The officer walked back to his own vehicle. Jake watched in the rearview mirror as he talked and laughed on the radio.

Seconds ticked past, becoming minutes, and the cop continued to shoot the breeze on the radio.

A second patrol car pulled to the curb in front of Jake,
the headlights bright in his eyes. The officer didn't get out
but simply sat there, no doubt watching Jake as if he might
make a break for it any second now.

Nearly ten minutes had passed when the first cop swag-
gered back up. "Maybe they do things different in New
Mexico, but around here, boy, a red light means stop."

"The light was green."

The officer puffed up. "You calling me a liar?"

Jake clenched his jaw to keep his temper under control.
"No." *If I was, you wouldn't have to ask.*

After scribbling out a ticket, the cop handed it over to
him to sign. Still gritting his teeth, Jake did, then extended
his hand for his copy and the documents.

The cop held them out, then let go an instant before Jake
could take them. The license fell to the floorboard, while
the ticket and the proof of insurance drifted down, one
landing on his leg, the other on the seat.

"Have a nice night," the cop said with a good-old-boy
grin before he walked away.

Jake muttered a suggestion for something that was
physically impossible as he retrieved his license. Then he
glanced at the ticket and swore again. A one-hundred-
twenty-five-dollar fine for something he didn't do.

But it was better than the life prison sentence Charley
was serving for something he didn't do.

He stuffed the ticket into the console, then made it back
to the motel without further incident. After a productive
four or five hours' work, he went to bed, tired, ready for a
good night's sleep…and lay there wide-awake.

Too bad Kylie had turned down his invitation. He would feel a damn sight better if he'd been able to spend the past few hours indulging in—what had she called it?—*wild sex.*

And he had no doubt it would have been wild. She might think of herself as dull, but that was only because the previous men in her life hadn't unlocked her passion. He wasn't being smug or arrogant to think that he had. He'd been there for that kiss. It had been one hell of a kiss.

One hell of a buildup to one hell of a disappointment.

But there was always tomorrow.

Eventually he dozed off, his sleep fitful, his dreams vivid. After each dream, he woke up, loath to remember the details, and each time he fell asleep again, only to dream again. Finally around eight o'clock he gave up and stumbled to the shower.

He'd had the dreams, part reality, part nightmare, for months when he was a kid. Climbing the steps to the Franklins' porch, knowing in his gut that something was horribly wrong, ringing the doorbell. Seeing a blotch of red paint on the white door, touching it, smearing it. Realizing it was blood.

Sometimes Therese was all right. Sometimes her body was as bloody and lifeless as her parents'. Sometimes when he ran outside with her, screaming for his father, Charley was nowhere to be found. Sometimes he was standing over the bodies, a butcher knife in his hand, blood flowing over his clothes, laughing, crying, sobbing words Jake couldn't hear for his own silent screams.

The Franklins were the first dead people Jake had ever seen. He'd never been to a funeral, never lost a relative or a friend. He'd seen dozens of photographs of violent death since then, but nothing compared to that reality. Ten years old, and he'd lost his breakfast in the Franklins' driveway. It still haunted him.

Once he was showered, shaved and dressed, he checked his e-mail and grinned. At least something was going his way. The night before, he'd contacted a friend, a cop who'd worked one of the earlier cases Jake had written about, and his buddy had come through with the current address of the court reporter from Charley's trial. She lived in Glen-pool, a small town south of Tulsa. Now if his luck would just hold…

He picked up the room phone, then set it down again and took out his cell phone instead, punching in the number included in the e-mail. He wouldn't put it past Roberts to have illegally wiretapped the motel phone.

His luck held. Of course she had the original of the transcript, Ruby Stockard said as if offended he could think otherwise. She had every transcript of every trial she'd covered in her twenty-five years as a court reporter. He made arrangements to meet her around lunch, then grabbed his backpack and left the room.

He hadn't driven more than twenty yards when an all-too-familiar sight morphed into another too-familiar sight: the cop behind him turned on his light bar, then hit the siren long enough for one shrill *whoop*.

Derek did his own swagger to the truck. "Can I see your license and proof of insurance?"

"Why? Did Officer Lard not get a good enough look at them last night?" Jake groused even as he handed them over.

"You've got a broken taillight. That's a defective-vehicle violation."

"I didn't have a broken taillight last night." If he had, no doubt the fat cop would have written him for it.

"Well, it's broken this morning. You wanna take a look?"

Jake climbed out and walked to the back of the truck. Sure enough, the red plastic covering over the light was smashed, as was the bulb itself. Courtesy of the fat cop once he'd seen the motel room lights go out?

"You saying that ain't broken?"

Jake scowled at Derek. Was a poor grasp of the English language a requirement to get hired by the Riverview Police Department? "Just write the ticket. I've got an appointment."

"With who?"

"That's personal." Sounded better than *None of your damn business*. Though, of course, the kid would find out when he followed Jake to Riordan's office. "Just give me the ticket."

Derek complied, handing over a slip of paper that was going to cost Jake eighty bucks to fix. What were the odds he could convince the IRS that the increase in his car insurance and the repair costs were a business expense, directly attributable to the book he was writing?

Five minutes later he was parked half a block from Kylie's office. He was tired and hungry, his head was starting to hurt and he was an hour early for their appointment. He opted for breakfast first, choosing Olivia Jane's Tearoom, right in front of his truck.

The place was fussy, with lace tablecloths, delicate tables and chairs and flowers everywhere. He was the only male customer, but he was accustomed to being the odd one out. He was reading a left-behind copy of the *Riverview Journal* and waiting for his food when someone slipped into the chair opposite him.

"Good morning."

He lowered the paper to find Kylie sitting there, and, like that, his headache was gone. She was dressed more casually today in a white shirt, khaki trousers and high-heeled boots, but she still exuded an effortless elegance. Her hair was in a braid again, but instead of diamonds she wore dangly turquoise earrings to go with the turquoise-bead bracelet of her watch.

She didn't look as if she'd had any trouble sleeping last night, he noted wryly. Her eyes were bright and alert, and there wasn't a line anywhere on her face.

"Good morning."

"You're up early."

"Not by choice."

"Livvy should give you a free breakfast for braving what is traditionally women's territory."

"I'll go anywhere for food." He folded the paper and laid it aside. "How did you know I was here?"

"Lissa saw you. She was just in to pick up some muffins. I told her I'm taking the next few days off." She hesitated. "I didn't tell her why."

The waitress brought his meal, then took an order for hash browns and toast from Kylie. He spread butter over the pecan waffle, smothered it with syrup, then cut off a wedge and offered it to her. She hesitated, then leaned forward, her hand over his to steady the fork, and slid the bite into her mouth. Her fingers made his skin tingle. Her tongue sweeping away a drop of syrup on her lip made other parts of his body tingle.

"What's on the schedule for today?"

"I've got to go to—" Movement outside distracted him as Derek walked past the plate-glass window, staring hard inside. "Tulsa," he substituted. "The taillight on my truck suffered from spontaneous breakage while I was asleep last night. I have to get it replaced."

She glanced outside, too. "You mean one of Chief Roberts's men broke your taillight intentionally?"

"It wasn't accidental."

"They can't do that!"

"Sure they can. Just like they can give me a ticket for it the first time I drive. Just like they can give me a ticket for running a red light that happened to be green." He chewed a bite of ham, then washed it down with coffee. "It's called harassment, darlin', and it's damn hard to prove."

"I'll speak to the senator—"

"No." He didn't want her speaking to Daddy on his behalf. Besides, he suspected Daddy was the one who'd suggested it to Roberts, though not in so many words. Riordan needed deniability. Just a hint here or there was enough for an old friend like Roberts to understand.

"But—"

"Forget about it. It's okay. So…you want to ride along to Tulsa with me? I'll be making a few other stops, too." Guilt nudged at him for not confiding the primary reason for the trip. But what if she innocently told Lissa that she would be in Glenpool, paying a visit to the court reporter? What if she not so innocently told Riordan or the chief? How easy would it be to make that original transcript disappear by the time his noon meeting with Ms. Stockard rolled around?

He *would* tell her. Once they were on the road. Once she lacked the opportunity to tell anyone else.

It wasn't distrust. It was caution. For Charley's sake.

"Sure," she agreed. "That's why I took time off."

To spend time with him. He was looking forward to that more than to getting his hands on the transcript. Getting into bed with her…

He was looking forward to that most of all.

* * *

They were at a garage in Tulsa, waiting for work on the pickup to be completed, when Kylie's cell phone rang. She'd expected an interruption long before this, but apparently nothing had come up that Lissa couldn't handle.

A glance at the phone showed that it was the senator calling. Another glance at Jake showed that he guessed as much. Giving him a taut smile, she flipped open the phone and walked to the opposite side of the waiting room. "Hello, sir."

"Lissa says you took a few days off. Are you sick?"

"No. I just needed a break."

"With Norris? Coy says you had dinner with him last night."

Chief Roberts couldn't possibly have known that for a fact, though, she admitted, it was an easy assumption to make. "Checking up on me, sir?"

"No. Keeping an eye on that troublemaker. What were you doing with him? I told you to stay away from him."

She faced a framed poster on the wall showing a shapely brunette draped over the hood of a Corvette. Reflected in the glass, she could see Jake watching her, his expression controlled. Was he curious? Of course. Concerned about what she was telling the senator? Probably. Distrustful? Likely.

She couldn't blame him if he didn't trust her, but that didn't stop the knowledge from stinging just a bit. The words she was about to say made it sting even more. "Remember your motto, sir? 'Keep your friends close and your enemies closer.'"

There was a moment's silence, then he chuckled. "I taught you well, didn't I? Everything you know."

Not hardly. She had to live her life, Jake had told her

the night before, to take the blame for her failures and the credit for her successes. Her father had *always* taken credit for her successes.

"I need to ask you something, sir." She swallowed hard, clearing the lump from her throat. "Who told you that Therese Franklin doesn't want Jake Norris writing this book?"

The senator was too smart to answer straight out. He knew as surely as she did what he'd told her. He also knew she wouldn't be asking if she didn't have reason to suspect otherwise.

"Why?" he demanded. "Has that bastard been to see her? Has he upset her?"

She closed her eyes. He'd lied to her. He wasn't going to admit it, but he didn't need to. *She pleaded with me*, he'd told her, and it was nothing but a lie.

"No," she said at last. "He hasn't upset her at all. She's quite excited about talking to him. In fact, she's quite excited about the book."

"No, no, no. She told Harold—"

Unable to listen to another lie, Kylie did two things she'd never done before. "I've got to go, sir," she interrupted and then she hung up on him.

Chilled from the inside out, she returned to the row of hard plastic chairs and sat down next to Jake, her phone clasped tightly in both hands. He gently peeled her left hand free, then held it in his own hand. "It's okay," he said.

Her first impulse was to tug her hand free. The second was to hold tightly to him. "It's not okay! He lied to me!"

He probably thought she was naive. People lied. Politicians certainly lied. But this wasn't a politician making a promise to a constituent that he couldn't keep. This was her *father*, and he was lying to her.

And he was lying to cover up something worse. A mistake, misconduct or malfeasance, Jake had suggested.

Or murder.

She remembered the day she'd come home from school to find her father there—unheard of in the middle of the afternoon. He'd put his arm around her and tried to gently break the news that her mother had died. She'd known it was true, had known it was just a matter of time, but she hadn't wanted to believe him so strongly that she'd made herself ill. It had been too big a shock, too ugly a fact to face.

She felt something similar now.

She'd stared at the tiled floor so long that the lines were blurring when Jake bumped his shoulder against hers. "You want to talk?"

She glanced at him and shook her head, then, of its own accord, her mouth opened and words came rushing out. "He told me that *he* talked to Therese, that she pleaded with *him*, that he promised her… Now he says it was Judge Markham she pleaded with, and even that's just so much bullshit."

The profanity was alien to her. She'd heard it a lot but never said it. It felt good saying it now—strong and angry and so fitting.

Abruptly she twisted to face Jake, still clinging tightly to his hand. "What is he hiding?"

His dark eyes were sympathetic. "I don't know."

"I need to know," she whispered.

"What if you don't like what you find out?"

That was a polite way of asking, *What if you find out he's guilty of far worse crimes than you suspect?* Could she handle it? If it meant complete disillusionment? Bringing shame on the family name? Losing the admiration and respect she'd always felt for her father? Losing *him?*

"I don't know," she murmured. "But I already know too much. I have to know everything."

He laced his fingers through hers, then lifted her hand and pressed a kiss to it. "We'll find out everything. You and me. And we'll deal with it. Okay?"

He was saying she could lean on him, draw strength from him, and at that moment she believed him. But even if the offer was rescinded, if something came between them, she would still deal with it. She was strong. Just not very strong at that instant.

"Okay," she whispered, shifting her weight against him. "You and me."

It was close to lunchtime when they left the garage, but instead of asking about a restaurant Jake headed south on Highway 75. Before she could question him, he glanced her way, dark glasses concealing his eyes. "We're going to Glenpool. I called the court reporter this morning, and she agreed to have a copy of the transcript ready for us at noon."

There was the issue of trust again—or distrust. She watched the countryside roll by for a time before quietly commenting, "You could have told me earlier. I wouldn't have told anyone."

"I had to be sure."

She accepted that with a nod. They were strangers…though she'd never been so intimate with a stranger in her life. He could trust her, but he would have to figure that out for himself.

As they passed the tank farms located just north of town, she began talking. "Did you know that, in the heyday of Glenpool, this small area produced more oil than anyplace else in the world? They pumped so much that they couldn't ship it all out. They dug big ponds and used them as holding tanks until they could get it on a train. Then the pipelines went in, taking it directly to the Gulf coast where—"

"Hey." Jake reached across the cab and claimed her hand, resting it on the console between them. "There's nothing to be nervous about."

She swallowed. "Easy for you to say. This doesn't involve your father and everything you've believed about him your whole life."

For a moment his thumb, stroking the back of her hand, went still, and his jaw tightened. Then he exhaled loudly. "Whatever your father did or didn't do, just remember—it's on him. It's his responsibility. The blame or credit is his. Not yours. Not mine."

She managed an anxious laugh. "So don't hold it against you if he winds up in trouble?"

"Or yourself. This is one instance where you can't protect his reputation." Pulling into the turn lane, he slowed for a left turn, then made a right into a parking lot. "Ruby Stockard's husband's office is here. That's where we're meeting."

The end office in the strip mall bore the name of Stockard Insurance across the windows. Inside, a white-haired woman stood at the counter, straightening a sheaf of papers. Neither her name nor her face was familiar to Kylie, but twenty-two years was a long time, and she'd been just a child. She could have met Mrs. Stockard a hundred times and not remember.

"I'll wait here," she said as Jake opened his door.

He looked as if he might object, then thought better of it. "I'll make it quick."

"Quick" was relative. Mrs. Stockard was chatty, and she kept the papers, now rubber-banded inside a manila folder, under her control while she talked. When she finally handed them over, she shook hands with Jake, then walked to the door with him, where she patted his arm while saying goodbye. The woman was affectionate.

Or maybe there was just something about Jake that made women want to touch him. Kylie certainly did.

He wore jeans again today that fitted as if custom made for his slender hips and long legs, along with the same disreputable boots and a sunny yellow polo shirt. It was a color she loved but couldn't wear, but with his dark hair, eyes and skin, it looked incredible.

When he climbed back into the truck, he brought with him a bit of cool fall air and the fresh, musky scent of his cologne. It was an enticing fragrance—strong, masculine, sexy. "What kind of cologne are you wearing?" she asked as he settled in.

He looked down at his shirt and sniffed. "Eau de fabric softener, soap and shampoo."

Of course. The sexiest scent she'd smelled in ages, and it was all him.

He set the folder on the console, then backed out of the space. "Where would you like to have lunch?"

She rattled off a list of options, leaving the choice to him. He chose Mexican, and they headed back toward Tulsa in silence. They'd turned onto the Creek Turnpike before he finally spoke again. "You can look at it."

She looked at the folder. She'd been sneaking glances at it for miles but hadn't reached for it. Had been curious but leery, too. Now she reached for it but for a moment simply held it in her lap.

"Okay," he said. "You don't have to look at it."

His tone was even, without inflection, but it sent guilt flushing into her face. Deliberately she removed the rubber band, opened the folder and read the opening arguments. She would have recognized her father's—he had a distinctive voice. Tim Jenkins's statement hardly qualified for the term.

Between reading, she gave directions—*Exit on Elm; turn right on Main*—until they'd reached a small mall on the bank of the Arkansas River. They chose patio seating, placed their orders, then went back to reading. She passed each page on to Jake as she finished and when she was done she sat back and waited.

He read the final page, tapped them on the tabletop to straighten them, then looked at her. "Nothing much of interest there."

She shook her head in agreement. The trial had been short, the only witnesses presented by the prosecution. The only motive for the murders—Charley Baker's affair with Jillian Franklin—had been brought up but not proven. The senator had presented no real evidence against Charley, and Tim Jenkins hadn't made a single effort to defend his client.

"Tim Jenkins is lucky Mr. Baker didn't get a new trial based on ineffective counsel," she said as she idly dipped a chip into salsa. "How did he ever make this the stepping-stone to the career he has now?"

"It was a small trial in a small town in middle America. He rewrote history—made it out to be such a solid case that a conviction was inevitable, that the only possible victory was keeping Charley from getting the death penalty. And people believed him. Nobody bothered to see whether his claims were true." Jake's grin was cynical. "People lie, Kylie. Lawyers, judges, the guilty and the so-called innocent. Truth and honesty aren't valued commodities in our society."

And authors lied, too, she thought as she gazed across

the river. They claimed backgrounds they didn't have and sold as fact stories they'd created out of thin air. But she had no reason to think Jake had lied, not yet.

While she *knew* her father had.

"Why did Judge Markham destroy the county's copy of this?" she asked. "There's nothing here."

"Except proof that the case against Charley was weaker than they claim. That Jenkins did a lousy job of representing him." Jake pulled a pair of dark glasses from his backpack and slid them on. "I don't think the purpose of destroying the transcript was to hide something. They were just screwing with me—trying to *dissuade* me."

Her hand was unsteady as she reached for the manuscript. She'd used her father's word when talking with Jake the night before, and he'd picked up on it. He was observant.

She put the pages back inside the folder, replaced the rubber band and laid it on the empty chair to her right underneath her purse. "Have you always lived in New Mexico?"

If her change of subject caught him off guard, it didn't show. "No. We moved around a lot. My mother and I settled there after she divorced my father."

"What about him? Did you see him very often?"

He shook his head. "Not at all until I was grown. She liked to pretend he didn't exist. When she remarried, she persuaded her husband to adopt me. She didn't even want me to have my father's name."

"Are you close to him now?"

He took a long drink of his tea before his mouth settled into a grim line. "Yeah, pretty much. Though it was hard to make up for the eight years we didn't have any contact."

"And are you close to your mother now?"

"I love her, but she's a little self-centered. Like Tim Jenkins—" he nodded toward the transcript "—she rewrites history. She denies even to herself that the first marriage even happened. She passes me off as my stepfather's son…which is pretty stupid, considering that they're both blond-haired and blue-eyed and I'm half Indian."

When she'd looked up his photograph on the Internet, she'd thought he looked Latino or Native American. Everything about him was so dark…except his grin.

What was it like for him growing up with his mother steadfastly denying one half of his heritage? Knowing that she hated his father so much she pretended he'd never existed?

"Families," she said with a soft sigh. "Can't live with 'em, can't exist without 'em."

That grin appeared again. "And yet we'll have one of our own someday."

We'll each *have one of our own.* That was what he should have said. But Kylie couldn't stop a bit of yearning to hold in her arms a dark-eyed, dark-haired baby with his daddy's charming grin.

No, no, eye and hair color didn't matter. It was just the usual maternal longing a woman her age felt—for *any* baby, not one belonging to any particular man. She had a nurturing spirit and thought she would be a good mother someday. When the time was right. When the man was right.

"Okay," she said, stubbornly pushing away that thought. "You're handsome. You have a job you like that I assume supports you comfortably. You believe in monogamy and you want children. Why aren't you married?"

"I've never been in love." He laid his hand over hers where it rested on the tabletop, his fingers warm and comforting and creating a tingle that was intensified by his next word.

"Yet."

Heat seeped through her, turning her blood sluggish, parching her lungs, making her want…things. *Yet. Him.*

Ridiculous. It was one little word…accompanied by one steamy look.

He was a stranger…whom she wanted to get intimate with. Whom she already felt intimate with.

He wasn't destined to be a long-term part of her life…unless one of them made it so. Unless he stayed or she left. She couldn't imagine him staying. Couldn't imagine herself leaving. Couldn't imagine a future with the man who was going to destroy her father.

And couldn't stop wondering…wishing…

"That's not entirely true," he said as the waitress delivered their food. "There was Regina Lyn Broward. She moved in next door one summer and proved there was such a thing as love at first sight. I was twelve and she was fourteen—and she broke my heart when she moved away again."

Kylie forced a smile. "So you've done the heartbreaking ever since."

He lifted her hand for a casual kiss to the palm before releasing it in favor of a fork. "Yeah. But don't worry, Kylie," he said with a grin and a wink, "I won't break *your* heart."

Until then, she hadn't been worried. Not at all.

Suddenly she was.

Chapter 5

They were just a few miles out of Riverview and had run dry on casual chatter when Jake recalled their conversation from the night before. "You said you live in Oklahoma City and Riverview."

She nodded. "The senator keeps an apartment in the city for when the Senate is in session. He also prefers to do most of his entertaining there unless—" Her cheeks colored slightly before she went on. "Unless he's looking to *really* impress people. Then he invites them to 'the mansion.' That's what he calls it."

Most people referred to it as the Colby mansion, Jake knew. Obviously the senator saw no need for the reminder that he'd married into the fortune and got no credit for it.

"Mom's poured a good deal of my stepfather's money into turning their house into a showplace, but we were pretty poor before him. We lived in some pretty shabby places—

trailer houses, rent-by-the-week apartments where we shared the bathroom with strangers, rental houses that should have been condemned." He grinned. "I'd be impressed with an invitation to the Colby mansion."

"*Showplace* is a good word for it," she said drily. "Along with *ostentatious. Pretentious.* It's a beautiful place, but it's certainly not what comes to mind when you think of 'home, sweet home.' But if you'd like a tour, I think that can be arranged."

He would like a tour—partly out of curiosity. Every time they'd driven past the house when he was a kid, which was just about every time his mother had gone to town, Angela had wondered what it was like to live there. The house had reminded her of all she was lacking and had become the symbol of the unfairness of life.

The author in him would like the tour, too, to compare the luxury in which Jim Riordan had lived all these years to the stark desperation of Charley's cell.

Most of all, though, the man in him wanted to see where Kylie lived. Where she'd played as a child, where she'd received her training to become the perfect politician's daughter, where she'd slept, where she'd dreamed. Where she slept now.

"I'd like that," he said. "I'm guessing you're talking about before your father returns home from vacation."

She glanced at him. "You're guessing he wouldn't let you set foot on his property? You're right. However…the house belongs to me. The only say the senator has in who comes and goes is what I allow."

Surprised, Jake stared at her. He didn't routinely look into a subject's assets unless it had some bearing on the story. So Phyllis Riordan, the perfect politician's wife, had left the family mansion to her daughter instead of her husband. It made him wonder what else she'd denied Riordan in death. Made him wonder whether their marriage had been based on mutual love and respect, ambition, connections…or something else.

And it made him realize that Kylie Riordan was more than just a well-paid political aide. The Colby mansion had been built at the height of the first oil boom, with no expense spared. He couldn't begin to estimate how much it was worth now, and it was *hers*.

Good thing his ego was strong enough to not let a thing like a fortune get in the way of what he wanted.

As they passed a sign announcing Riverview City Limits, Derek in his patrol car pulled out of a parking lot and into the lane behind them. "Do you think he sat there all morning waiting for us to return?"

Kylie turned to look, then smiled brightly and waved. In the rearview mirror, Jake watched Derek grimace before backing off a few car lengths. "Our tax dollars at work," she said with a sniff.

"He's dating Therese Franklin."

"Really. I didn't know. Though I can see the appeal. He's got this macho need to be manly, and she's so fragile and in need of protection."

Jake recalled the way she'd apparently calmed Derek in a matter of seconds at the cemetery. "Not so much in need as you think. Now that she's out from under her grandparents' suffocation, she might do just fine."

"They loved her dearly," Kylie pointed out, then relented. "But they were a bit overprotective. They made it impossible for her life to be normal."

Just as Kylie's parents had loved her but had failed at giving her a normal upbringing.

They were stopped at the red light he'd been ticketed for running the night before when she sighed and looked his way. "What about the tour? Want to do it now?"

"Maybe later." He swallowed over the sudden knot in his throat. "There are two other houses I need to see now."

"The Franklin and Baker houses?"

It was hard to pull enough air into his lungs, to force a nod. He stared at the street ahead, seeing not the pavement and buildings lining either side but the dirt road, the *Y*, the two vastly different houses.

When she laid her hand gently on his arm, his muscles twitched. "Would you like some company?"

Relief rushed through him, but he kept it under control with a wry grin. "Yeah. Sure."

The three miles passed in a blur, his body warming until he had no choice but to roll down the window, the rushing in his ears becoming too strong to attribute to the breeze coming in through that window. By the time he turned off the paved road his grip on the steering wheel was so tight that his fingers were cramping.

He followed the road until it split, then turned to the right. A rusted gate hung crookedly in the open position, leading into what had once been a manicured lawn. Now it was overgrown with weeds and clover, and clumps of cedars had grown up wherever they could take root.

The driveway was hardly visible. He navigated it as much from memory as by sight. At its end, he stopped. Shut off the engine. Simply sat.

He didn't want to be there. Didn't want to remember finding Jillian and Bert Franklin's bloodied bodies. But twenty-two years had passed, and he hadn't forgotten yet. He never would.

The house was two stories and had once been painted white, though little color remained but a few graying flecks. The dark green on the shutters was faded, too, to a dull, flat gray. Some hung drunkenly and a few lay on the ground. The gardens Jillian had hired a staff to care for had gone to seed, consisting now of roses grown wild and a few perennials that had managed to survive.

"It must have been a lovely house in its time."

Startled, Jake glanced at Kylie. She had unfastened her seat belt and her hand was on the door handle, poised to open it and climb out. Clearly she expected him to get out, to go closer, to walk around and look. He didn't want to, but he did it anyway.

"This is about where Charley Baker parked that morning," he said as he walked around the truck to her side. "It was a Saturday morning. He and his son, C.J., were going into town. Both their mailbox and the Franklins' were down at the bottom of the hill. There was a package for Therese that wouldn't fit inside the box—her birthday was the next week—so the mailman had attached it to the door with a rubber band. It had just started to rain, and Charley tried to be a good neighbor by bringing the package up here so it wouldn't be ruined."

C.J. hadn't cared about being a good neighbor. He'd been anxious to finish the errands they were running because Angela had promised him and his friend a trip to the movies that afternoon if he got all his chores done. He stared at the ground, where part of a flagstone path barely showed through the weeds, and tried again to remember that friend's name. He drew a blank.

"The Franklins' cars were there." He gestured toward a somewhat clear area at the rear of the house where paving stones had marked off a parking court in front of the detached garage. "Charley gave the package to C.J. and told him to run it up to the door."

The rain had been coming down hard, and he'd tried to shelter the box inside his jacket, but it had been too big. In the seconds it had taken him to reach the front porch the ink had smeared Therese's name and address on his shirt.

He'd rung the doorbell, but no one had answered. While he'd waited, the rain had stopped as quickly as it had come. One second it had been pouring; the next there were just a few sprinkles glinting as the sun came out of the clouds. He had bent to lean the box against the door, where the Franklins couldn't help but find it, and when he'd stood up again he'd seen it. A dark red smudge, sticky in the morning humidity, out of place on the white door.

"There was blood on the door," he went on quietly, finally moving away from the truck and following the stone path to the front of the house. "C.J. touched it, and when he did the door swung open a few inches. He heard sounds inside—breathing. Sniffling. He pushed the door all the way open and he saw Therese."

"In a bloody nightgown, sitting next to her mother's body," Kylie filled in for him.

The image had become symbolic of the murders, though no one had actually seen it but him. No one had discussed the killings without mentioning poor little Therese and that blood-soaked gown. Riordan had made reference to it repeatedly in both his opening and closing statements. It was the most enduring memory of the case.

Kylie hugged her arms across her middle and shivered in spite of the afternoon's warmth. "That poor kid."

"She doesn't remember anything."

"I meant C.J. He was just a boy. What a horrible thing to see. And if the sena—" She broke off and bit her lip before rephrasing it. "If Charley Baker *is* guilty, he knew what his son would find. He deliberately sent that little boy to discover two murdered bodies."

Jake stiffened, then consciously eased the muscles in his jaw, his neck, his hands. "Charley and C.J. were very close. He swears on his life he never would have done that to him."

"And you believe him."

"Can you imagine the nightmares the kid had? Still has? What kind of father would purposely subject his own son to that?" He'd heard the answer to the question before: the kind of man who would kill his lover because she wouldn't run away with him. Who would kill her husband because he'd walked in on the murder. Who would leave a three-year-old girl alone in the house with her parents' lifeless bodies for at least ten or twelve hours.

A cold-blooded killer.

But that *wasn't* Charley. Jake believed that with everything in him.

God help him if he proved himself wrong.

They stopped where the path made a left turn to end at the broad porch steps. There was a sturdy padlock on the door, and the downstairs windows were covered with plywood to protect them from vandals. The second-floor windows had been broken, no doubt by kids tossing rocks, leaving those rooms exposed to the wind and the rain. The place looked abandoned. Bereft.

"C.J. went inside, careful not to step in the blood, not

to touch anything. He wasn't thinking about preserving evidence. He was only ten. But he didn't want the blood on him. Didn't want the evil on him. He saw Bert sprawled in the middle of the kitchen floor and he grabbed Therese, held her tight and ran out screaming for his father."

"Did Charley go inside?" Kylie asked, climbing the steps one at a time.

"Yes."

"He checked the bodies?"

Jake nodded. He hadn't actually seen it. He'd thrown up in the driveway, then huddled inside their beat-up old truck, clutching Therese as if she might try to run away. She hadn't. Though she'd hardly known him, she'd clung to him, her little hands gripping his shirt, leaving bloody prints there.

"And he didn't touch anything either," Kylie mused. When he raised one brow, she shrugged. "You said earlier his fingerprints weren't found anywhere in the house."

He watched her walk the length of the railless porch, then return to the steps. Twenty-two years ago, there had been wicker chairs, a swing at one end and a glider at the other, and big clay pots of flowers had stood along the edge. Now there was no sign of the furniture, likely carried away by thieves, and only shards of the pots remained on the ground where they'd fallen or been thrown by the same vandals who'd broken the windows.

"How well did Charley know the Franklins?" she asked as she came down the steps again, then started around the house.

Jake would have preferred to wait for her at the truck, but that would have defeated his purpose in the drive out there. He followed her, albeit reluctantly. "Not well. The

Franklins were friends of your parents. Charley worked at the glass plant, his wife at the truck stop." They'd lived in different worlds that happened to have collided all those years ago.

With a little help from the senator and his pals.

At the rear of the house a low stone wall separated the parking court from a patio where the Franklins had entertained on warm summer evenings. The crumbling remains of a brick barbecue stood in one corner; a fountain occupied the opposite corner, with a statue of some kind of woodland sprite in the middle of the pool. Only its legs remained intact; the torso, head and wings lay shattered below.

Kylie paused in front of the fountain, her brow wrinkled. "I've been here before. It was hot—summertime, I guess— and Therese and I were wading in this pool and my mother was fussing and Therese's mother said…" She closed her eyes as if that might help her better recall the memory, then opened them again with a regretful shake of her head. "I was only five when they died. I don't remember…"

Abruptly she shivered, then turned to survey the area. "Where is the Baker house?"

"On the other side of that pasture. Through those trees."

"Can we walk over there?"

When he nodded, she started through the knee-high weeds that had taken over the drive without seeming to notice them. What did it say for her upbringing that one of her earlier memories was of her mother fussing at her? And what would Phyllis Riordan say if she saw her daughter now, tramping through the weeds with a man her father had told her to stay away from, on her way to the former home of a convicted murderer?

When they reached the road, she kept her gaze on the rutted ground. "Why do you believe Charley's innocent?"

This would be a good time to tell her, *Because he's my father. Because I know him. He's not capable of this. Because he wouldn't have wished these nightmares on me. Because he's a good man.*

But he didn't offer any of that. Instead he shoved his hands in his pockets. "Gut instinct."

"But you said yourself—people lie. People accused of horrific crimes, in particular, lie."

Not Charley. At least Jake didn't think so.

"Since the book where the guy got a new trial, I've been contacted by a lot of people in prison. They told me their stories. They proclaimed their innocence. They wanted my help." He kicked a clod of dirt that rolled a few feet before breaking into smaller clumps. "I didn't believe most of them. But my gut says Charley's telling the truth."

"Is your gut ever wrong?" She stopped walking and turned to face him, hands on her slim hips. The breeze rustled through her hair, blowing a few loose strands across her face that she patiently swiped away.

When the next wind whipped them again, this time he reached out, brushing them back, tucking them behind her ear. His fingers lingered on the dangling turquoise earring, then slipped down to her jaw. "On occasion. It didn't warn me that Regina Lyn Broward was going to break my heart."

"What does it tell you about us?" She looked solemn, as if it mattered what his instincts said.

"That I'd be a fool to get involved with you." He saw a flicker of emotion in her brown eyes, something that looked—felt—like disappointment. It faded into a hazy, smoky gaze when he went on. "That I'd be a bigger fool to walk away from you."

It wasn't wise. It wasn't ethical. It wasn't logical or reasonable. But what did emotion have to do with all those things? *The heart wants what it wants.* He'd read that somewhere, probably on a sappy greeting card, and it was true. Of all the women in the world for him to fall for, the worst one under the circumstances was Jim Riordan's daughter. But he was falling anyway.

"Funny," she murmured as she took a step toward him. "That's what my gut says, too. And the senator says I should always trust my gut."

He got a faint whiff of her scent as she touched her mouth to his, then he forgot to breathe. She rested her slim, delicate hands on his chest, leaned against him for support and kissed him sweetly, needfully. Her teeth nipped at his lip, then her tongue dipped inside his mouth, and his body grew hotter and harder than he could ever recall being.

He raised his hands to her face, cupping his palms to her cheek, and tilted his head to deepen the kiss. Heat surged through him, and lust, hunger and, practically lost in the intensity, a small faint warning. Did he want to be a fool with his heart intact or a bigger fool, wiser but sadder for the experience?

His body's answer was clear: he just *wanted.* Now.

He would worry about the future when it came.

She was the first to pull away. She studied him a long time, the yearning slowly fading from her eyes before a slight smile curved her lips and she set off again. After a few steps she extended her hand, and after a few more steps he caught up with her and took it.

For her, he was willing to risk being the biggest fool in the world.

* * *

The road to the Baker house climbed a gentle slope that left Kylie winded by the time they reached the top…or was that the fault of the kiss? Considering that she ran most mornings, the answer seemed apparent, but she chose to ignore it.

While most of the surrounding land had been cleared into pasture, trees grew thick around the house, screening it on all sides. They were mostly scrub oaks, gnarled, their leaves turned brown. They would cling to those leaves well into winter, until the last one fell to join the years' worth blanketing the ground.

Doubtlessly the Franklins had considered themselves lucky the trees existed to block their view of the neighboring house. It was small, its wood siding ill-fitting, its dark brown paint drab. Instead of a porch there was merely steps leading directly to the front door. The windows were narrow, the screens torn and rusty. It wasn't what came to mind when she thought "home, sweet home," either. Looking at it just made her feel sorry for people she'd never known.

"Welcome to the Baker mansion," Jake said flippantly, leading the way through the weeds to the steps. He fished his keys out of his pocket and inserted one in the lock.

"Where did you get the key?"

"From the owner. He lives about fifty miles from here in Buffalo Plains. After the Bakers moved out, he never could rent it again. He blamed Charley."

"He must have rented it to the Bakers sight unseen," she murmured as the door creaked open.

Jake stepped back so she could enter first. "Charley never made much money and he never cared where he lived as long as his wife and son were with him."

Nice for Charley. Maybe not so nice for the wife and son.

Kylie took a cautious step inside and found herself in a hall. On the left a doorway opened into a small, square living room, with the kitchen visible through its other doorway. On the right was a bedroom. Remnants of furniture remained—a ratty couch, a coffee table splintered into pieces, a rusted iron bed frame.

Halfway down the hall another door opened into the bathroom. Rust stained the fixtures, and the mirror that had hung above the sink lay in pieces on the floor, their surface too heavily coated with dirt and age to reflect anything. Next to it was a second bedroom—C.J.'s, judging from the single bed and the poster for the Dallas Cowboys that curled on the wall.

The Franklin house had given her a feeling of sadness—because Bert's and Jillian's lives had ended so violently, Therese had been robbed of her parents and C.J. had been robbed of his innocence. But this small, dark house carried sadness as well as a sense of despair. Even in its best days the house had been shabby. The Bakers hadn't had much; they'd worked and struggled and they'd lost everything while they lived here—had wrongfully lost it, Jake believed.

She left the bedroom that was little more than a closet and turned into the kitchen. The appliances were gone, wires and lines hanging from the wall to show where they'd once been. The sink sagged at an awkward angle, the cabinets in poor shape to support its weight. It would fall before too long, wrenching free of its pipes. The entire house would probably fall before too long, and no one would care or even know.

"It wasn't the worst place they ever lived, but it was hardest for Angela," Jake said, his voice taking on that aloof quality she'd heard too much of at the Franklin house. The tone was flat, as if the only way he could tell the stories was without emotion. How hard was it for him spending months wrapped up in the sorrows of other people's lives?

"She wanted something different. A kitchen where the cabinet doors stayed shut once you shut them." He demonstrated by closing one of the upper cabinet doors. The instant he withdrew his hand, the panel slowly swung open again. "A sink with a garbage disposal. A tub with a shower. A place for a washer and dryer so she wouldn't have to lug the dirty clothes to the Laundromat every week. The deputy and the assistant D.A.—"

Coy Roberts and her father.

"—claimed her unhappiness was why Charley turned to Jillian Franklin."

Kylie started to lean against the counter behind her, thought better of it and went through the connecting doorway to the living room instead. A mouse skittered out from under the couch, setting the fabric asway, and disappeared through a hole in the corner. "And why did Jillian turn to him?" Bert Franklin had had money, influence and power. To a lot of women in their social circle those topped their list of important qualities.

Jake grinned. "Because he was good-looking?" Then the grin faded. "Some women like to slum. Your mother chose to marry a man who had no money, no family name to speak of."

"My mother loved my father," Kylie pointed out. "Did Jillian love Charley?"

He crossed to the window and stared out, hands in his hip pockets. "I can't find any evidence that Jillian even knew Charley. Yeah, they were neighbors, but they were separated by pasture and woods and the entire social spectrum. Charley says he only spoke to her a time or two. Angela says Jillian was rude every time she tried to strike up a conversation with her. Can you imagine your parents being friendly with a common laborer and a truck-stop waitress?"

"Only if the senator was stumping for votes," she murmured. As for socializing or being neighborly…it never would have happened. Colbys and Riordans did not make meaningful connections outside their small circle of equals.

Jake tested the window frame, then turned and leaned against it, arms folded over his chest. "How *did* Phyllis Colby of *the* Colbys wind up married to a nobody?"

It was a fair question but one that made Kylie uncomfortable nonetheless. She wasn't even sure why. Because of the implied criticism? Because her mother and father *hadn't* seemed a likely match? Because she didn't want to include them in a conversation about slumming and nobodies?

"The senator was just out of law school when they met," she said at last. "He was already active in politics, working on campaigns, making a name for himself within the party. My grandfather introduced them—Grandfather was a senator himself, you know. He liked my father's ambition. My mother liked his blue eyes and his smile."

"So she became a snob after the marriage?"

A sudden chill passed through Kylie, and with the surge of its energy she started for the door. Jake followed. "She was always a snob, actually," she admitted as she carefully descended the steps. "She'd lived a privileged life. I think she made an exception for the senator. She expected great things of him and wanted to be a part of them."

She *had* loved him. Kylie was sure of it.

Wasn't she?

Back out in the afternoon sun, the chill faded. She breathed deeply, clearing the mustiness and sadness from her lungs, then gestured out back to a sagging corral. "Did the Bakers have any animals?"

"Just a dog and a horse. C.J. refused to leave them behind, so Angela reluctantly trailered them out west when they left."

She walked in that direction, but when she saw a pond in the near distance she bypassed the corral and continued across the field. It was a beautiful afternoon—the sky pale blue, everything else golden and scarlet. Oklahoma in winter wasn't a pretty sight, but in autumn it could be gorgeous. At that moment, with the house behind her and Jake beside her, it *felt* gorgeous.

The pond was large, maybe a hundred yards across at its widest point, and the surface was marred with tiny ripples created by the wind. Piers from a long-gone dock marched fifteen feet into the water, some crooked, all of them rotted. Trees on the back side sheltered the pond from the north winds; the gently undulating land hid the houses and Jake's truck from view.

A low sandstone boulder stood near the water's edge, so perfectly positioned that it might have been placed there with sun-worshipping in mind. She sat down, gazed across the water and listened to the breeze, the birds, the quiet lap of miniature waves against the shore.

"So…" Jake sat beside her, his shoulder bumping hers. "Is it Colby or Riordan tradition for the father to choose his daughter's suitors? Or both?"

She wanted to say no, of course not. She was a grown woman, fully capable of making such personal decisions for herself. But hadn't the senator chosen the man she'd almost married? Wasn't he even now trying to win her over to David Vaughan's side? And hadn't he endorsed both men for reasons that had everything to do with politics and nothing to do with her?

He'd always been quick to approve or disapprove of her boyfriends, she realized, all the way back to her junior prom date. And when he'd disapproved, she had soon ended the relationship.

How intensely would he disapprove of Jake Norris?

"The senator would like to make it a tradition," she said at last, uncomfortable with how close she'd come to allowing him just that.

"But maybe there's a bit of rebellion in his daughter after all." Jake's voice was quiet, his tone teasing as he bumped against her again.

"Maybe a very small bit," she conceded. After all, as Jake had pointed out, she was with *him,* wasn't she?

Drawing her feet onto the rock, she rested her arms on her knees, her chin on her arms, and tilted her head to the side for a better look at him. His hair was too short to be ruffled by the wind, and his gaze was fixed on some distant point. "Are looks enough?"

Slowly he turned his head to look at her. Funny that they both had brown eyes but his were so much *more* brown. They were shades deeper than her own and hinted at a complexity so much deeper than her own. "What do you mean?"

"When I asked what drew Jillian to Charley, you said he was good-looking. Is that enough?" After all, Jake was extremely good-looking. She imagined women had been coming on to him since he was old enough to shave—even before then, if she counted Regina Lyn Broward. *She* wanted to come on to him…but not because he was handsome. Because there was some indefinable something between them. Because he attracted her in a way no man ever had.

Trying to ignore the heat that flushed her face, she cleared her throat. "After the initial attraction, the initial lust, there must be something else. Shared interests, mutual goals, affection, the promise of a future."

Jake's smile came slowly and raised her body heat several more degrees. "Haven't had many meaningless affairs, have you? The initial lust is all that matters in an affair, Kylie. We're not talking about marriage or a long-term relationship. It's just sex."

She didn't have much experience with "just sex." She didn't think she was wired that way emotionally. Even with Jake, when they eventually surrendered, it wouldn't be "just sex" to her. Not even if he left town the next day and she never saw him again.

That thought made her gut clench. How silly she was being, she chided herself. She hardly knew the man…but she felt as if she did. There was no chance of anything more than lust between them…but it felt as if there was. She *felt*—and that was the point. None of the men she'd dated had ever made her *feel* quite the way he did. Everything seemed sharper, clearer, more *real* with him.

Her pulse pounding, she deliberately forced her attention back to the conversation. "But you don't kill your lover for refusing to run away with you if it's just sex."

"According to the authorities, you do if you find out that what you thought was love was really just convenient sex."

"So, according to them, Charley was in a relationship and Jillian was having a meaningless affair. Then it seems rage or rejection would have been better motivation for killing her than wanting to run away with her." She watched a hawk soar in lazy circles over the pond before alighting in a tree on the far side. "Did he have an alibi?"

"Yeah. He worked late Friday, had dinner at the truck stop where Angela worked, then went to a bar to have a few drinks while waiting for her to get off."

"There was nothing about that in the transcript." The defense attorney hadn't offered an alibi or, as far as that went, any real defense at all.

"Charley got exactly what he paid for with his lawyer," Jake said with a thin smile.

Since Tim Jenkins had been court-appointed, Charley had paid nothing. Except his life.

"We can check out his alibi."

"I intend to," Jake said. "The bar was out by the glass plant, a little dive that's been there probably since this place was named Ethelton."

"Buddy's," Kylie said, earning a surprised look from him. She faked a haughty sniff. "I don't go there, but it *has* been there forever. Want to go now?"

He glanced at the sun in the western sky, then his watch. "Actually, I'd rather take you up on your offer. Show me where you grew up, where you learned to be such a prim and proper young woman." After standing up, he extended his hand and pulled her to her feet and achingly close. "After that, maybe I can show you a few ways to be *im*proper."

Her breath caught in her chest. She'd been taught to keep her poise in any situation, but at that moment she couldn't remember any of her mother's lessons. How to talk. How to hide what she was feeling. How to move. She didn't want to be poised. Didn't want to be calm, cool and in control. *Did* want to learn every improper thing he could teach her.

Her silence—and, likely, the heat radiating off her in waves—made him chuckle. He took a step back, claimed her hand and started across the pasture toward his truck. "I've flustered Kylie Riordan. Bet that's a first."

Then he gave her a grin and a wink. "Bet it won't be the last."

By the time they reached the truck the sun had disappeared behind dark clouds moving in rapidly from the northwest. Jake unlocked the doors as the wind freshened, bringing with it the smell of rain. Good thing they were leaving. This place was sad enough in bright sunlight. Rain—like he'd run through that morning so many years ago—would make it damn near unbearable.

He backed out, then headed down the hill. The visit had gone better than he'd expected. He'd known seeing the houses for the first time in twenty-two years wouldn't be easy, but it could have been worse. He could have been alone.

At the bottom of the hill he stopped and checked for traffic. The sky was dark behind them; the rain would definitely overtake them before they reached town. Off to the right a pair of headlights identified a fast-moving vehicle in the distance, but it was too far away to be of concern.

"I love rain," Kylie remarked as he turned onto the paved road. She had rolled her window down, and the wind was whipping her hair, working strands free of its braid. "When I was little, I used to take refuge in a corner on the porch where the rain couldn't reach me and watch it."

"I used to go out and play in it, splashing through mud puddles and getting soaked to the skin."

She gave him a faint smile, enough to tell him that perfect little daughters didn't indulge in such undignified behavior.

"I bet you wore dresses and patent-leather shoes and big floppy hats," he remarked, switching the wipers on as the first drops hit the windshield. "You never ran, never got dirty, never slid down the banister or did anything that might muss your appearance."

"I run three miles a day four or five days a week."

He grinned. "I knew there was a reason I liked your legs."

As raindrops began to blow in, she sighed softly and rolled the window up. "You're right. Most of my play when I was little involved dolls and tea parties. I never stepped in a mud puddle and I never got soaked to the skin unless I was in the shower. I was in school before I got my first pair of pants and in college before I got my first jeans. And I looked absolutely adorable in my big floppy hats."

"I bet you did." He couldn't relate to the kind of upbringing she was describing. Angela may not have been the best mother, but she believed in letting kids be kids. No adults in miniature bodies for her, thank God.

Lights flickered behind him, and he glanced in the rearview mirror to see a vehicle approaching faster than seemed safe in the rain. He steered closer to the right shoulder, leaving the idiot plenty of room to pass. "Did you miss running and splashing in puddles and climbing trees? Or did you like playing with dolls and having tea parties?"

"Maybe I missed it a little. But my mother didn't encourage that kind of behavior, and truthfully, I was a very girlie girl."

"Now there's a news flash," he said drily as he checked the mirror again. The vehicle was an SUV, black with dark-tinted windows, and was now less than a few car lengths off his rear bumper. Kids, probably, acting stupid as kids often did. Still, he eased his foot off the accelerator and let the truck slow a few miles off his previous speed.

At what seemed the last chance before a collision became inevitable, the other driver swerved into the opposite lane. Jake swallowed a sigh of relief and eased his fingers' hold on the steering wheel. Then suddenly the SUV swerved, clipping the left rear of Jake's truck. The impact shuddered through the truck, and he gripped the wheel hard. Across the cab, Kylie grunted as the seat belt stopped her forward motion, but he couldn't spare a look to see if she was all right.

The truck spun in a tight curve, skidding on the wet pavement before coming to rest on the westbound shoulder, facing the direction they'd just come from. The SUV slowed to a stop in the middle of the road, then the driver backed up a few yards. Again it stopped, the powerful engine idling for a moment, then the driver shifted out of Reverse and drove off.

"Are you okay?" Jake asked, watching the taillights in the mirror until they disappeared.

"Y-yeah, I, uh, think so. Are you?"

"Yeah. Fine."

"I can't believe— That moron— He didn't even stop to see if we were injured!"

Slowly he forced his fingers to uncurl. He rubbed his shoulder where the seat belt had burned before it'd locked in place, then gave her a wry look. "He didn't intend to hurt us."

Her face was pale, her eyes wide with delayed fear. "I'm sure he didn't *intend* to hit us, but—" Something in his expression stopped her. For a long moment she stared at him, then a muscle in her jaw twitched. "You think he *did* intend to hit us."

"It's a maneuver cops use to stop a vehicle in a chase, called a PIT maneuver. It's sort of a controlled crash."

Her face got even paler. "Cops…as in Derek West."

He shrugged.

"Oh, my God."

It was little more than a whisper, but it made him want to wrap his arms around her, hold her close and promise her nothing else would happen. The problem was, he couldn't make such a promise. Only her father could.

Leaving her to reach the realization that her father and his friends had arranged an accident that involved *her*— an accident that could have been serious, because even a controlled crash went out of control sometimes—he unfastened his seat belt. "I'm going to check the damage. Wait here."

The temperature that had been comfortable before the rain was chilly now, especially when he was drenched by the time he reached the rear of the truck. There was a pretty good dent there, but the damage didn't seem too bad. He would have to replace the panel and maybe the bumper, but the tire and wheel well didn't appear to be affected.

This book was costing him in ways he hadn't expected, he thought grimly as he straightened—and came face-to-face with Kylie. Rain ran down her face and dripped onto her blouse. She'd removed the band from her hair and combed it free of the braid, so it hung around her face like damp gold. She looked damned beautiful. She wasn't just a goddess but a goddess of the sea.

"I thought I told you to wait inside."

She was looking at the truck. His words brought her gaze to his face. "I called the highway patrol. They're sending a trooper to take a report." Her throat worked as she swallowed, then that muscle in her jaw twitched again. "I'll pay for the repairs."

"The hell you will."

"Don't worry. I'll bill them to my father." She started toward the cab but made it only a few yards before spinning around and marching back. "Why would they do this? What if there'd been a ditch or an embankment here? You could have been hurt. You could have been killed! What are they hiding?"

He sluiced the rain from his face with one hand, for all the good it did, then returned her stare. "Who really killed Jillian and Bert Franklin."

Maybe they knew or maybe they didn't have a clue. Having an unsolved double homicide wasn't good for either the elected or the appointed officials of the county. Maybe Charley had merely been a scapegoat.

She wanted to argue with him—he could see it in every stiff line of her body—but she kept her mouth clamped shut. Hugging herself tightly, she walked a few feet away, her back to him, her gaze locked on nothing.

He moved to stand behind her, hands resting on her shoulders. "Whoever it was picked his spot. This is the only section of road between here and the highway that *doesn't* have a ditch or an embankment. There aren't any trees or fence posts close to the road. There was no other traffic. I imagine it's about as safe a place to run someone off the road as you're going to find."

The wind and the rain muffled her voice. "I can't believe you're not angry."

"I'm angry. Hell, between this and the two tickets I got, my insurance rates are going to double. But we're okay, Kylie." He slid his arms around her from behind and rested his chin on the top of her head. "Mostly what I am is more determined than ever. I want to know what they're hiding. Who they're protecting."

After a moment she settled her hands on his wrists. "So do I," she whispered.

Chapter 6

They returned to the truck to wait for the trooper. Leaning over the floorboard, Kylie wrung water from her shirt, then squeezed it from her hair. She was wet, cold and sick to her stomach, but she didn't complain. She didn't want to talk, to put her thoughts into words.

Most likely her father had given Chief Roberts the order to scare Jake off. Regardless of intentions, Jake could have been killed. *She* could have been killed. And for what? To protect the men's secrets? To protect misconduct, malfeasance, a murderer?

She was shivering inside and starting to shake outside, too, when red-and-blue lights flashed behind them. The car parked on the shoulder, and a figure in a bright yellow slicker strode to the driver's door. Jake rolled down the window, and Kylie found herself the object of Coy Roberts's piercing stare.

"What the hell are you doing here?"

Bedraggled as she was, she drew her shoulders back and fixed an unwavering look on him. "I don't appreciate your tone, Chief, or your language. What I do and who I do it with is none of your business, no matter what the senator might say."

His ears turned red in the dim light as he forced what was meant to be a humbled look. "I'm sorry about that, Kylie. When I heard that you'd been involved in a hit-and-run accident, naturally I was concerned for your well-being."

More likely concerned that her father would be furious with him for not orchestrating their campaign against Jake more carefully. Of course, the senator had given her orders to keep her distance. She had talked her way around last night's dinner, but he wouldn't have expected her to go to the Baker and Franklin houses with Jake. He wouldn't have expected her to be in the truck with Jake when he was run off the road.

"What happened here?" Roberts asked, trying to look and sound official.

"Ask Der—"

Without looking in her direction, Jake extended his hand to stop her. She bit back the words.

"A black SUV pitted my truck," Jake said evenly.

"Pitted—" Rain dripped off the brim of Roberts's hat but didn't blur the smug arrogance of his smile. "Sounds like you've been watching too much *Cops* on TV, Norris. Why in the world would anybody pit you? Most likely some kid was just driving too fast and clipped the back end of your truck when he passed you. You get a license number?"

Jake shook his head.

"A description besides 'black'?"

"Two doors. A Chevy, I think. Windows tinted so dark you can't see in."

"Doesn't sound familiar. You know, that kind of tinting is illegal around here."

Jake's smile was thin. "And of course no one ever does anything illegal around here, do they, Chief?"

The amusement disappeared from Roberts's thin face, replaced by disgust. He looked away, then gestured down the road. "Here comes the trooper. He'll take care of this."

Take care of this. When did that phrase take on an ominous meaning? Kylie wondered.

Roberts turned to leave, then stepped back into sight. "I'll tell your daddy you're okay, Kylie."

"I'll tell him myself," she retorted.

He returned to his car, made a U-turn, then switched off the emergency lights. A moment later another car parked where he'd been. The trooper took the report, agreed with Roberts about careless kids, then left. Long after he'd disappeared into the night, Jake started the engine. "Well, hell."

An appropriate sentiment.

They didn't talk on the way into town, not until she gestured to the intersection ahead. "Turn left here."

"Do you mind if I go by the motel and change clothes first?"

"Sure." There was a thought to warm her: Jake stripping down to bare skin, rubbing a towel over his body… She was surprised steam wasn't rising from her own clothes.

He parked next to his room but didn't invite her in. Because it was still raining? Because the Tepee Motor Court was no place for the senator's daughter? She would prefer the first. It would be nice to think that *someone* didn't care who her father was.

Even if she was just kidding herself.

He returned in under five minutes, wearing another pair of faded, snug-fitting jeans and a black T-shirt under an open slicker. Again without conversation, he drove back across town to the Colby house. He didn't need directions. He'd probably looked it up his first day in town.

She did direct him past the front gate to a smaller service gate on the south side of the property. The narrow blacktop lane became stone where it joined the main drive. To the right it curved around to the front of the mansion. To the left were the detached garage and the cottage she called home.

"You live here?" Jake asked as he parked near the door.

"You think I'd want to live there?" she responded with a nod toward the mansion. In the early dusk, it looked huge, hulking, empty—because it was. The housekeeper was already gone for the day.

"Here, take my jacket—"

Before he could shrug out of the slicker, she opened her door and slid out. "You keep it. I'm already wet."

It was just a few yards to the door and the overhang that offered protection. She unlocked the door, shut off the alarm, then led the way inside.

The cottage had been built at the same time as the mansion to provide luxurious accommodations for family guests. When Kylie was little, Grandmother Riordan had occasionally taken up residence there, an event that had never failed to displease Phyllis. She'd made an exception in her snobbish ways for her husband, but she'd never liked spending time with his family. Typical tensions between in-laws? Or had she considered the other Riordans beneath her even if she *had* married their son?

Until meeting Jake, such questions had never occurred to Kylie.

She switched on lights as she moved from the foyer into the hall, then the living room. "Make yourself comfortable. Take a look around. I'll be right back."

Hoping to minimize the dripping, she hurried to the master bath, where a glimpse of herself in the mirror made her grimace. She looked like a drowned rat—hair lank and clinging to her skull, shirt revealing every bit of lace and ribbon on her bra, trousers splashed with mud and boots that would never be the same. After discarding it all in a pile, she briskly rubbed a towel over her, chasing away the chill, trying to bring some color back into her skin.

Wishing for time for a hot bath, she towel-dried her hair, then combed it straight back with a scowl. It would take more than a bath to make her look her best. This and dry clothes was all she could manage in limited time.

She padded into the bedroom, put on panties and a bra, then ducked into the closet for clothes. When she returned with a pair of jeans and a sweater in hand, she saw Jake at the bedroom door and came to a sudden stop. "Wh-what are you doing?" she asked, her voice hoarse.

"Following your directions. Taking a look around." His voice was hoarse, as well, but he'd lied. He wasn't looking around. The only thing he was looking at was her.

That quickly, the last of her chill evaporated and heat flooded her skin. Suddenly the jeans folded over her arm felt too coarse, the sweater too warm. As her hand fell limply to her side, the garments slid to the floor, landing with a whoosh on the rug.

She could pick them up. Ask him to leave. Get dressed. Meet him in the living room and take him on the promised tour next door. She could pretend she wasn't standing there half-naked, that he wasn't looking at her as if he wished she was completely naked. She could be smart, sensible, the way she'd been for twenty-seven years, and walk away from him.

And how did walking away from him constitute smart? No man had ever intrigued her the way Jake did. No man had ever made her lust the way he did. So what if he wasn't staying and she wasn't leaving? Not all good things had to be permanent. They could have a lovely, luscious affair that ended when he returned home. It didn't have to be accompanied by regrets.

But *not* having an affair with him was something she would regret. Not exploring this sizzle, this need. She would always wonder what she'd missed.

So she did the smart, sensible thing—and walked *to* him.

"There's not much to see," she said, erotically aware of how much he wore and how little she wore. Her nipples were tight beneath the lace of her bra, and lower, heat and dampness swirled through her. "The house is comfortable but small."

He swallowed hard and shifted his weight from one foot to the other. The movement drew her gaze down, over the cotton shirt stretched taut across his chest, to the faded denim of his jeans, past the zipper that was distorted by the swelling beneath it, down long, muscular thighs. "I…I can go…back out if…if you want."

She smiled. "Do I look like I want you to go?"

Something softened in him—certainly not his erection, and not the muscles that practically vibrated with tension. Relief, maybe, that she wanted what he did. That he hadn't gotten that quite impressive erection for nothing.

She stopped in front of him, a few feet separating them.

The bed was to her left, the sitting area with its fireplace behind him, the bathroom with its oversize whirlpool tub behind her. Choices that she cared nothing about. All she wanted was to touch him, to be touched by him.

He brushed her hair, lifting its cool, damp weight, twining it around his fingers, then drew her to him. His first kiss was sweet, only the touch of his mouth to hers, and wicked because it promised so much more. His tongue slid between her lips, and she opened to him as her hands sought his shoulders for balance, for support, for pure pleasure. Even through his shirt his skin was hot, the muscles ridged and growing more so as his tongue delved deeper into her mouth.

Releasing her hair, he pulled her until their bodies were touching, chest to thigh. His hard length rubbed against her belly, making her quiver. It was a delicious sensation, a tingle that heated her blood and made each breath a struggle. When his fingers slid featherlight along her spine, shivers washed over her. When they dipped inside the low-cut band of her panties to cup her bottom and press her hard against him, she gasped.

He ended the kiss, lifted his head and looked at her, his expression serious, intimate. She felt his gaze slide lower, past her mouth, down her throat, to her breasts, and her nipples tightened again, achy and in need of his mouth. He reached out with one hand and undid the front clasp of her bra without more than a brush of knuckles against her skin. He didn't push the lace and satin away, though, but left that to her.

She lifted her left breast, pulled the fabric free, then lifted the other breast and did the same. The thin straps slid down her arms, then the bra landed somewhere behind her. He caught her hands, brought them back to her breasts and stroked her fingers over her nipples. Heat tinged her face and down her throat—a little embarrassment, but mostly arousal. He liked watching her touch herself, and she liked that.

But she wanted to touch him, as well. Freeing her wrists from his hold, she gathered the hem of his shirt and peeled it over his head. His chest was broad, smooth, brown, so soft and so hard. She drew her tongue across his nipple and it hardened instantly. When she sucked it between her teeth, he grunted, and when she slid her hands to his groin, he shuddered.

She tried to unfasten his jeans so she could *really* touch him, but her fingers fumbled over the button. "Oh, damn," he muttered, grabbing both of her hands in his and holding them away from his body while he undid the jeans. Wriggling loose, she freed his arousal from soft denim, briefs, and drew a low, guttural moan from him.

Stroking his, hot, heavy, twitchy flesh in her hands, she whispered, pleaded, "I need you inside me."

Jake didn't need a second invitation. He gently pulled her hands away, then toed off his boots, stripped off his jeans and briefs and took his socks with them. When he turned to the bed, she had removed her tiny pink panties and was lying there, hair across the pillow, long, lean body trembling, waiting…for *him*. Sweet hell, she was beautiful—blond and gold, sleek and muscled, soft and feminine. Her breasts were swollen, her nipples aching little nubs, and the curls between her thighs glistened with need, tempting him. Sea goddess aroused.

His erection throbbed painfully, but instead of joining her on the bed he bent to retrieve his jeans. "Let me get …" Plastic crinkled as he pulled the strip of three condoms from his pocket. He'd gotten them when he'd changed clothes. After that kiss out at the house and the way she'd gotten all still and aroused when he'd offered to teach her something improper, he'd figured better to be prepared than not.

When he turned back, she was leaning on one elbow, retrieving a small box of condoms from the night table drawer. He grinned. "A woman after my own heart."

Taking the condoms from him, she ripped one open, then rose onto her knees to put it in place. First, though, she took him in her mouth for a long, lazy, intimate kiss that made his skin burn. She drew hard on him for a couple minutes before pulling back and deftly unrolling the condom over the length of his erection.

"Right now I'm just after this," she murmured, stroking him, pulling him with her as she lay back. "We'll talk about your heart later."

Right now *this* was enough. He worked his way inside her, a tight fit that felt incredible. Every move she made, every breath she took, everything she felt, he felt, too. It was snug, hot, wet, and he could stay there forever.

Though he wasn't going to last nearly that long.

He tried to stay still, to endure the sensations until they reached unendurable, but she tempted him with the wiggle of her hips, the tensing of her muscles deep inside where he filled her, her delicate little bites on his nipples, her tongue thrusting inside his mouth. Unendurable came sooner than he'd expected, forcing him to move, to pull out, then push in, long and slow and deep for about two strokes, then long and fast and deep. Pressure built, stimulation so intense that his skin, his body, felt raw. Every touch, every breath, was accompanied by pain, and every pain was filled with pleasure. The harder he pumped, the harder she met him, whimpering, swearing, pleading. He was so close, ears rushing, heart pounding, blood boiling, but he held back, waiting for her, waiting—

Her body went rigid, bucking up off the bed, and her frantic gasps turned to a low moan. Inside she tightened around him, tiny little spasms of exquisite pain, more than he needed, more than he could bear. His vision going dark, he lifted her hips tighter against his and, with a groan to match hers, he came. Hard. Long.

He didn't know how much time passed—enough for the shudders to fade away, for his muscles to protest too much flexion, for his heart and lungs to decide he wasn't dying after all…though what a hell of a way to go. The sweat was cooling on his skin, and beneath him Kylie was relaxing, too. One delicate hand stroked along his spine from shoulder blade to hip, and a sweetly enticing smile curved her lips.

"I guess I don't have to ask if it was good for you, too," she teased softly.

He slid to the side, removing most but not all his weight from her, disposed of the condom, then tucked her against him. "It was acceptable."

"Uh-huh. Any more acceptable and you'd need CPR."

He grinned and nipped her shoulder. "It was incredible. I kneel at your feet, goddess. You are amazing. Outstanding. Fantastic. Super—" He broke off with a grunt when she elbowed him.

"Don't overdo it. But keep that kneeling at my feet in mind for later. That sounds fun."

His body stirred. Oh, yeah, that sounded like *great* fun.

With a soft sigh, she adjusted the pillow they shared, then gazed past him to the windows. Darkness had fallen early, thanks to the rain, and the temperature had dropped with it. Despite daytime highs in the sixties and seventies, it was still fall, with winter on the way.

He couldn't think of a better way to stay cozy through a cold winter than making love with Kylie.

A chill settled over him—because the temperature *had* dropped, he knew, and not because he wasn't likely to see Kylie much, if at all, once he left Riverview. Once he uncovered the truth about her father, she would likely never want to see him again.

He maneuvered the comforter out from beneath them, then covered them both with it. She sighed again as she huddled into its warmth. He stroked her hair, mostly dry now, letting it sift through his fingers, and considered what to say. His first impulse was to make love to her again and say whatever had to be said later. His second was to make love to her again and forget whatever had to be said. His third was to make love to her again and somehow change what had to be said. He went with number four.

"Regrets?" His gut tightened as he waited for her response. *No*—that was the only answer he wanted. *None at all.*

Another sigh. "Yes…no…some."

Well, hell, he'd had to ask.

"Not about this." She lifted one hand to indicate the bed and their naked bodies. "I just regret that we are who we are."

That she was the senator's daughter. That he was the author who believed the senator guilty of taking a man's life. That he had set into play events that could destroy her father's reputation and the daughter's illusions she treasured.

And she had no clue that the man her father had cheated of life was *his* father.

Phyllis Colby Riordan would be spinning in her grave

to know that her precious daughter had been intimate with a poor trailer-trash convicted killer's son.

Even without a grave, Jim Riordan would spin out of control if he found out.

Not that there was any reason for him to find out. Kylie knew how to keep a secret, and Jake certainly did.

In the dim light she offered him a rueful smile. "I'm sorry. I didn't mean to spoil the mood."

He kissed her forehead, then grinned. "You can't spoil my mood, darlin'. I just had incredible sex with a goddess. Life doesn't get much better than that."

But it could. If they tried. If she didn't hold her father's downfall against him. If she could ever choose him over her father, it could be damn near perfect.

In the silence that followed, her stomach growled, bringing a flush to her face and a rare giggle to her lips. He laughed, too. "If I feed you, do I get to come back to bed with you?"

Her amusement faded into seriousness as she laid her palm to his cheek. "As long as you're in town."

He didn't know how long that would be, but even if it was months, a niggling little fear inside doubted it wouldn't be enough. The way he was feeling right that instant, nothing less than forever would be enough.

So he would change the way he was feeling. Remind himself regularly that it was just an affair. Remember who she was, who he was, who he *really* was. Remember it wasn't his heart she wanted. Just his body.

And the truth.

They dressed, checked the refrigerator, then ordered pizza and hot wings delivered. Kylie hadn't seen anything wrong with a salad or a frozen dinner, but Jake had over-ruled her. He wanted *real* food. Food with lots of calories and fat and sticky, gooey goodness.

After cleanup—consisting of refrigerating the last two pieces of pizza and throwing everything else in the trash—she dangled her keys from her finger. "Still want that tour?"

Something passed through his eyes, something…distancing. But it disappeared when he grinned and said, "Sure. Who doesn't want to see how the better half lives?"

"Hardly better," she corrected him as she took a hooded trench coat from the closet. "Just different."

"Honey, I've been poor. Being rich has to be better. It certainly makes a lot of people think they are."

Like her parents. Both Phyllis and the senator had nurtured a sense of entitlement, and they'd tried to instill it in her. How many times had her mother told her *You're a Colby* or *You're a Riordan* as if that truly mattered? Dozens. Hundreds.

She belted the coat around her waist as Jake thrust his arms into his slicker. With the hoods pulled up for pro-tection from the rain, they left the coziness of the cottage for the stone path that wound through gardens to the mansion's rear entrance. "Ordinarily I'd take you in the front door for the full effect," she said as they removed their coats, followed by their soaking shoes, in the utility room. "It's impressive."

She wasn't sure Jake would agree. She wanted him to. It was her family home. Colbys had bought the property, earned the fortune, built the house and lived in it for gen-erations. It was a part of who she was, and she wanted him to…to not be turned off by it.

From the utility room they cut through the kitchen to the hallway that ran front to back, dividing the house in half.

Along its length hung photographs not of early Colbys but of the oil wells that had made them rich, each bearing a brass plate with well name, location and date drilled. The furniture beneath the photos—two uncomfortable chairs and three demilune tables—were antiques. Most of the furnishings in the house were old and valuable, too much so for a young child to play on or near.

Ordinarily when she gave a tour to a friend she did a spiel about the history, the family and the more unusual treasures. Not with Jake. He was smart enough to recognize the rooms for what they were and curious enough to ask any questions that came to mind.

The front entry *was* impressive: a huge foyer, the ceiling reaching three stories high, painted with a gold-leaf mural of sky, clouds and angels. The double doors were unusually wide, stained glass in both doors, the sidelights and the arch overhead. The house faced south, and when the sunlight streamed through those windows it was breathtaking.

They walked quietly through the ladies' parlor, the gentlemen's parlor, the library, the music room and a nursery filled with plants, where six of the eight walls were floor-to-ceiling glass. Side by side they climbed the broad, curving staircase that swept to the second floor, where the corridor held the family portraits missing downstairs. On one side was her father's suite and a guest suite; Jake hardly glanced at either.

On the other side was her childhood rooms, where she'd lived from the time she was born until she graduated from college. She opened the door into the bedroom and let him enter, then leaned there and watched him. He walked the perimeter of the room, touching mementos, studying photographs, taking in and probably analyzing the first twenty-two years of her life.

At the window seat he picked up a pink-and-cream-striped pillow. "Until tonight, I would have said pink wasn't your color. By the way, you look lovely in pink. You look lovelier in nothing but tiny pink panties."

Her cheeks heated to match the color under discussion, and she shifted awkwardly. It wasn't fair that he could make one reference to seeing her in panties and raise her temperature into the red zone.

Wicked amusement lighting his eyes, he tossed the pillow back onto the bench. "I'm guessing Mama Phyllis decorated this room. It sure doesn't look like you."

"No," she agreed. "It doesn't."

"You did call her Mama, didn't you? You didn't have to refer to her as 'the senator's wife'?"

"Actually, I called her Mother. She wasn't a Mama or Mom sort of person."

With a nod, he moved on, scanning the books that filled the shelves. She was too far away to read the titles, but she remembered them. "Histories and political autobiographies," she said. "My mother's idea of light reading for a child."

There was that nod again—mostly inscrutable but with a bit of disapproval and a bit more of sympathy. This time when he moved on he stopped on the opposite side of the bed. Bending his knees slightly, he brought them in contact with the mattress, sending a tremor across the bed. "You ever have sex in this bed?"

She laughed. "I doubt I ever even *thought* about sex in that bed."

Hands in his pockets and a bad-boy grin on his mouth, he bounced the mattress again. "Want to rectify that?"

She strolled across the room to stand across the bed from him. "Let's see, wild and wicked sex in my childhood bed in my childhood home…I don't think so."

"It would be fun."

"I have no doubt." Just the image of him naked, hard and sweaty on the pink sheets where she'd dreamed childish dreams was enough to warm her to the core.

Still grinning, he turned away and opened the door behind him. Behind it was a short hall, with a door on the left to the bathroom, one on the right to the closet and one straight ahead leading into another room the size of her bedroom. He glanced into the bathroom, also pink, and the closet, pink and white and obscenely large for a child, then opened the third door. Reaching past him, she switched on the lights, then glanced around.

"Welcome to the playroom," he murmured.

"That was what Mother called it. After I turned ten, I called it my study."

"Pretentious little brat, weren't you?"

Shelves and cabinets lined most of the walls, and thick carpet covered most of the floor, except in the craft corner, where cabinets, a sink and worktables shared space, and the dance corner, with its mirrors and ballet barre. In both those areas the floor was hardwood. Cushy leather chairs were grouped around a large-screen TV, video games and a stereo, and a solid oak table, salvaged from some long-razed library, provided a study area, a row of yellow glass lamps marching down the middle to gleam warmly on the wood.

Jake saw it all from his place in the center of the room, then moved to her favorite area. It was the outside corner, with large windows on each wall that bathed the space with light. Her easel stood there, balancing a painting done long ago, and her supplies filled a battered armoire. She'd kept a canvas drop cloth on the floor to protect the aged wood, but the senator had instructed the housekeeper to get rid of it ages ago. She would have expected him to get rid of the painting, as well.

She was surprised to realize that she wasn't nervous when Jake stopped in front of the easel. Showing one of her pieces to her father had always made her queasy. But Jake wouldn't be critical. Whether he liked the landscape or thought she was a no-talent hack, he would be encouraging. He understood creative longing and the need to express it.

He studied the canvas a long time before glancing at her. "You shouldn't have stopped."

Had she told him she hadn't painted since college? Or did he just know it intuitively, because she was so good at taking orders from the senator? "Maybe I'll take lessons again," she remarked lightly as she joined him.

"You don't need lessons. You need to paint. You need to pick up a brush and create. You have the space. You have the brushes. Buy some paints and paper and *do* something, and if your father says anything, tell him to go f—"

She cut off his words with a kiss, hard but brief, then smiled. "Maybe I will."

For a moment he looked as if he wanted to argue, but instead he turned to gesture around the room. "This is where you grew up, isn't it? In these four walls. Where you had your tea parties and read your books. Where you were safe from the world, from behaving like a normal kid, from fun."

"It wasn't so bad." She would rank her childhood as average in quality. She wished a few things had been different, but overall she had no resentments.

He shook his head. "I was luckier being poor." Taking

her hand, he led her out into the corridor again. "What else is there?"

She waved her free hand in the direction of the smaller stairs that led to the third floor. "More rooms, mostly used for storage. Generations of Colbys living in the same house have amassed an unbelievable amount of stuff, and they've kept it all for posterity."

"And what is that?"

She'd hoped he wouldn't notice the door at the end of the hall. It was closed—always was—and was the one room in the mansion where permission was required to enter. "That's the senator's study."

Interest lit Jake's eyes. He looked from the heavily carved door to her, then back again. He wanted to go inside. She could feel it in the tension radiating from him, along with her own tension. *Don't ask. Please don't ask.* She couldn't invite him into her father's domain. It would be a violation of his privacy, a betrayal…but hadn't she already betrayed him? Just thinking that the senator was involved in wrongdoing in the Baker case, that he could be guilty of sending an innocent man to prison, was a betrayal, wasn't it?

Not if it was true.

Her nerves were stretched taut when Jake's fingers tightened around hers and he started toward the stairs. "It's an impressive place, but I see why you live out back."

Relief danced through her, easing the knots in her muscles.

"Of course, you'll have to move in here eventually," he went on. "When you marry. Have kids."

Her foot slipped, and she grabbed the banister to stop from falling. "Sorry," she murmured, face red, when he helped her catch her balance. "I suppose that's the plan." In fact, her father had pointed it out when she'd announced she was moving into the guest cottage. *If that's what you want. But of course you'll be back to raise your family here. It's family tradition.*

Raise her children in a showplace instead of a home. Raise them in rooms filled with furniture they couldn't bounce on, climb on, eat crackers on. Spend the first three years of their lives saying *No* and *Don't touch*. Send them to the playroom so often that it became the center of their worlds.

Raise her children…with someone else. Not Jake.

Subdued, she retraced their steps, turning off lights, leaving only the ones the housekeeper normally kept burning. While Jake waited on the steps, she reset the alarm, locked the door, then pulled the hood over her hair before facing him. "I believe I'll take you up on *your* offer now."

"What offer was that?"

"'Show me where you learned to be such a prim and proper woman,'" she mimicked, "'and I'll show you a few ways to be *im*proper.'" She wet her lips, tasting lipstick, rain and a faint hint of him. "I want to be improper. Show me, Jake. Please."

Chapter 7

The sky was still dark when Jake lifted his head with a groan. He knew immediately where he was—Kylie's bed—and knew, too, it was an ungodly hour to be awake. What had awakened him, though, he couldn't say. Everything was still, quiet, except for the drip of rain outside the window.

Then the mattress shifted behind him, and he realized the heat against his back had been gone for some time. He rolled over and saw Kylie sitting on the edge of the bed. She was dressed in light colors—pants, shirt, both fitting snugly, and a loose jacket—and her hair was pulled up in a ponytail. She was tucking something from the night table into her jacket pocket, but she stilled when he moved. "Sorry," she whispered. "I didn't mean to wake you."

"What are you doing?" he whispered back.

"Getting my pepper spray." She held up a narrow canister. "Ten percent. It's kind of illegal, but Chief Roberts gave it to the senator for me, so I don't think I'm going to get into trouble."

"Why do you—" Breaking off, he cleared his throat and spoke aloud. "Why do you need pepper spray at—" he squinted at the clock on her side of the bed "—five forty-five in the morning?"

"I'm going for a run. Go back to sleep. I'll be back in less than an hour."

Sleep sounded really good. His heart didn't even develop a normal rhythm until sometime after nine in the morning. But instead of settling in again he pushed back the covers, sat up and rubbed his face with both hands. "I'd better go."

Rising, Kylie pressed a button on the wall that brought the lights up a few watts. "You don't have to get up just because I am."

He eased to his feet, stretched out the kinks, then tried to remember what he'd done with his clothes the night before. His shirt was somewhere near the front door, along with his jacket, and he distinctly recalled leaving one boot in the hall.

"I trust you alone in the house," she said. "I have no secrets."

Grinning, he turned to face her. "You've been keeping at least one secret, darlin'. Despite your cool, elegant exterior, you're not prim and proper at all. The heart of a wicked woman beats inside your body."

She retorted, "Only when there's a wicked man inside there, too," flushing deep scarlet. Increasing the lighting another twenty watts, she bent to scoop up his jeans and hand them over.

He found his boxers dangling from the doorknob and

stepped into them, aware she was watching, then tugged on his jeans. "Chief Roberts's goons have probably noticed I haven't been at the motel all night. Hopefully they don't know where I am. If I leave now, while it's still dark and sane people are still asleep, maybe they won't find out. And if they don't find out, they can't tell your father."

She bent again and this time came up with one boot and two socks. "I don't care—" Abruptly she broke off, her nails digging into the scuffed leather upper of the boot.

"I care." He gently pried the boot from her fingers, sat down and put on both socks and the boot. She was standing just a few feet in front of him, stretchy fabric encasing her body like a second skin. He slid both hands over her thighs, the fibers slick and cool, then gripped her hips and pulled her close. Nuzzling the hem of the tank top from the waist-band of the pants, he pressed a kiss to her middle.

"What we're doing out there—" he jerked his head in the direction of the windows "—Riordan and Roberts and everyone else is going to know about. But this…" He kissed his way to her breast, then mouthed her nipple through the heavy material, making it harden, making her stiffen and catch her breath. "Right now this is between you and me."

She threaded her fingers through his hair and tugged him closer, her body radiating heat and tension as a tiny whimper escaped her. At the moment he wished there was *nothing* between him and her—no clothes, no reputations, no privacy issues. But with a sigh, he released her, gently pulled her hands free, then stood up. "I'd better go while I'm still able. Is it still raining?"

It took a few deep breaths for her to regain her compo-sure. "No. It's just drippy."

Drippy. Humid. Soon into her run, she would shed that

jacket, probably tying the sleeves around her waist. Sweat would collect on her skin, and her ponytail would lose its bounce as the dampness weighted it. Her clothes would get damp, too, clinging to her even more than normal, and her breathing would grow labored, just like yesterday evening. Last night. Early this morning.

Doing his best to ignore the swelling in his groin, he went down the hall. A dim lamp in the living room cast enough light to locate his missing boot, along with his shirt and jacket. He pulled the shirt on, then braced himself against the wall to shove his foot into the boot. By the time he'd laced it, Kylie was standing near the front door, waiting.

"What's your agenda for today?"

He glanced at her as he shoved his arms into the slicker. It was just one of his quirks, but he didn't like the word *agenda,* not applied to him. Granted, it had once been a perfectly acceptable word, but somewhere along the way it had taken on a negative connotation. *He has an agenda* was no longer a simple statement but an implication of underhandedness.

"I'd like to talk to some of Jillian Franklin's friends."

She nodded. "My mother's friends. I can introduce you to them. Do you want to meet for breakfast in a few hours or do you need more sleep?"

Though he'd gone to bed hours earlier than normal, he hadn't slept nearly all that time. Still, with a shower, coffee and food, he would be all right. "Breakfast."

"Eight o'clock? At the Pancake Palace?" When he nodded, she rose onto her toes, brushed a kiss to his cheek, then opened the door.

He walked through the fog to his truck, watched her stretch for a moment, wondering how difficult it would be to persuade her to try exercise of another kind this morning, then drove off as she jogged away in the other direction. The gate opened as he approached, then swung shut behind him.

He didn't see another vehicle until a hundred yards from the motel entrance, when a police car pulled into the lane behind him. Keeping one eye on the rearview mirror, he parked next to his room, then got out and openly watched the officer, who stopped a few feet away.

"Awful early to be out and about," the man said as he got out of his car, the engine still running, the headlights reflecting off Jake's truck.

"Or awful late. Depends on your perspective."

"Where have you been?"

Jake pulled his room key from his pocket and examined it a moment before lifting his gaze to the cop. "Out and about."

The officer bristled. He wasn't tall—three, maybe four inches shorter than Jake-but he was solid. With broad shoulders, thick arms, thick legs, no neck and a shaved head, he looked as if he could break Jake in two without much effort. Judging by the muscle twitching in his jaw and the way his hands clenched and unclenched, he was thinking about it. "Don't get smart, Norris—"

"I can't help it. I was born smart."

"You don't want to mess with me."

"You're right. I don't." He'd never been much of a fighter. He preferred to talk his way out of ugly situations—it was less painful. "If you give me a legitimate reason for wanting to know where I've been, I'll tell you. But if you're just asking because the chief told you to keep an eye on me, screw you *and* him."

He waited expectantly, but when the cop didn't say anything, he slowly pivoted and started up the steps. Turning his back on the guy took more nerve than he wanted to acknowledge, but he made it to the stoop without incident, inserted his key in the lock and opened the door.

"You're not gonna find anything," the cop said belligerently.

"Then tell your boss to stop worrying and stop harassing me."

"Charley Baker was guilty as sin. He was just a no-good drunken Indian. Everybody who knew him knows that."

Shaking his head, Jake went inside, closed and locked the door. All of No-Neck's last words were wrong. Charley *wasn't* guilty. Even though luck had never been with him, he'd been a hardworking man, a good husband and father. He hadn't been given to drunkenness, and *nobody* in Riverview had known him.

He showered, checked his e-mail and made a few notes, but it was hard to concentrate for long. Every thought about the trial transcript, the visit to the houses, getting run off the road and the tour of the mansion led to a thought about Kylie, and that led to remembering and wanting and needing. She'd gotten under his skin damned fast, but he figured it would take one hell of a long time to get over her. How weird was it that they were so obviously bad choices for each other and yet not even forty-eight hours after meeting they were in bed, getting intimate, and it had felt so *right?*

It was destiny, his mother would say. They were fated to be together…at least for a time.

Problem was, he was starting to want more than *a time*.

He was starting to think about the future. Long-term. Permanency. Forever.

Rolling his eyes, he caught a glimpse of the time and

hastily packed up his backpack. The Pancake Palace was only two blocks away; with a surge of energy, he slung the pack over his shoulder and set off on foot. If the cop saw him, let him follow. If he didn't, let him sit back thinking Jake was locked inside his room.

The emptiness in his gut started to tingle as he approached the restaurant. *Hunger,* the practical part of him said.

You bet, the impractical part agreed.

But not for food.

It was five minutes till eight when Kylie left the house for the second time that morning. She'd picked up her car from the downtown street after her run and was halfway to it when she noticed her father's Jag sitting in front of the garage. Alberto, the elderly housekeeper's husband who oversaw the grounds, gave her a smile and a wave as he hosed soapy water from it.

Mechanically she smiled and waved in return. "Good morning, Alberto. Is the senator coming home today?"

"He's already here, Miss Kylie. He arrived from the airport an hour ago."

She turned to gaze at the house. An hour ago she'd been pounding along the pavement, maintaining a steady pace, controlling her breathing…and thinking about Jake. How amazing he was. How wrong he was for her. How much she didn't care that he was wrong. She hadn't spared a single thought for her father, but if she had she would have been glad he was out of town, glad there were several days left on his fishing trip.

Why had he come home early? Because Chief Roberts had told him she'd been involved in an accident? Oh, sure, fatherly concern had brought him rushing home, where he'd then made no attempt to contact her or check on her well-being.

More likely he was here because Roberts had told him she was spending time with Jake. More likely his goal was damage control.

She checked her watch, then started along the path to the house. Alberto's wife, Rosalie, was in the kitchen when Kylie entered. She greeted the woman with a warm smile, asked about her father, then went down the hall and upstairs. The nearer she got to the senator's study, where Rosalie had directed her, the slower her steps got. Was she up for this? Did she really want to confront him just now?

Yes. At the ornate door she rapped, then waited for her father's distracted command to enter. With a steadying breath, she did so.

Of all the opulent rooms in the mansion, the study was the most opulent of all, filled with priceless antiques, art and Persian rugs. The mahogany paneling and cabinetry were so rich that they warmed the entire space, the leather chairs so buttery-soft that sitting in them was like sinking into a toasty cloud. A stained-glass border decorated every window; handmade glass tiles surrounded the fireplace; and leather-bound first editions lined the bookshelves.

It was impressive.

Her father sat at the centerpiece, a massive desk that had once belonged to some czar or king, his cell phone to his ear. He waved her to a chair across from him, then ignored her while he ended the call. When he laid the phone down, he fixed a stare on her.

Resisting the urge to squirm, she smiled. "Good morning, sir. You're back early."

"Of course I am. How could I finish the trip on schedule after what Coy told me?"

"What was that, sir?"

He leaned forward, a tactic that most people found intimidating. Kylie was no different. "That you were with Norris yesterday—all day. You were with him when I called you. You went out to the Franklin place with him."

And I spent last night with him, she wanted to say. *I brought him into this house, showed him my room, showed him your room.* Wisely, though, she kept her mouth shut.

"What are you doing, Kylie?"

She clasped her hands loosely in her lap, forcing them to remain relaxed. If her fingers knotted, he would notice. If anything at all was indicative of stress, he would see it and use it. "I'm keeping an eye on Jake. As I told you yesterday—"

"Yeah, yeah, keep your friends close and your enemies closer."

"You didn't have a problem with it then."

"I thought we were discussing one meal. A couple hours of your time. Coy tells me it's been a hell of a lot more than that. Exactly what is it you think you can accomplish by hanging out with this guy?"

"I'll know what he knows." *I'll find out whether you're the man I always believed you were or if you're no better than the common criminals you used to prosecute.*

Her father had always been her hero. He'd come from nothing, pulled himself up, gained power and influence. As district attorney, he'd upheld the law; as senator, he'd made the law, and he'd done it all for the greater good.

At least that was the story he and her mother had told her. The first part was definitely true. He'd come from nothing, had been the first in his family to graduate from high school, had put himself through college and law school with the G.I. Bill, scholarships, loans and working more jobs than any three people could have handled. Then he'd married into the Colby family. It was easy to gain power and influence when your in-laws had it in spades.

The upholding-the-law part…it appeared that was questionable.

He didn't look very heroic this morning. His gray hair was neatly combed, as always. He wore a conservative white shirt, steel-gray suit and burgundy tie—practically a uniform for him-that fitted as if custom-made, which, tie aside, they were. He was clean-shaven, and his skin had a healthy glow after days in the Florida sun.

But he looked worried. On edge. Trying, as always, to hide it but failing. Jake's purpose in town concerned him.

Because he had something to hide.

"Norris has an agenda."

"Of course he does," she said evenly. "He's here to research a book, to gather as much information about the Charley Baker case as possible—a task that you're not making easy for him."

The senator's brows arched. "Me? I've been out of town."

"And in regular contact with Judge Markham and Chief Roberts." She sat straighter in the chair, her expression bland, her voice emotionless. "Chief Roberts has been abusing his authority by assigning officers to harass Jake. Someone removed the old newspapers from the library archives and persuaded the publisher to make his copies unavailable. Judge Markham says you told him to destroy the trial transcript. And Therese Franklin never asked you to stop this book."

The temperature around the desk dropped a few frosty degrees as her father stared at her. His mouth opened and closed a few times, then settled into a harsh line. "I cannot believe my own daughter is sitting here in my study, in my house, saying these things to me. I don't control Coy Roberts's every move. If his officers are harassing Norris, then I can only assume that Norris has done something to warrant it. I don't know what's going on with the newspapers and I would never condone the destruction of court records. If Hal Markham told you I did, he's a damned liar."

Kylie gazed at him, stiff and still. Some part of her had hoped the senator would deny everything, but in her fantasy she'd believed him. Now, for the first time in her entire life, she didn't believe him. She wanted to. He certainly sounded indignant enough to be telling the truth.

And what he said made sense. Chief Roberts was a grown man, capable of independent thought and action. There were plenty of explanations for the disappearance of the microfilm from the library—mischief, theft, misplacement. The newspaper owner sending everything to Houston could just be coincidence. And Judge Markham could have lied, could be senile, could have misunderstood. But…

"What about Therese?"

His blue gaze, always alert, sharpened. Was he trying to remember exactly what he'd said to her about Therese on Wednesday? She could help him. She remembered it verbatim. *She pleaded with me, Kylie. She begged me to not let Norris do this, and I told her I would do my best to dissuade him.*

The senator apparently decided to bluff it out. "I told you—she called Hal about Norris, all upset and asking him to put a stop to Norris's snooping around. He asked me for help, and I told him I would do what I could to persuade Norris to drop it."

Ice crept through Kylie. He sounded so sincere that if she hadn't taken part in the conversation herself, she would have believed him. Her lungs tightening in her chest, she murmured, "Dissuade."

Her father frowned at her. "What?"

"You said you would dissuade him. Not persuade."

"You're right. That sounds more like me." He gestured impatiently. "You remember the conversation. Why are you asking me?"

"You said she pleaded with *you*."

Shadows passed through his eyes, along with the slightest hint of guilt, but both were gone so quickly she might have imagined them. "No, I didn't. I haven't talked to that girl since her grandfather's funeral."

You said it to me! Kylie wanted to shout. *You lied to me!* And he was lying again, boldly, well aware that she knew it and not caring.

If you repeat something often enough, people will begin to believe it. More of her mother's words of wisdom. Did he think if he denied the conversation she would ignore what she knew for fact and accept his version instead?

"You're letting that bastard stir up trouble, Kylie," her father went on. "Worse, you're *helping* him. You say you're 'keeping your enemy close'—" derision curved his mouth "—but I don't believe you. You're infatuated with this man and you're helping him destroy innocent people all for the sake of his dirty little book. Has he seduced you yet? Has he told you how beautiful you are, how special you are? Because I guarantee you it's coming. He'll get you into bed and twist you around his little finger, and you'll believe his lies and forget all about the people who matter. I forbid you to see him again."

Kylie stood, smoothing her skirt, filling her aching lungs with air before giving him a thin smile. "I'm not a little girl, sir. You can't forbid me to see anyone. As a matter of fact, I'm meeting Jake for breakfast this morning and I'm already late. As Lissa told you, I'm taking a few days off, so I'm not going in to the office today, but I'm sure I'll see you soon."

Leaving him flustered and openmouthed, she walked to the door, then turned back. "By the way, sir, you don't have to worry about him seducing me. *I* seduced *him* last night. Three times. Right there in my own bed." With another chilly smile, she walked out, down the hall and the stairs, through the house and to her car. She waved at Alberto as she passed, exited the gate and drove on autopilot to the Pancake Palace.

There she started shaking. She couldn't shut off the engine. Couldn't release her grip on the steering wheel. Couldn't catch her breath. Shivers wracked her, but sweat popped out on her forehead. Her chest was tight, her vision tunneled, and rushing filled her ears, drowning out everything but the pounding of her heart.

A second beat joined in, louder, more solid. Eyes shut, she tried to block it out, but it was persistent. So was the voice calling her name. Jake's voice.

She managed to turn her head and saw him bent beside the car, rapping on the window. His gaze was worried, his mouth moving in words she couldn't comprehend. It took her several tries, but eventually she stabbed the button that unlocked the door, and he jerked it open.

"Kylie, are you all right? What's wrong?" he demanded, crouching beside the car, reaching in to peel her fingers from the wheel.

The panic receded, the quaking slowing to occasional tremors. She drew a shaky breath, wiped the sweat from her face, then turned off the key. "I—I—"

"Come here, darlin'." He undid her seat belt, then lifted her from the car and into his embrace. One arm settled around her waist; his other hand stroked slowly, reassuringly, up and down her spine. He murmured soft words— *It's okay, you're all right*—that meant little but sounded good. *Nothing* was okay…except this. His arms. His comfort. His voice.

After a time, she lifted her head, calmer, steadier, and gave him a wobbly smile. "I'm sorry I'm late."

"Hey, no matter. It gave me time to mainline a gallon of coffee." He studied her, his dark gaze intense, then snuggled her to his side. "You need food."

She considered it a moment. Yes, she did. Food might fill that gnawing, throbbing emptiness inside her.

Inside the restaurant, she felt a moment's relief that no one was paying them undue attention…and a moment's regret that Jake had dropped his arm from her waist when they'd walked in the door. He gestured toward a booth along the front window where a cup of coffee cooled between two menus, and she gratefully slid onto one bench. Her feet bumped his backpack on the floor.

The waitress brought another cup, filled it with strong black coffee and took their orders before Jake spoke again. "What happened?"

She stirred sweetener and powdered cream into the coffee, then grimaced. "My father came home this morning and he looked me in the eye and he…" She felt disloyal even thinking the words, doubly so for saying them out loud.

"He *lied*."

* * *

"Jillian Franklin was a bitch."

The pronouncement came from Serena Whitley, on whose porch they sat. It didn't take Jake by surprise—in his experience, people often spoke ill of the dead—though it made Kylie blink.

"I thought you were friends."

"Oh, we were," Sheila Browning said. "But that doesn't change the facts. She was greedy, manipulative—"

"The biggest flirt you ever saw," Paula McCormack chimed in. "She loved being the center of attention."

"Male attention," Serena clarified drily.

"And she made sure she got it. She dressed provocatively—"

"Behaved provocatively."

"Looked at every man as if she just might devour him."

"*Did* devour more than a few, according to rumor." Serena lifted her coffee cup in salute to her friends, and all three women laughed.

Jake imagined the women knew exactly what kind of look they were talking about. In fact, the newly divorced Paula had looked at *him* as if he were dessert more than once.

So these were Phyllis Riordan's best friends since high school. They were lovely, spoiled and pampered, and he'd bet their tongues could be more lethal than any weapon known to man. There was a brittleness about them, a subdued meanness that simmered just below the surface. Was that how Phyllis had been? Probably, which meant poor Kylie had struck out with both parents.

"How was her marriage?" he asked, forcing his attention back from Kylie, sitting at his side.

The women exchanged glances, then shrugged in unison. "Bert was nearly twenty years older than Jillian," Serena said. "How do you think it was?"

"Was she his second wife?"

"No. He was a confirmed bachelor until she decided he wanted her. How does that saying go? He chased her until she caught him?"

"She had affairs?"

Another group look, another group shrug.

Jake gazed across the lawn to the street. Was that where Riordan and Roberts had come up with the theory that Charley was having an affair with Jillian? Because according to rumors she'd had more than a few? "Do you know who she supposedly slept with?"

Look, shrug, then Paula said, "It was rumor, honey. Frankly I didn't want to know."

Had her husband been one of them? In filling him in on the way over, Kylie had briefly covered Paula's recent divorce—after thirty years of infidelity and insults, she'd taken her husband to the cleaners. He'd managed to hold on to his family home and his name, but that was about all.

Jake shifted in the wicker chair, making it squeak. "What about Charley Baker?"

Serena's smile was sultry. "He was a handsome man. Tall. Dark. Muscular. He was Indian—I guess we're supposed to call them Native American now."

She'd managed to surprise him. He would have guessed that the people who lived in these few blocks of Riverview never knew the common folk existed. "You knew him?"

"Oh, no. He worked for my husband—Jack used to own the glass factory—and I saw him at the trial. I can see how a woman would be tempted."

"Was Jillian tempted?"

"Coy Roberts said so. Kylie's daddy said so." Paula's apple-red lips pursed, then relaxed. "But *she* never said so. I don't think he was her type."

"Because he was Indian?" Jake asked.

Leaning forward, Paula brushed her hand seductively over his knee. "Don't be silly. Because he didn't have any money. Jillian loved money. She married for it. Rumor had it that when she died, she left a *whole* lot of it in an account in her name only at First Security Bank."

And that was significant because Bert had been president of First National. "Where did rumor say this money came from?"

"Nobody knew," Sheila replied.

"Maybe it was family money," Jake suggested.

Serena snorted. "Her family didn't *have* any money. That was why she married Bert in the first place. He had plenty of money, and she was all too happy to spend it for him."

"Maybe she was saving money that he gave her," Kylie said. She'd been pretty quiet all morning—pretty shaken by her run-in with her father.

Jake felt guilty for the disillusionment he'd seen in her eyes more than once through breakfast. He wasn't to blame for whatever Riordan had done, but he felt as if he was. He only hoped Kylie didn't blame him, too. Didn't come to hate him.

"He gave her a lot of money," Serena agreed, "but she spent a lot. There's no way she could have saved that much. We're talking six figures."

"Saving for a rainy day?" Jake asked drily.

Serena gave him a cynical smile. "Honey, with money like that, she was saving for a damn global flood."

After a moment's silence, he looked at each of the women in turn. "Do you believe Charley Baker killed her?"

This time the women didn't exchange glances. Serena sipped her coffee. Sheila examined her manicure. Paula gazed off into the distance. Finally, though, came the shrugs, first from Serena.

"I like to think he did. Better to have *someone* locked up than to never know."

Next Sheila, who nodded in agreement.

Then Paula. It took her a moment to refocus her gaze, first on Kylie, then Jake. "I think other people had better reasons to want her dead...but I'm not a cop or a district attorney. What do I know?"

Her hunch was probably better than the cops' or the D.A.'s. After all, she didn't have something to hide—at least, he was guessing, nothing criminal.

He thanked the women for their time, stood and followed Kylie to the steps. Halfway there, she turned back. "I remember going to the Franklins' house. Is that something my family did a lot?"

Once again there was no shared look or shrug. The others let Serena answer, and she did so with a studied level of indifference. "No more than the rest of us, I suppose. Most of that summer, we were all out there once a week or so for cookouts in the backyard, letting the kids swim in the pond, drinks by the fountain."

Most of that summer, Jake mused. "What happened to stop the visits?"

Serena met his gaze, hers steady and sharp. "They died."

With a nod, he took Kylie's arm and walked to the car with her. She fastened her seat belt, waited until he'd pulled away from the curb, then spoke his thoughts aloud. "They died in late September. That's not summer."

To most mothers—and all three of those women had

children—summer ended when school began, a full month before the murders. Had Jillian and the others had a falling-out before her death? Something like…oh, getting caught with one or more of their husbands?

Could that possibly be all Jim Riordan was hiding? An affair?

How much would it have cost him? Possibly his marriage. His father-in-law's support. His wife's fortune. His political ambitions. Was that incentive enough to send an innocent man to prison?

Jake tried to consider the question without his dislike for the senator coloring the answer. Whether he succeeded, though, was questionable, because he kept reaching the same conclusion. *Yes.* For a man like Riordan, whose own daughter came second to his ambition, absolutely yes.

"What now?" that daughter asked.

"Where would we find Therese Franklin?"

"Turn right at the corner. She does transcription for the local hospital, and when her grandparents got so frail, she began working from home. Even though her grandfather died and her grandmother's in an assisted-care facility, she still works there." Kylie's voice softened. "I wonder how hard it will be for her to learn these things about her mother."

"She doesn't remember her parents at all. She doesn't feel connected to them."

"But they're still her parents. That must mean something."

A familiar tickle of guilt edged along his spine. "She wants to know."

For the first time since he'd left her house at dawn, Kylie's smile was genuine. "I'm not suggesting you should back off or sugarcoat the truth for her. I'm just wondering."

"Maybe someone who's learning a few tough things

about her own parents can help her adjust." He regretted the words as soon as they were out, because her smile faded and the somber expression returned.

Grateful that Therese's house was so close, he pulled to the curb a moment later. As they got out of the car, a police car turned onto the street at the far end of the block and approached them at a crawl. The driver—Chief Roberts himself—rolled the window down and fixed a steely stare on them. Jake stared back for a moment, then stepped onto the sidewalk and started across the yard. Realizing that Kylie wasn't following, he backtracked, found her returning the chief's scrutiny glare for icy glare, caught her hand and pulled her along with him.

As Jake rang the doorbell, he swore he could feel the moment Roberts turned the next corner—could feel the anger and animosity evaporate once he was out of sight, though he was still well aware of Kylie's own anger and animosity. His hand throbbed from her grip. He gave it a shake, drawing her attention back from the now-empty street, and said mildly, "Hey, I write with that hand."

"Sorry," she murmured and let go as Therese opened the door.

"Jake," Therese said with real pleasure. "I was hoping to see you again. And Kylie. This is a surprise. Come in, please."

The house was located in the right part of town, but was half the size or less than its neighbors. It had good bones, but everything Jake saw on the way to a small, sunny room at the back looked as if it was home to someone still living in the 1940s. Her grandparents, apparently, hadn't seen reason to change a thing over the years, and now that she lived there alone, neither had she.

Therese, looking like a wingless fairy in a swirly pastel

dress that reached practically to her ankles, offered them coffee or tea, but they declined. She saved the files on the computer that occupied one corner, then perched on an ottoman in front of the sofa where he and Kylie sat. "I didn't realize you two had met. Though it's logical, of course. Surely you would want to speak to the senator, and to do that you have to go through Kylie."

"I haven't spoken to him yet," Jake said drily. "Can I ask you a personal question?"

Therese smiled. "You're writing a book about my parents' murders. I can't imagine any other kind."

"What kind of estate did your parents leave?"

"The house. Some commercial rental property in Oklahoma City. Stocks. Life insurance. Some jewelry that had been in my father's family for generations. Some cash."

"Were you their sole heir?" The first rule of a murder investigation, his cop friend had told him, was to look at who would profit from the death. Obviously a three-year-old was beyond suspicion, but if someone else had benefited...

"Yes, I was. My father's close family was gone, and my mother apparently saw no reason to share with her family." Her face turned pink as she hastily continued, "Not that my grandparents would have wanted to inherit anything. It broke their hearts when she and my father died. They were named my guardians and were allowed access to the money to support me, but they never used any of it. Granddad continued to work and pay the bills right up until his death."

"He worked all his life at the glass factory, didn't he?" Kylie asked. At Therese's nod, she went on. "Did he know Charley Baker?"

"I have no idea. My guess would be yes—it's not that

big a place—but he and Grandmother never discussed what happened."

"How was your inheritance set up?" Jake asked.

"My grandparents had control, with a court-appointed trustee overseeing, until I turned twenty-one, when everything came directly to me."

"Do you know if there was money from a bank account of your mother's?"

Her gaze turned distant as she considered it. "There was a lot of money. I honestly don't know where it all came from. But my grandparents' lawyer must have a copy of the will and records on the various accounts. I can ask him."

"Who is it?"

"Tim Jenkins. They'd been using him since long before he became a big criminal lawyer." Abruptly she seemed to realize that it was her parents' murder that had made Jenkins a big criminal lawyer and shuddered.

Jake felt the weight of Kylie's look and met her gaze. How convenient. Of course, Jenkins should have given Therese a copy of all the records regarding her parents' estate. What had he told her? *Don't worry your pretty little head. I'll take care of everything?* Had he suspected four years ago that problems might arise in the future or had he just been extraordinarily cautious? Or extraordinarily guilty?

"What about your parents' personal papers? Bank statements, bills, receipts—the sort of thing we all keep?"

Before she could answer, the phone on the desk rang. "It's probably just my boss at the hospital," she said with a dismissive gesture. "The machine will get it. As far as I know, everything is still—"

The answering machine clicked on, and Derek West's voice floated into the room. "Pick up the phone, Therese…come on, I know you're there. I know who else is there, too. Damn it, Therese, I *told* you—" He broke off, then exhaled loudly. "Sorry. I didn't mean— Look, just call me as soon as you get this message. Okay?"

After the machine disconnected, an unnatural silence settled over the room. Therese was blushing, but there was also a hint of annoyance beneath the color. Jake kept his voice low, his tone conversational. "What did he tell you?"

"Not to talk to you. To just forget about all this." Her smile was unsteady. "People have told me what to do and what to forget my whole life. I didn't even know my parents had been murdered until I was in high school. I'm not going to spend the rest of my life knowing nothing about them or why they died just because everyone thinks I'm too fragile to handle it."

Define everyone, Jake wanted to request. The chief? The senator? Judge Markham? Tim Jenkins?

"I've been through this house, taking care of my grandfather's affairs, getting my grandmother's in order, and there's nothing of my parents' here. I know the furniture, the clothing, the dishes—all that stuff is still at our old house. Once the sheriff was finished with his investigation, Grandfather locked up that house, and as far as I know, no one's ever been inside since."

"Do you have the key?" Kylie asked.

Jake's muscles stiffened as he half hoped Therese would say no. He didn't want to go back to the Franklin house, didn't want to go inside and remember that Saturday morning all too clearly. The house had smelled of death, and in his imagination it still would. He would still see the blood, still feel the evil.

But if Therese gave them access, he would go inside and

smell the smell, feel the feelings. For Charley, he would do anything.

She sat motionless for a long time before rising from the hassock and going to the fireplace mantel. She brought back a carved wooden box, set it on her lap and lifted the lid. On top was a photograph that she held a moment or two before handing it to Jake.

Bert and Jillian Franklin, standing on the dock at the pond out behind their and the Bakers' houses. He wore shorts and a T-shirt that showed a paunch, and the sun lit the gray strands in his hair. She wore a bikini that showed not one extra ounce of fat and she held Therese, maybe two years old and in a kiddie bikini of her own, on one hip. Jillian was smiling for the camera, lovely, sultry, provocative. A *bitch*, her best friends had called her. Always rude, Angela had said, often in more colorful terms. Unfaithful to her husband and apparently guilty of some underhanded activity to fund her secret bank account.

And Therese's mother. It was easy to lose sight of that.

He passed the photo to Kylie, who studied it. "I remember..." Her voice trailed away, her forehead wrinkling as if she'd lost the distant memory she'd been seeking.

Next Therese removed a set of rings—the man's band plain gold, the woman's gold with a row of small diamonds, the engagement ring with small diamonds flanking a rock in the center. She took out a small gold cross on a delicate chain, a silver lighter engraved with Bert's initials and, finally, two keys looped together with a wire tie. "I always thought...someday I might go out there...after my grandparents were..."

With a sigh, she clutched the keys tightly for a moment before offering them to Jake. He wrapped his own fingers tightly around them. As Kylie handed the picture back, he asked, "Can I get a copy of that?" He had pictures of both Jillian and Bert, both dead and alive, but none that included Therese. He wanted the reminder that whatever else Jillian had been, she'd also been a mother who'd loved her daughter.

"You can have that. It *is* a copy. The original's upstairs in my room." She gave it to him, and he slid it inside his backpack, then stood.

"If Derek or anyone asks, tell them you gave us your permission to be there." He wouldn't put it past Roberts to have them thrown in jail just for the harassment value.

"I will." She smiled faintly. "I hope you find something of interest."

Jake was sure they would.

Chapter 8

"Tell me about C.J.," Kylie requested as Jake made a tight U-turn, then headed for Main Street. Listening to Therese, seeing the photo of her with the parents she couldn't remember, had made Kylie blue enough. Might as well get really down by hearing about the other child whose life had changed forever twenty-two years ago.

Jake kept his attention on the street ahead except for frequent glances in the rearview mirror. She didn't bother to twist around and look. If they were being followed, she didn't want to know. Didn't care.

"He's grown," Jake said, using that distant voice again. "He's not married. He sees his mother a couple times a month and his father three or four times a year. Not that a maximum-security penitentiary is an ideal place for family reunions. He likes his job, he travels a lot and it would mean everything to him to see his father cleared."

"What was it like for him after his father was arrested?"

Finally Jake spared her a wry glance. "What do you think? It was the best time of his life." He signaled to turn west onto Main. "It was a tough time. He had nightmares about discovering the bodies. He didn't believe for an instant that his father was guilty. His mother lost her job the same afternoon Charley was arrested. The kids at school made life miserable, and he got his ass kicked a couple times trying to defend Charley. His dad was in jail and wasn't getting out, they had no money and no hope of getting any and pretty much everyone in town wanted them gone. So they left."

Who was to blame for all that? Certainly not C.J. The boss who'd fired Angela. The kids who'd targeted C.J. Their parents for not teaching them better. The school for not protecting him better.

The senator and his associates.

Or were they accomplices?

"Do you ever get depressed by all this?"

Jake looked at her long enough to send the car drifting across the highway's center line. When she gestured, he steered back into their own lane, then shrugged. "It's other people's lives. Other people's sorrows."

She knew he was pretending uninvolvement. She'd heard his voice, expressionless and removed from the moment, when he talked about events. She was convinced it was how he protected himself, because it was something she'd learned to do, too.

"But don't you get worn down? You can tell the story. You can get the truth out there and give your readers an understanding of what happened, of what these people have gone through, but in the end you can't *change* any of it. The victims you write about are still dead. Their families are still mourning them."

"But I tell their stories and that's enough. And, on one lucky occasion, I did change things."

The new trial, the acquittal. Surely that was what Charley Baker, as well as his son, was hoping for—to clear his name, to get back the life taken from him twenty-two years ago. And it looked as if that might actually happen.

At the cost of the senator's career.

Jake well might give C.J. Baker his father…while taking away Kylie's. Already their relationship had been damaged. No matter what eventually happened, she and the senator couldn't go back to life as usual. He couldn't climb back onto that pedestal she'd put him on, couldn't regain the respect he'd thrown away in the past few days.

Could she continue to work for him? Did she even want to? She honestly didn't know. She'd worked for him nearly half her life, had gotten a college degree that he could use, had gone straight from her part-time job during school to a full-time career without considering any other options. Now she might be all out of options. She might have no choice but to find a new job, a new home, a new town.

"You're looking kind of worn down," Jake commented as he turned off the highway onto the road that led to the Franklin house. He slowed to a stop, then twisted to face her. "Do you want to go back to town? I can do this by myself."

His last words didn't sound very positive. She didn't blame him. She wasn't looking forward to spending time inside that house and she knew less about the case and the people involved than he did. She'd never met Charley Baker…though she thought she would like to. She would like to judge for herself what kind of man he was.

As if she had any expertise at that.

"No," she said, and relief flashed through his dark eyes. "It'll go quicker with two of us. I want to go. It's all just...sad."

As he pressed the accelerator, he mused, "I wonder how much money Therese has. Sounds like a lot, but you'd never guess it to look at her."

Kylie feigned an indignant look. "I'm not sure whether that's a compliment or an insult *or* how it applies to me. Do I look like I have money?"

He grinned. "Darlin', you look rich from the top of your head to the tips of your pink-painted toes. I took one look at you in the senator's office and thought you were *way* too well paid for a mere aide. Of course, that was before I knew who you really were."

"That was your first thought?" She smacked his forearm. "That I looked overpaid?"

"Actually, my first thought was that you looked like a goddess. And that I have a real weakness for brown-eyed blondes. And that you have damn fine legs. I didn't get to 'overpaid' until after you damn near froze me with your haughtiness."

"I wasn't haughty," she protested but not vehemently. She had learned haughtiness from the best teacher in the world—her mother.

"I didn't know which I wanted more," Jake went on, "to tweak you or kiss you."

"You've managed to do both quite nicely over the past few days." Gazing out the window, she recognized the place where the black SUV had run them off the road the day before. Jake was right. They'd chosen the safest place to do it. But something still could have gone wrong. He could have been injured or killed. Would the senator have felt even a moment's guilt then?

Or did he have prior experience with involvement in a person's death?

The closer they got to the Franklin house, the thicker the air in the car became. It came from Jake and wrapped itself around her, making her wish they could turn around, go back to her house and spend the rest of the day having hot sex instead. But she didn't make the suggestion and neither did he.

The gate still stood open. The house still stood empty and abandoned. He parked where Charley had parked, and they followed the path that C.J. had followed to the porch, where Jake stopped at the bottom of the steps.

Kylie stopped, too, and watched him stare at the house. *Other people's sorrows*, he'd said, but they touched him, too. A certain level of empathy was required in his job; if he didn't care about the people he wrote about, how could his readers?

She didn't know how long they stood there—long enough for her to grow warm under the midday sun. Five minutes? Ten? It didn't matter.

Finally Jake straightened his shoulders and fished the keys from his pocket. He raised his foot to the first step, and wood splintered above them, accompanied by a small *crack*.

She raised her gaze to the small hole in the wall next to the door, for an instant too puzzled to realize what she was looking at. Then came another *crack*, and another hole, and Jake shoved her to the ground. She hit hard, jarring her shoulder, weeds and paving stones scraping her bare legs, his weight squeezing the air from her lungs.

"Son of a bitch," he muttered as he half crawled, half scuttled to the end of the porch, dragging her with him, and around the corner into the scant shelter where the porch met the house.

"What the—"

A third *crack* interrupted her, followed rapidly by a fourth, and understanding dawned. Dear God, someone was *shooting* at them! With a *gun!*

The tremors started in her belly and worked their way out until she was shaking from head to toe. Jake's body pressed hers against the concrete foundation, and she pressed her face to his back, murmuring—whimpering— a frantic prayer. *Oh, God, oh, God, oh, God.*

The fourth shot was followed by silence, then moments later the distant sounds of an engine revving, of tires squeal- ing. Long after the sound faded away, Jake rolled over to face her, gathered her in his arms and just held her.

He was shaking, too, she realized and felt better for her own reaction. She burrowed closer to him, trying to crawl right inside him, and held on tightly until her fingers went numb and her muscles began to ache.

"They tried to kill us," she whispered.

Slowly Jake sat up, looked toward the woods from which the shots had come, then eased to his feet. He helped her up, too, supported her until her legs were steady, then brushed the dirt and dead grass first from her, then himself.

"I don't think so," he said at last.

"They took four shots at us!"

"And missed by a yard every time." He pulled her back to the steps and climbed the porch without hesitation this time. "This one—" he pointed to the first hole "—was a couple feet above our heads. This one was six feet to the right. When we moved to the right, he fired the next two several feet to the left. He wasn't trying to hit us."

She stared at the evidence. "Just to scare us," she murmured. "Well, he did a damn good job. I'm scared."

Jake turned once again to stare at the woods. "We weren't followed when we left Therese's."

"You're sure?"

He gave her a dry look. "I've had enough run-ins with cops lately. I'm sure."

"So…did they just guess that we would come back here?"

"I doubt it. Remember what Derek said in his message to Therese? 'Call me as soon as you get this.'"

And Therese, who'd been told her entire life what to do, had probably called him as soon as they'd walked out the door. And if Derek asked, Jake had told her to tell him she'd given them permission to search her parents' house. Even without being asked, she wouldn't have thought twice about sharing the information. She never would have believed he might take a few shots at them.

Kylie was having a little trouble believing it herself. Okay, she admitted ashamedly, she could believe Coy Roberts would risk having one of his men shoot at Jake. But at *her?* What if his aim had been off? Wouldn't it enrage her father if *she'd* been shot?

The senator viewed every election as a battle. He had a battle plan, a war chest and a motto. *If you're not for me, then you're against me.* And he showed no mercy to those against him.

Did he consider her one of the enemy now?

"I'm going to take you back to town," Jake said grimly. "You can clean up and go to work, go shopping or do nothing at all, but you can't stay here."

When he tried to grab her hand, she clasped them behind her back and took a few steps away. "The hell I can't. I'm safe with you—"

"Apparently not," he said with a snort.

"Then maybe you're safer with me. You're not staying here by yourself. You need me here." And she needed to be there. Needed to see for herself whatever he found. Needed to know he wouldn't be tempted to sugarcoat the truth for her.

Scowling, Jake loomed over her. "So far, they've just been screwing with me. Getting run off the road, getting shot at— they just wanted to scare me off. What if they get serious? What if the next time they're really trying to stop us?"

She drew a deep breath to level her voice. "Then I'll need to know so I can do something about it. My father's not the only one in the family with influence. He's a Riordan. I'm a Colby. I know senators, representatives, the governor. The daughter of the head of the Oklahoma State Bureau of Investigation is a sorority sister of mine. The attorney general is my grandfather's godson. I call him Uncle Frank. If they seriously try to stop us, I can get someone to stop *them*."

He was wavering—she could see it in his eyes, in the flare of his nostrils, the set of his mouth. He wanted to send her away for her own safety…but he could use her.

Finally he ran his fingers through his hair, then plucked a weed from her hair. "All right." His tone was grudging, but that was all right. He would get over it.

One of the two keys fit the padlock on the door; the other went to the dead bolt. He unfastened both, hesitated, then turned the knob.

The door opened with a creak on rusty hinges, casting a wedge of light into the foyer. Dust covered the wood floor and floated on the air, drifting along with a strong musty odor. Twenty-two years without disturbance. Even the vandals who would destroy anything had done nothing more than break out the upstairs windows. Even they had realized this was a desolate place better left alone.

Jake entered first, his boots leaving distinct prints in the dust. Kylie was a few steps behind him. Her palms were damp and her chest was tight.

Jillian had spared no expense on the house. The flooring, beneath all its dirt, looked like aged heart of pine. A top-quality Persian runner extended the length of the hall, and there were antiques everywhere.

There was also, just inside the arched doorway into the living room, an ugly dark stain on the floor, soaked into the very fibers of the wood. *Blood.*

"Jillian died right there," Jake said numbly. "Stabbed eleven times in the neck, chest and abdomen. The authorities said the number of wounds indicated rage, and the fact that her face was untouched suggested the killer loved her."

If something that warped could be called love, Kylie thought as she walked past him into the shadowy room. She avoided the bloodstain and glanced at the photos that covered most flat surfaces. Bert and Jillian on tropical beaches, on a sailboat, in snowy mountains. In London, Paris, Rome. A wedding portrait, a first anniversary photo, a pregnant Jillian, a newborn Therese.

In the photographs they looked like the typical happy family…and maybe they had been. Just because Kylie could never be happy with a spouse who was unfaithful didn't mean Bert hadn't been. He'd had a beautiful wife and a daughter whom he'd clearly adored. Maybe he'd seen her infidelity as a fair trade-off.

Another arched doorway led into the dining room, where one chair was knocked to the floor and a sterling candlestick lay on its side in the middle of the table, next to a vase of long-dead flowers.

"The theory is that Charley came to the house to persuade Jillian to leave Bert and run off with him." Jake circled the opposite side of the table, stopping in front of one boarded-up window. "She refused, they argued and he stabbed her. Bert came in, saw what he had done and ran through this room, trying to make it to the back door, where his car was parked just a few yards away. Charley caught him in the kitchen, stabbed him once in the heart, then left."

Kylie was shaking her head by the time he finished. She stepped around the fallen chair and continued through yet another arch into the kitchen. Another stain marked the floor there, near a marble-topped island beneath a pot rack.

"There are so many holes in that theory." She opened a door into a butler's pantry with every small appliance a cook could ever need, then closed it and leaned against it to face Jake. "Charley was charged with second-degree murder in Jillian's case because he didn't come here intending to kill her and with first-degree murder for Bert because he killed him while in the commission of a felony."

Jake nodded. "The weapon was presumably the butcher knife missing from that set." He gestured to a wood block at the back of one counter that held eight knives in its nine slots.

"So he comes here, they argue, he comes into the kitchen, gets a knife and kills her in the living room. And he does this while Bert is home and liable to walk in any minute."

Nodding again, Jake wondered if she was as cool as she appeared. Was her skin crawling at all? Did she feel the evil or was the place simply sad to her?

"Then Bert does walk in. He sees what Charley's done and is horrified. He fears for his life and he tries to flee the house. Alone."

"Leaving his three-year-old daughter upstairs. No way. She was everything to him. He would have died to protect her." Just as Charley would have died to protect *him*. "What if the murder had nothing to do with Jillian? They came up with a theory and manipulated the facts to fit it. But instead of Bert dying because he saw Jillian killed, what if it was the other way around? If Bert was the target and Jillian was the witness?"

"If someone killed him, she walked in, screamed, ran— maybe trying to get upstairs to Therese—and he caught her and killed her." She shrugged. "It makes more sense than Bert intending to abandon Therese with a murderer in the house."

Jake massaged his temple with one hand. "Even so, the rest of their theory holds up—gets even stronger, in fact. They'd say Charley killed Bert to get him out of the way, thinking that would leave him a clear field with Jillian. But she still rejected him, even after he killed for her, so she had to die, too."

Kylie heaved a sigh, then pushed away from the door. "This isn't helping us with what we came here for. I'm going to start in Jillian's bedroom. See if she kept any mementos of an affair with Charley or anyone else."

His first impulse was to go with her, but he restrained it. He was doing okay. He could handle searching the downstairs rooms by himself.

There was a built-in desk near the pantry, clearly Jillian's domain. A fabric-covered bulletin board held recipes, a phone number or two and a few photographs of Therese, and the drawers were filled with pens, paper clips and other supplies. Cookbooks lined the shelves above. He flipped through each one, looking for a note tucked inside, but found only loose recipes.

Down the hall on the left was Bert's study, a large room with dark paneling and burgundy drapes. The bits of light leaking in around the boarded windows were barely sufficient to illuminate his way across the room. A porcelain coffee cup sat on the desk, dried residue darkening the inside, and a checkbook, a stack of bills and a pen rested on a leather pad. Bert had been in the middle of paying bills when he'd died. What a way to spend his final minutes—tedium, then terror.

Jake searched the desk and the credenza, then opened the top drawer in the file cabinet. Every folder was neatly labeled, but the lighting was too bad to make out the faded type. In the pantry he located a box of trash bags, emptied the contents of the file cabinet into one, then left it near the front door.

There was a library, a sunroom, a utility room and four closets on the first floor. None of them held anything of interest. He climbed the stairs to the second floor and followed the faint sounds Kylie was making to the master suite. It was brighter up there, with no boards over the windows, no glass in the frames. On the downside, instead of a thick layer of dust, everything in the room was crusted with dirt. Leaves littered the carpet and the bed, and water damage showed near each window.

Kylie had gathered a small pile of items on the bed—a jewelry box, some framed photos, a red leather address book. He flipped through the book before dropping it back and turning to look for her. "Find anything?"

Her voice came from the closet. "Birth control pills in Jillian's bathroom and condoms in the back of her nightstand drawer."

"To protect from pregnancy with her husband and disease with her lovers?" He moved to stand in the closet door. It was bigger than his bedroom back home and was filled to overflowing: rod after rod of clothing, shelves of shoes and purses, a built-in dresser housing drawers filled with scarves, stockings and lingerie—the sexy, wispy pieces he would expect of the photographed woman in the bikini.

"That would be my guess. Jeez, her friends weren't exaggerating when they said she spent a lot of money. She must have been a favorite customer at every high-end shop within driving distance." Kylie was on her knees, pulling out drawers, feeling beneath them, looking behind them. When she finished with the last, he offered his hand and helped her to her feet. She took a step away, stubbing her toe against the dresser, knocking a strip of wood at the bottom loose. She looked at it, looked at him, then knelt again.

The molding fitted easily back into place when she pushed on it and came away easily when she pulled. She removed it completely and held it up to the light coming in the door so he could see there were no nails, no glue. The piece on the end nearest him didn't so much as wiggle when he nudged it; neither did the one at her end.

Bending low, she looked into the space underneath the bottom drawer, then gingerly reached in. When she pulled out a folder and offered it to him, his stomach knotted.

The folder contained bank statements, filed with the most recent on top, for a savings account in the name of Jillian Franklin and showing a mailing address of a post office box in the nearby town of Bristow. The final statement was for the month before her death, and the amount was well over three hundred thousand dollars.

"Wow," Kylie murmured. "What was she doing? Prostituting herself? Robbing banks? Stealing Bert blind?"

Jake scanned the activity for the final month—four deposits, no withdrawals. It was the same for the previous month—same dates, same amounts—and the month before that and the month..." Or maybe blackmailing someone. Considering the different dates and amounts, maybe four someones."

She had reached out to steady his hand so she could see, too, but suddenly her own hand trembled too badly. He knew she was wondering if her father was one of those four—knew she was afraid he was.

Jake wished he could make all this easier for her, but he also knew what it was like to be disillusioned by a parent. Angela had let him down—and Charley—more times than he could count. There wasn't anything he could do to make it less awful for Kylie besides be there for her when she wanted to talk, when she needed to vent.

Abruptly she turned away, moving to the corner of the closet where two dozen or more jackets and coats hung. "There's a door at the end of the hall that leads to the attic," she said, her tone brittle. "Why don't you check up there while I finish here?" She began patting down each coat, checking the pockets and the lining for anything out of the ordinary.

"Kylie—"

"I'd really like to get all this stuff and get out of here. This place gives me the creeps."

He considered pushing it but agreed with her. He would feel more comfortable delving into the details of the

Franklins' lives back in his motel room. "All right. If you need anything…"

She smiled tightly but didn't stop her search.

The stairs to the attic were narrow and steep, and the space itself was narrow and gloomy. It held a few pieces of furniture covered with canvas cloths and a dozen boxes of Christmas decorations. Therese's cradle and crib were in one corner, next to a stroller, a walker and a wind-up swing. Maybe she would want those things one day. He would like to have something from his childhood to pass on to his children, but they'd moved too often to lug along anything that wasn't essential, and Angela hadn't been sentimental about baby things.

He'd bet Kylie's baby things were on the mansion's third floor. Her family kept everything for posterity, she'd said. That would be just as good.

He grimaced. He'd known the woman for less than seventy-two hours and he was thinking about having kids with her? Damn, he was an idiot…but it felt as if they'd been together forever. There was just something about her—some connection. And she felt it, too. She never would have spent last night with him if she didn't. Sex with someone she'd just met was as much out of character for her as it was for him.

The only records stored in the attic were clearly marked and all premarriage. Jake peeled the brittle tape from a few boxes and looked inside, but they were exactly what the labels said, and none of them looked as if they'd been tampered with since they were first stored.

Dusty, hungry and wanting to wash the smell of the house from his skin, he returned to the second floor, glanced inside two guest rooms, then stopped at the nursery. It had been painted in pastels, lavishly decorated and filled with everything the pampered daughter of a wealthy couple could desire. The covers on the bed were rumpled, and a pink teddy bear lay facedown on the floor beside it, fallen there, no doubt, when Therese had gone looking for her parents.

Therese. In a bloody nightgown, sitting beside her mother's body.

He shuddered, backed out of the room and called Kylie's name.

She came out of the master bedroom with her finds in a wicker wastebasket. She looked dusty, too, and as if a shower would hold great appeal. Maybe they could wash each other's backs.

They left the house, locking it up securely, carrying their cache to the car. As she waited for him to stow the trash bag in the trunk, she gazed across the yard to the garage. "Should we check that out?"

He glanced that way, too, and said shortly, "No. We've been here long enough for one day."

She looked as relieved by his answer as he felt.

Once back in town, he drove straight to the motel, then faced her. "Want to come in?"

She gestured toward herself. "I need to clean up."

"Yeah, me, too. So…you want to come in?"

Her smile was sweeter for its rarity. "I don't think so. Why don't you come over to my place when you're done? We'll be more comfortable going through this stuff."

"Will the senator be there?"

"Probably not. He doesn't spend much of his days at the house when he's in town. But even if he is…I own the place. What can he say?"

Jake was pretty sure she'd never had to use that small

fact against her father in all the years since her mother had died. He was sorry she'd even thought of it now. "All right. I'll bring lunch with me."

She nodded, and they each got out of the car. Swinging his backpack over his shoulder, he started toward the steps, but she stopped him.

"You'd better keep this with you."

He turned back to find she'd opened the trunk and was lifting the basket out. "I trust you with it." He didn't believe she would destroy or conceal evidence from him.

"Thanks." She smiled briefly before turning grim again. "But the senator has keys to my car and my house, so I'd feel more comfortable if you kept it."

How hard had that been? he wondered as he returned to heave the trash bag from the trunk. He took the basket, too, brushing fingers with her in the process. "I'll see you in a while."

With a resigned nod, she slid behind the wheel, then drove off.

Chapter 9

For the second time in six hours, Kylie showered, applied makeup and dithered over what to wear. Earlier she'd chosen the slim denim skirt because it made her legs look good. Now she chose jeans because they hid the scratches and bruises she'd gotten when they'd been ambushed.

Despite her words, she'd worried on the way home about inviting Jake over when the senator was back in town. Seeing that the Jag was gone had eased the knot in her stomach, but she still felt a certain discomfort about it. *Don't poke the bear*, the saying went, and virtually parading Jake Norris at the Colby home was sure to poke the senator.

But it *was* her home. If the senator didn't like it, he could move out.

Jake arrived before she'd had the chance to put on her shoes. She padded barefoot through the house, undid the locks and opened the door. In faded jeans and a red T-shirt, he looked incredible. And he held a brown paper bag that smelled incredible.

"If you'll take this…" He gave her the bag, then returned to his truck to get his backpack and the Franklins' belongings.

Since it was a pretty day, she laid out the food—barbecue from a joint on the north edge of town—on the patio table, along with a beer for him and pop for her. While they ate, they talked about the little things that would hold no real interest to anyone but them. He liked NASCAR and had been known to pass entire days fishing. She didn't like sports, though she occasionally played tennis. He skied, but she had a problem with altitudes in excess of eight thousand feet. He liked rock music, country and classical, and she would rather plug her ears than listen to one note of Bach.

Simple stuff. Meaningless stuff. The stuff relationships were built on.

Well, that and good sex.

After lunch they settled in the living room, the dozens of file folders stacked on the coffee table. Bert Franklin had been meticulous in his record-keeping—a good thing for a banker. Every bill, statement and tax report was filed and labeled. He'd taken care of the household expenses, and Jillian had taken care of spending thousands every month on clothing, meals and gifts. He'd kept her personal checking account well funded and paid her credit card bills in full every month.

And she'd kept her personal savings account well funded *and* well hidden.

After a time, bored with finances, Kylie picked up the red leather address book and flipped through the pages.

"Anyone there who shouldn't be?" Jake asked without looking up from his own stack of papers.

"Seems to be the same names you would find in my mother's address book. The Whitleys, Coy Roberts, my father, the McCormacks, the Markhams, the Jenkinses, the Brownings. Several mayors are here, the district attorney the senator worked for, the newspaper owner, most of the town council from that era." Frowning, she slowly paged through the book again. "Odd, though. Only the men are listed. It doesn't say Phyllis and Jim Riordan—just Jim. Mark McCormack. Clyde Browning."

"Maybe she was really old-fashioned or she associated status with the men rather than their wives."

That fit with Kylie's mother. She'd never missed a chance to refer to herself as Mrs. James Riordan...except on the occasions when his status wasn't enough. Then she'd been Phyllis Colby Riordan.

"But presumably she was friends with the wives. I list my married friends in my address book as Jane and John Doe or just Jane Doe." She turned to the *R*s again and studied the entry for her father, and a chill shuddered through her, obvious enough for Jake to lay aside what he was looking at.

"What's wrong?"

She shook her head, then flipped a few pages, then a few more. Her face growing hot, she closed the book and looked at him. "The number she had for my father is his private number at home. It rings only in his study. She also had Judge Markham's private number. Tim Jenkins's number, not for his office here in town but for the Tulsa office. Mark McCormack's extension at work."

"And you recognize these numbers because...?"

"I'm the senator's aide. It's my job to know how to reach his friends."

Jake leaned against the chair at his back and rested one arm on his bent knee. "It may not mean anything."

"Sure. A married woman has the private numbers of a bunch of married men in her private address book, but it doesn't mean a thing." Her voice was quivery but not with tears. She was afraid, disappointed and angry. If her father had had an affair with Jillian, she would…would…

Would never understand. She might forgive, but she would never forget. Marriages were sacred partnerships, and there was never any justification for one partner to turn to someone else. If he'd wanted to have an affair, he damn well should have divorced her mother first.

But he would have lost everything.

Hand shaking, she tossed the address book onto the table, then sifted through the folders for the one she'd found in Jillian's closet. "You mentioned blackmail earlier. What would she be blackmailing them with? The affairs?"

Jake shrugged. "Some people get caught in affairs and it's no big deal, like Paula McCormack's husband. It took her thirty years to do something about it."

She scowled at him. "Just for the record, one time is one too many for me. I believe in monogamy with a capital *M*."

He grinned. "Just for the record, so do I. But…" He got to his feet with easy grace and dropped down on the couch beside her. "We may be the exceptions to the rule in this town. Jillian apparently found four men with too much to lose. Their wives, their kids, their reputations, their ambitions."

And when it came to ambition, the senator topped the list.

"She was an equal-opportunity blackmailer." He tapped the top bank statement. "Looks like she had a sliding scale based on their ability to pay."

The deposit amounts *were* different: four thousand,

twenty-five thousand, fifteen hundred and five hundred. "So we need to figure out which four men had the most to lose and could pay this kind of money every month for—" she flipped through the statements "—nearly three years."

"Three years," Jake repeated drily. "Gee, why does that sound significant?"

For a moment she didn't understand what he meant, but when she thought back to the murders, several numbers came to mind. Twenty-two—how many years ago it had happened. Twelve—how many hours they estimated Therese had been alone with her dead parents. Three—Therese's age at the time.

"Oh, God," she muttered, sickened by the thought. "One of those men is Therese's father? Maybe my father?"

Jake laid his hand over hers, his fingers warm and strong for her to cling to. "It's a possibility, that's all. Jillian could have blackmailed them with nothing more than the affairs. She may have told each man he was Therese's father and one of them really was. She could have told them that knowing that Bert was really the father. Anything's possible, Kylie. We don't have enough evidence to lean toward any one theory. Hell, we don't have any *proof* that an affair or blackmail ever took place."

And no way to get it. If four of Riverview's upstanding citizens had been blackmailed over their indiscretions, they certainly weren't going to admit it now, when it had been buried with Jillian the past twenty-two years. Their consciences obviously weren't going to nag them into confession at this late stage.

The only way to prove one of them guilty was with their cooperation-giving her and Jake access to their decades-old bank records, offering to take a polygraph exam or agreeing to donate DNA for a paternity test. And all that would prove them guilty of was having an affair and possibly fathering a child.

But if they'd had a lot to lose twenty-two years ago, they probably still did—maybe even more.

She didn't even know which four she would approach if she could. Her father, definitely. Might as well put a few more rifts in their relationship. Probably Judge Markham. Like the senator, Markham had married into his money. As for the other two, any of the men in the book was as likely as the others.

Jake bumped his shoulder against hers. "Want to take a break?"

"Why? Are your eyes crossing?"

He looked at her with his eyes, indeed, crossed. When she burst out laughing, he pulled the folder from her hand, dropped it to the floor, then maneuvered until she was lying beneath him on the couch. "Actually…" He brushed a kiss to jaw. "I was thinking…" Another to her ear that made her shiver. "That we could do something…" The third kiss trailed along her jaw to the corner of her mouth. "That you've never done before…"

His tongue slid inside, parting her teeth, meeting her own tongue, and his fingers stroked deep into her hair. Heat stirred inside her, flaring to life, robbing her of breath, tightening her lungs. She raised her hands to his body, first his face, then his chest, his arms, his middle, unable to decide what she wanted. Finding warm, soft skin where his shirt had ridden up, she knew and slid both hands beneath the fabric, gliding them across his ribs, caressing muscles and nipples and making him gasp.

When he lifted his mouth for badly needed air, she gave

him her sultriest smile. "What is it you think I've never done before?"

He blinked, clearing the haze from his eyes before he offered his own sultry smile. "Been to Buddy's."

It was her turn to blink a time or two before she laughed again. She'd never met a man who could turn her hot and needy with no more than a look and in the next minute make her laugh. It was a gift she appreciated. *He* was a gift she appreciated.

She thrust her hips against his, rubbing against the length of his erection. "You want to go to Buddy's? *Now?*"

"Well…" When she rubbed again, his eyes damn near crossed for real. "I guess it could wait an hour…or three or five."

He kissed her as if he had nothing else to do, nothing more on his mind—long, sweet, lazy kisses that heated her blood and made her nipples taut. Ache throbbed through her, causing her to move restlessly beneath him, to push halfheartedly at his clothes, wanting more, needing more…soon. For the moment it was enough to luxuriate in his kisses, his touches, his mouth trailing heat wherever it touched.

Her shirt was open, her bra unclasped, and he was sucking her nipple between his teeth when she murmured, "Do you have a condom with you?" Her stash—what was left of it—was in her room. She just wasn't sure she could make it that far.

Bracing himself on one arm, he dug into his unusually tight jeans pocket to display one between two fingers. "I'm always prepared," he said with a grin.

Always. Not just for her. He was a single man, free to have sex with every willing woman who came along, and he was prepared for it. She should be grateful—it showed he was careful, conscientious, not stupid. But she didn't want to think about him with other women. She didn't want to know that when he left Riverview he would be "always prepared" for someone else.

The condom disappeared inside his fist as he brushed his other hand across her hair. "Hey. For *you*," he said quietly. "I don't sleep around, Kylie. Only with a woman who matters, and you're the only one who's mattered in a long time."

She smiled faintly. "I don't have a claim on you."

"The hell you don't." He bent, scowling, until his nose was millimeters from hers. "You've got a stronger claim on me than anyone I've ever known, and I've got the same claim on you."

He sealed his words with a kiss, hot and hungry, demanding the same response from her, and she gave it willingly. They shed their clothes without stopping the kisses and caresses, positioned the condom without pulling apart and joined together there on the sofa…and again on the floor…and again in the bed…

The western sky was tinged pink and lavender when they finally left the house. Kylie noticed—with relief, she insisted, not guilt—that the Jag was still gone. Where had the senator been all day? At a war council with a few of his friends? Plotting to save his career?

Did any of his worries concern her? she wondered. Did he know he'd disappointed her? More importantly, did he care? Or, in his eyes, was this all about *him?*

Everything else in their lives had been. Why should this be different?

Buddy's was located a half mile from the glass factory, a quarter mile from the truck stop just off the Turner Turnpike where Charley Baker's wife had waited tables. Kylie had never been to either the bar or the truck stop and had set foot inside the glass factory only once, when her fourth-grade class had taken a field trip there.

Most of the faces inside Buddy's were familiar, though she couldn't put names to them. She'd seen them around town—at the gas station, at Wal-Mart or the grocery store. For the most part, they lived on the east and south sides of town, went to their own churches, frequented different restaurants.

The bartender was big, muscle gone to fat, with a gray ponytail hanging halfway down his back. Tattoos covered most of both arms, along with a snake that writhed up his neck toward his jaw, but the white T-shirt and apron he wore were impeccably clean. "Can I help you?"

"A Bud and …?" Jake glanced her way.

"Coke."

The man filled their order, then studied them with a narrowed gaze. "You're that writer," he said after a moment. "And you're the Colby girl."

Conscious of her mother's manners, she extended her hand. "Kylie Riordan."

He looked around as if to make sure no one was watching, then shook it before turning his attention back to Jake. "You're writing a book about Charley Baker."

"Did you know him?"

"Sure. He come in here every other Friday night like clockwork. Payday, y' know."

"You've been working here that long?"

The man grinned. "I've been working here every damn day since I bought the place. Goin' on thirty years now. My name's Leonard Scott."

"Not Buddy?" Kylie asked.

"Hell, Buddy's been dead since I was a pup. His son and then his grandson ran the place before I took over."

Jake shifted to sit on a stool. "You remember the trial?"

"Sure. Figured they'd call me to testify, seein' that Charley was here at the time the sheriff claimed he killed them people, but they didn't."

"You remember him being here."

Leonard nodded. "Like I said, every other Friday night like clockwork."

"Who did you tell?"

Leonard excused himself to fill an order for the waitress, then returned with a damp cloth in hand, wiping the counter methodically. "Coy Roberts. He was a deputy back then. That lawyer fellow, Jenkins." The wiping slowed, and his gaze darted sideways to Kylie. "And your father."

She shouldn't have been surprised. She'd received enough shocks regarding the senator in the past few days, but she still felt a jolt, still felt the impulsive need to defend him. Its death left a bitter taste in her mouth.

A prosecutor could *not* withhold from the jury information that might clear the defendant. It was unethical. If it could be proven that the senator, Roberts and Jenkins had conspired to hide Charley's alibi, their actions would be criminal.

"I wasn't the only one that told 'em," Leonard went on. "The waitress back then—she was kind of sweet on Charley, not that she ever did anything about it—did, too. And a couple of old boys that he sometimes drank with. They're all moved on, though. Patsy Sue took a job down in Texas. And them old boys were like Charley—they never stayed in one place long."

Jake drained his beer, then shook his head when Leonard offered another. "Can you take a few minutes to write out what you just told me and sign it? Just so I can have it for my records."

"I ain't much for writing," Leonard replied. "But if the Colby girl wants to write it for me, I'll sign."

Kylie smiled tautly in agreement, and Jake removed a pad and pen from his backpack. Sure, why shouldn't she personally write out the statement that would put another nail in the senator's coffin?

Jake was up to see the sunrise Saturday morning, but only because he hadn't yet gone to bed. Kylie had nodded off sometime after midnight, curled on the sofa beneath a throw, wearing an old OSU Cowboys T-shirt and a sweet smile, and he'd sat on the floor sifting through more Franklin records, entering information—interviews, theories— into the computer and spending way too much time just watching her.

Now he was tired, his butt was numb and his back ached from the awkward position. Careful not to disturb her, he eased to his feet and stretched until his spine popped, then went to the kitchen.

She didn't keep much food in the house, no ice cream, no cookies, no potato chips—three of the basic food groups as far as he was concerned. But he did find some packets of instant oatmeal and zapped the water in the microwave to stir up two. Bowl and spoon in hand, he undid the locks on the front door and stepped outside to watch the sky lighten in the east.

The air was chilly, the stone damp beneath his feet. The streetlights burned with a faint buzz, but there was no traffic, no sign of life anywhere.

Except on the opposite side of the parking court.

Jim Riordan was walking from the rear of the house toward the garage. He wore khaki trousers and an emerald-green polo shirt, the color a good match with his tanned skin and white hair. A bag of golf clubs was slung over one shoulder, and he carried a travel mug of coffee in one hand.

Jake would have recognized him anywhere. He'd found dozens of photos of the man—attending parties, accepting honors, holding press conferences, vacationing in exotic places. Living extravagantly while Charley passed day after endless day in a one-hundred-and-ten-square-foot cell. Riordan had married well and made others pay the price for his sins. Life had been good to him.

When he saw Jake, Riordan came to an abrupt halt. Slowly he began moving again, closing the distance between them in a manner that was meant to intimidate. But Jake had faced stone-cold killers before. He wasn't easily intimidated.

Or was that *other* stone-cold killers?

Stopping six feet away, Riordan looked him over from head to toe, and Jake knew what he saw looked bad. His hair stood on end, his shirt was unbuttoned and his feet were bare. As if the early hour wasn't enough, he couldn't make it any more obvious that he'd spent the night there if he'd tattooed it on his forehead.

Even though, ironically, he'd done nothing more than work…and watch Kylie sleep.

"Jake Norris." Riordan's tone was glacial as he eased the golf bag to the ground. "Why, you've just made yourself right at home, haven't you?"

Refusing to respond, Jake scooped the last of the oatmeal from the bowl, then balanced it on the edge of the planter next to him. He was tempted to button his shirt and

run his fingers through his hair, to make himself present-
able—not for the senator but for Kylie's father. He resisted
the urge, though, shoved both hands into his hip pockets
and waited for Riordan to go on.

"You look a hell of a lot like your father."

Now the ice was Jake's, spreading through him, turning
his blood sluggish. Of all the things he might have expected
Riordan to say, that wasn't one of them. He tried to hide
the fact that he was having trouble breathing, but the gleam
in the bastard's eyes showed he knew just how big a bomb-
shell he'd dropped.

"You look surprised— What should I call you? Jake
seems so deceptive. C.J.?" He chuckled. "I used to think
that stood for Charley Junior, that coming up with something original was too taxing for your mother's feeble mind.
I never knew it was Charley Jacob until yesterday." Then
even the faintest hint of humor disappeared and everything
about him turned hard. "Did you really think I wouldn't investigate the man screwing with my career?"

Jake had expected him to say *daughter,* to just once put
Kylie ahead of his damn precious career. Nothing, apparently, came before it.

"It wasn't even hard to find out," Riordan boasted. "You
did a piss-poor job of hiding it. It took my investigator less
than six hours to track Angela Baker and her brat from here
to New Mexico. I have more information on you than you
could possibly gather on me."

Finally Jake found his voice. "I was ten years old when
my mother legally changed our names—eleven when my
stepfather adopted me and changed it again. I wasn't hiding anything."

"I wonder if my daughter would see it that way. I don't

know. I think Kylie would expect the man who's screwing her to tell her who he really is first."

Jake's fingers curled into a fist. He would dearly love to punch that smug look off the bastard's face—would like to make him damn sorry for using the word *screwing* in the same sentence with Kylie. But how much trouble would assaulting the senator on his home turf bring him? More than he needed.

"Kylie's learning a lot of new stuff since I came to town," he said mildly.

Riordan's face flushed an unhealthy red, and a vein throbbed in his forehead. "She doesn't believe your crap. I'm her father. She's idolized me since she was old enough to walk."

She had, but Riordan had never returned the favor. He should have adored his daughter, treasured her, not used her to achieve his goals. Not disillusioned her. "And now she knows her idol has feet of clay…and the morals of a common criminal."

The red turned crimson and the vein looked ready to burst. It took a moment's deep breathing for Riordan to get it under control, took another moment for him to summon up the brash, ballsy arrogance. "You think she's on your side in this? You think she gives a damn what happened to your worthless father twenty-two years ago? You're wrong. She's on damage control. She's playing you for a fool, Norris. She's loyal to me—always has been, always will be. She's been keeping me informed of your every move. I know what you know."

"Right," Jake said flatly.

"I know you talked to the bartender at Buddy's yesterday. Went out to the Franklin house with the key Therese gave you. Met with those three bitches Phyllis called her best friends."

Jake was ashamed to admit that, deep inside, he felt a moment's doubt. He knew Kylie had talked to her father about him on Wednesday morning, again on Thursday and yet again on Friday morning. Though they'd spent most of Friday together, she'd had chances to call him—when she was alone in the Franklins' bedroom, when she'd dropped Jake off at the motel to clean up, when she'd gotten ready for the bed. With a cell phone, the senator was never more than a button away.

"The cops you had following us could have given you the same information."

"Me? Have cops follow you? I don't have that authority. And even if I did, I would never abuse it that way. I'm a public servant. I would never take advantage of my position for personal gain." Riordan was wearing his politician's persona now, so sincere that even Jake would be tempted to believe him if he didn't know better. But the sly look that entered Riordan's eyes was more in keeping with what Jake did know. "Besides, I have no reason to rely on the police department to keep track of you. Kylie's much more efficient."

Riordan raised one brow. "You don't believe me? How about a little proof? I know you found out about Jillian's secret bank account. Over three hundred thousand dollars. Where do you think it came from? Blackmail?"

Jake's nerves tightened, and his jaw clamped so hard that his teeth ached. Kylie wasn't keeping her father informed. He didn't believe it. Wouldn't believe it. He'd seen how upset she was by all the negative things they'd uncovered. He knew how deeply this whole mess disturbed her. He'd pried her fingers from the steering wheel in the Pancake Palace parking lot, had practically pried her from the car. She couldn't fake that kind of emotion.

Unless, like her father, she was one hell of an actor.

He hated himself for doubting her, hated Riordan for making him doubt her. She'd risked her entire relationship with the father she admired to help Jake find the truth.

Unless there hadn't been any risk. If Riordan was behind everything she'd said and done...

But there was no way he would have condoned her having sex with Jake. He was her father, for God's sake. Not a loving one, but still...even Jim Riordan's ambition must have *some* limits, and surely prostituting his only daughter exceeded them.

It was almost as if Riordan read his mind. "Kylie and I have a very close relationship. Of course, you wouldn't understand that, seeing that your father's spent more than half your life in prison. Since her mother died, we've become even closer. There's nothing she wouldn't do for me. Hang out with a second-rate writer. Pretend to believe his outrageous accusations against me. Sleep with him."

The senator shrugged expansively. "*I* would have drawn the line there, but Kylie is devoted to my career. I told her Wednesday, 'You do whatever it takes to make that man believe you're on his side,' and the very next night she invited you into her bed. Three times, I believe she said."

Jake's stomach knotted and his palms grew damp. He couldn't fill his lungs without a struggle, couldn't hear for the buzzing in his ears. Maybe Riordan had made a lucky guess. Maybe Roberts had reported to him that Jake had spent the night there—though he hadn't seen any officers tailing him that night or the next morning, until No-Neck had caught up with him at the motel, wanting to know where he'd been.

In his experience, women just didn't discuss the details of their sex lives with their fathers. But Kylie's relationship with Riordan was unlike any father/daughter relationship he'd seen.

"What's wrong, Norris? At a loss for words?" Riordan chuckled. "You'd think, dealing with scum like you do—coming from scum like you do—you'd have a better sense of when someone's feeding you a line. Guess it's tougher to tell when you're thinking with your crotch instead of your head."

He made a show of looking at the Rolex on his left wrist. "I'd better get going or I'll miss my tee time. You want some advice? Forget this book, forget your worthless father and go back where you came from. This town ran you off once before. We'd be happy to do it again. Only you won't get off so easy this time."

Hefting the golf bag over his shoulder again, he strode off to the garage, keyed a code into the box on the near end, then ducked under the electric door as it raised.

Jake edged back into the recess of the door, coarse wood biting into his back. For a moment he just leaned there, controlling his breathing, blocking the racing thoughts from his mind, but the focus lasted only a moment.

Jim Riordan was a liar. He would do anything to protect his reputation and his political ambition. He'd already sent at least one innocent man to prison, had already broken his marriage vows with at least one affair. Why in hell would Jake believe anything he said?

He wouldn't. Didn't. There was another logical source for each of the bits of information Riordan had. In spite of No-Neck's dumb act, the police might have known Jake was at the mansion that night. One of Phyllis's friends could have mentioned the savings account to her husband, who'd passed it on to Riordan. Therese had likely told her cop boyfriend about giving them the key to the house. Anyone could have seen them at Buddy's.

All more likely than Kylie reporting to her father that they'd had sex, when and how many times. Unless Jake didn't really know her at all.

It had been less than ninety-six hours since they'd met. Not much time to go from attraction to hostility to desire to intimacy and a whole lot more. Not much time to know just how far he could trust her.

Not much time to fall in love with her, either, but he was too damn close to doing just that. His only defense was that it had been an intense four days. He felt as if he'd known her forever. He found himself at odd moments thinking about forever. Sharing his work with her, his home, his life. Having a family with her. Making the most of what destiny offered with her.

He smiled thinly. He wanted "forever" with a woman whose father he had to destroy in order to save his own. Destiny had one hell of a sense of humor.

But what he wanted wasn't the point. For several reasons, the book had to come first. He was contractually obligated to deliver a manuscript by next summer. He'd promised Charley he would find out the truth. He'd promised himself, regardless of what the truth was. If he proved Charley's guilt, it was better than not knowing.

But instead he'd virtually disproved it. He had a real chance at getting his father out of prison, at giving back the freedom Riordan and his pals had stolen. He could give Charley a shot at a normal life, could undo at least some of the wrongs done him.

That was what mattered. *All* that mattered. He couldn't let anything or anyone interfere with that, not even Kylie. Not if there was the slightest chance what her father said was true.

It sickened him that he might not be able to trust her. That he had to treat her as untrustworthy whether it was true or just another of her father's lies. Charley had too much to lose.

He had a lot to lose, too, some part of him protested. Kylie was the first woman he'd ever felt this way about. If he lost her...

He'd have a chance to make it right or to learn to feel this way about someone else. He was relatively young. He had a lot of time left. Charley, on the other hand, was fifty-eight years old. He never should have spent a day in jail, much less twenty-two years, and damned if Jake was going to risk his best opportunity to get out.

Grimly he went inside, leaving his oatmeal bowl in the sink, moving quietly to the living room. He packed away his computer and the piles of paper stacked around the sofa. He buttoned his shirt, put on his boots and socks, carried everything to the door, then returned to the sofa.

Kylie hadn't moved except to snuggle closer to the fat pillows that lined the back of the couch. The throw covered her at an angle, its fringed edge dragging the floor. Crouching, he straightened it, tucked it more securely around her, then brushed his fingers lightly over her hair, across her cheek, to her shoulder. Even in sleep, she smiled, freed one hand to cover his and murmured his name.

His gut knotted. He was making a mistake. Kylie wasn't like her father. She wasn't taking his side.

But she was Riordan's daughter, and Jake knew too

well what a child would do for a parent, right or wrong be damned. He was walking away from her on the off chance that her loyalty was greater than her honor. It was the worst wrong he'd done in a long time and he knew it, but he was doing it anyway. For Charley's sake.

Maybe someday she would forgive him. But he knew for sure that if he trusted her and she betrayed him, he would never forgive himself.

Gently he worked his hand free of hers, gave her shoulder a small squeeze, then stood and walked out.

Kylie knew the instant she awoke that Jake was gone. It wasn't just the stillness in the house. It was a change in the aura. She didn't *feel* his presence and she missed it.

Stretching, she rolled over and realized she lay on the couch instead of her bed. She'd sorted through Bert and Jillian's tax records until she couldn't stand it anymore, she recalled, and had lain down just to watch Jake work for a while. He'd looked so serious, sitting there on the floor, computer in front of him, papers all around him. At some point he'd kicked off his boots, unbuttoned his shirt and combed his fingers through his hair a dozen times or so, giving him an adorably tousled appearance. She could have just lain there and looked for hours if she hadn't fallen asleep.

The papers were gone now. So was the laptop. No empty water bottles lined the coffee table. In fact, there was no sign that he'd been there at all except for the elusive fragrance that drifted on the air.

Pushing back the throw, she got up and padded off looking for a note from him. It wasn't on the coffee table or the refrigerator. There was nothing on the door, propped on the bed pillows or against the bathroom mirror, and no message on her answering machine.

Why had he left without a word? That didn't seem in keeping with the Jake she knew. If he'd had someone to interview, he would have invited her along. If he'd simply gotten hungry and gone out for breakfast, he would have awakened her to go, too. After all, she'd gotten more sleep than he had.

Could it have something to do with the senator? Could he have noticed Jake's truck parked beside the hedge and ordered him from the property? Could he have done something more sinister?

Heart rate steadily increasing, Kylie went to the night table, thumbed through the phone book, then dialed the Tepee Motor Court. The clerk connected her to Jake's room, where the phone rang six times before she hung up. She retrieved her cell phone from her purse in the foyer, keyed through the screens until she found Jake's cell phone number under Incoming Calls and pressed dial. After four rings, it went to voice mail. "This is Jake. Leave a message."

She swallowed hard. "Hi, Jake. It's Kylie. I was just wondering what's up. Give me a call." Grimacing, she disconnected, then combed her hair back from her face. Would she sound as insecure to Jake as she had to herself?

It was no big deal. He'd probably gone back to the motel to shower and change clothes and he'd taken everything with him to keep it safe. Hadn't she told him she wasn't comfortable having the Franklins' records in her house or car? He hadn't left a note because he was a man, and men didn't think of those things, and he'd probably thought he would be back before she knew he was gone.

That all sounded logical, but she couldn't wrap her

mind around "logical," not after the past few days. Someone had already run him off the road and taken a few shots at him. What if their scare tactics had escalated? What if they'd been waiting when he'd driven out the gate? What if—

"Stop it!" she admonished. "You're worrying for nothing." She would shower and get dressed, and if she hadn't heard from him by then she would call again or drive to the motel.

An hour later she was in the process of doing both—dialing the number as she turned onto Main Street. Her palms were growing damp when the ringing ended abruptly. There was a moment's silence, then a hoarse, "Hello."

Relief flood through her. "Jake, it's Kylie."

Another silence. "Yeah. I figured."

"Did I wake you?"

"Yeah." Bedsprings creaked in the background, accompanied by a soft slither of sound. Bedsheets against bare skin.

"I'm sorry. I woke up and you were gone and I was worried."

"Sorry. I just needed to sleep."

His voice was husky, dazed, and his yawn sounded genuine, but she couldn't shake the feeling that something was wrong. There was no reason he couldn't have slept at her house—unless he was too old-fashioned. Hadn't he wanted to leave early Friday morning so no one would know he'd spent the night?

"Okay. I'm sorry I woke you. Call me later, will you?" Without waiting to see if he agreed, she hung up, stopped at a red light, then sighed. There was no point going to the motel now that she knew he was all right. She didn't need to run any errands, didn't have any chores awaiting her at home, really didn't have anything at all to do besides catch up on her work. She didn't want to spend the next few hours focusing on the senator's career, but even more she didn't want to hang around the house waiting on Jake's call.

The front door of Riordan Law Office was locked, the reception area lit only by the sun that filtered through the blinds. She locked the door behind her, ignored the light switches and went down the hall to her office. There she practically skidded to a stop.

The lamp on her desk was on, and her father sat at her desk, rifling through the drawers. A week ago she wouldn't have thought anything of it. This morning she couldn't stop suspicion from flaring. "Can I help you find something, sir?"

His gaze flickered over her. "That's hardly appropriate attire for the office," he said as he removed her date book from the center drawer and flipped through it.

She glanced down at her caramel-colored trousers and rust sweater set. Though she usually wore dresses or suits with heels to work, this was far from the most casual outfit she'd chosen, and he knew it. "Let me run right home and change into something more appropriate," she murmured sarcastically. Crossing the room, she sat in the chair that fronted her desk.

He tossed the date book on the desk on top of folders he'd removed from the file drawer. A moment later an envelope of photos of a college friend's newest baby landed there, too, along with a few magazines.

"If you're looking for something that has to do with Jake, you won't find it," she said evenly.

"I found these." He picked up a box from the floor and dropped it on the desk with such force that it slid to the edge, nearly toppling into her lap. Inside was the complete works of true-crime writer extraordinaire, Jake Norris.

She'd been so busy since placing the order that she'd forgotten about them.

"I wanted to see if I agreed with your assessment," she said, nudging the box back from the edge.

Giving a snort, the senator shoved the pile in front of him and knocked the box to the floor. "You're not paid to have an opinion, Kylie. I tell you what to think, and you think it."

She refused to pick up the box, or to rub the sudden emptiness that had appeared in her stomach. She had always thought they had a good working relationship, that he'd meant it when he said he valued her intelligence and her input. Did he really think of her as some sort of mindless drone who let him do all her thinking for her?

"Where is Norris?"

"Call Chief Roberts and ask him."

The senator's face turned dark. "I cannot believe what an idiot you are. Some half-breed Indian trailer-park trash pays you a little attention, and you start believing everything he says. You've betrayed me, your mother, the Riordan name. And the funny thing is, you don't even know who he really is."

His accusation of betrayal hurt, but she ignored it, just as she ignored the impulse to insist that of course she knew who Jake was. He was all about the truth. He wasn't hiding his own truths from her. But she knew her father well. *Know your enemy* was one of the commandments he lived by. If he said there was a secret in Jake's past, undoubtedly he had the documentation to prove it.

"You ever ask yourself why he's so determined to prove Baker's innocent?"

"Proving Charley's innocence isn't Jake's goal. He wants the truth." Though she kept her hands clasped in her lap, they started to tremble. "And the truth is, Charley *is* innocent, isn't he? He had an alibi for the time of the murders. He couldn't have killed the Franklins. You knew it. Roberts knew. Jenkins knew. And you took him to trial anyway. You prosecuted an innocent man, and they helped you do it."

The senator's gesture was sharp, dismissive. "That alibi wasn't credible. Leonard Scott didn't know the time of day. He damn sure didn't know what time Baker was in his bar. Charley Baker was guilty. Everyone knew it."

How many times had her father told that lie? Dozens. Probably often enough to convince himself at least part of the time that it was true. Often enough to believe that his mindless daughter would accept it as truth, too.

"Bullshit," she said bluntly. "He was framed. And you helped."

The senator's face took on an ugly red flush. "How dare you!"

"How dare *you!* You hold yourself out as a good man, an honorable man, and you don't know the meaning of the words!" Unable to sit one moment longer, Kylie surged to her feet, nearly stumbled over the box of books, grabbed them up and started to the door. She needed to leave, to get away before they destroyed their little family beyond repair. She was halfway there when her father spoke again.

"You think Norris is an honorable man?" he sneered. "You don't even know his real name. He's not looking for the truth, Kylie. He's trying to get his worthless father out of prison and he'll do anything, including screw you, to do it."

Her feet took root, ignoring her brain's insistent commands to continue moving. Her ears buzzed, and her vision tunneled on the doorway, only a yard away but too far to reach. The emptiness in her stomach grew, spreading welcome numbness through her, drowning out the buzz, softening the edges of the tunnel.

Jake was Charley Baker's son, C.J. The ten-year-old whose life had changed so drastically with the murders. The boy who'd been harassed, bullied and forced to leave town after his father's arrest.

Oh, God, he was the boy who'd found the Franklins' bloodied bodies, who'd rescued Therese from her nightmare, who lived with his own nightmares.

The quivering started deep at her core, forcing her to take the last step that separated her from the door. There she leaned against the jamb, grateful for the support. The sad stories Jake had told her about C.J. seemed so much sadder knowing they were about him. She wanted to go to him, hold him, help him. She wanted to share her strength with him, to hold the nightmares at bay for him.

And ask why he hadn't trusted her enough to tell her.

"See? You didn't know." The senator's triumphant crow filled the room. He'd stunned her, taken her breath away, and was delighted by it.

And that was the reason she called him by his current title rather than Father. He'd been an idol, a role model, a boss, the focus of her life, but he'd never been much of a parent. He wasn't capable of being a dad.

Rather than give the obvious response, she asked a question of her own. "Did you have an affair with Jillian Franklin?"

It was a tactic she'd learned over the years from the best reporters—catch him off guard. He would put his usual spin on his answer, but there was that instant before he regained control that could be telling.

Today it was. Emotion passed through his eyes—guilt, quickly eclipsed by anger that morphed into icy cold. "I loved your mother."

"That wasn't the question, sir." But it made the answer crystal clear. Dismay clenched her jaw. Had her mother known? Was that why the close friendship they'd shared with the Franklins had cooled so suddenly there at the end? Had Phyllis forgiven and forgotten or merely decided that a divorce was unacceptable?

He rose from the chair, rested his hands on the desk and leaned toward her. "No. I did not have an affair with Jillian or anyone else."

Too little, too late, too untrue.

She straightened, no longer needing the door's support. "Does it ever bother you, sir, that you sent an innocent man to prison? That you perverted the very law you were sworn to uphold? That you took a father away from a ten-year-old boy? That a murderer is still out there, living his life without fear?"

He bristled unconvincingly. "I never sent anyone to prison. I prosecuted the cases brought to me by the police and the sheriff's department. I presented the evidence they gathered, and the juries made the decision as to innocence or guilt. The *juries*. Not me."

Wordplay. Most politicians were good at it. He excelled.

"Have you ever regretted it, even just a little?" She wanted him to say yes. It wouldn't make much difference, but at least it was *something*. But if he admitted to regrets, he had to admit to guilt, and he was in full-bore-denial mode.

He fixed his gaze on her, steely and unforgiving. "My only regret is that my daughter has turned into the kind of person who could even think these things about me, much less say them. I have never been so disappointed in anyone."

She smiled sadly, offering one last comment before walking out the door. "The disappointment is mutual, sir."

Chapter 10

Jake slept another five or six hours after Kylie's phone call, but it was a restless sleep, broken by bad dreams. Bad memories. Jillian, beautiful, dead, laughing a sultry laugh, her blood-soaked dress clinging provocatively. Therese, small, defenseless, mute. Charley, blood dripping from his clothes and the knife clutched in his left hand, slowly morphing into Jim Riordan, with Kylie standing behind him, her expression stunned, hurt, bewildered.

He sat on the edge of the bed, rubbing his hands over his face. He needed a shower, a shave, food. A stiff drink sounded pretty good, too. After that, he had some hard planning to do. There were still a few people he wanted to talk to, Therese, her grandmother and Charley's priest among them. Then he was leaving Riverview.

Because he couldn't talk to the one person he wanted

to see most. Couldn't discuss theories or plans with her. Couldn't confide in her.

He couldn't even tell her—two days too late—that he was Charley's son. No doubt Riordan had already taken great pleasure in spilling the news. She wouldn't understand how he could make love to her without sharing that one fundamental part of who he was.

He showered, shaved, brushed his teeth and dressed in jeans and a T-shirt. Carrying the backpack by a strap, he stepped out the door, locked it, then turned and stopped.

Kylie sat on the second step, elbows resting on her knees, a book open in her hands. Hearing him, she closed the book, one finger marking her place, and his own face gazed up at him from the back jacket. He spared it only a glance, though. He was more interested in her face. She looked ragged. Shaken. Beautiful.

Sitting on the opposite side of the step, he let the pack slide to the concrete and mimicked her position. For a time he just sat there, unable to think of anything to say. Finally he forced a sorry smile. "Good book?"

"Sad book."

It was that. His first one—the story of a mother who'd killed her three children because God told her to. Suffering from severe paranoid schizophrenia, she was the saddest person he'd ever met.

She folded the dust jacket flap over to mark her place, then closed the book. "I talked to my father."

Jake turned his head away from her, squinting into the afternoon sun. "So did I."

"Really. He didn't mention it."

"But he did mention my father, didn't he?"

"Yes." Her answer was so subdued that it was nearly lost in the sound of traffic from the nearby street.

"So my secret's out." Was she angry? Hurt? Disillusioned now with him instead of Riordan? He wanted to look for answers in her face, but he couldn't. He just kept staring off to the west.

"You could have told me."

"People were unhappy enough when they thought I was just some writer asking questions. How different would it have been if they'd known I was Charley's son?"

"We're not talking about 'people.' We're talking about me."

The hurt barely identifiable in her voice made his nerves tighten. "Oh, yeah. You're Senator Riordan's daughter. You're special. You're entitled to know things other people don't."

"No," she said quietly. "I'm Kylie, the woman you turned to for sex, assistance and information. I'm nothing special. But I did think I was entitled to know your real connection to this book before you went to bed with me."

An ache started in his chest, and he absently rubbed at it. Guilt, no doubt, accompanied by need—to hold her, to be held by her. To ease her pain, to take away the wounded look he was sure darkened her eyes. But he didn't reach for her.

"You're right," he agreed. "I'm sorry. I haven't used my real name—my father's name—since I was ten years old. I wanted to tell you. I intended to. I just…" He shook his head and shrugged.

She shifted on the step to face him. He saw the movement peripherally but continued to avoid her. "What did the senator say to make you not want me anymore?"

The idea was so ridiculous that he would have laughed if not for fear he would choke instead. "I still want you. I can't imagine not wanting you. Hell, I'm about this far—"

he raised two fingers a millimeter apart "—from falling in love with you."

"But you don't trust me. He made you doubt me."

He was ashamed to answer. He trusted her more than anyone else in the world. He was ninety-nine percent sure he could trust her with his life. But ninety-nine percent wasn't good enough to trust her with Charley's life.

Finally he turned to look at her. "He said you're simply following his orders. That he told you to do whatever it took to make me believe you were on my side—hang out with me, pretend to believe me, sleep with me. That you were keeping him informed of everything we were doing, everything we learned. He knew every move we made yesterday. He knew about Jillian's bank account, how much money was in it and that we suspected she was blackmailing her lovers."

Her features were expressionless. "He's probably known about that for years."

True. Even if Riordan hadn't been one of Jillian's blackmail targets, Tim Jenkins, the Franklins' attorney, would have known of the account and likely would have shared it with him.

But there was one thing Riordan knew that he could have learned from only Kylie or Jake, and Jake damn well hadn't told him. "He knew the first time we made love. Where. How many times."

Her face flushed, though anger seemed more likely a reason than guilt. She stood up, the book falling unnoticed to the ground, and the air between them damn near shimmered with tension. "You know he's lied. I told you he lied to me. And yet you believe him on this."

"No. I just…"

She waited, but when nothing else came she smiled thinly, so sadly that he felt its pain in his chest. "You just don't believe you can trust me."

He didn't say anything. Couldn't.

For a long time she just stared at him as if she didn't know him at all. Then her shoulders drew back, and her chest rose with a deep breath. "For the record, Jake, the only order the senator gave me was to stay away from you. I chose to spend time with you anyway. I chose to sleep with you. I chose to accept the evidence that my father has done some terrible things. I haven't passed on information about you. I haven't told him what you're doing or what you're learning.

"I admit, I did make a mistake in telling him that I'd slept with you three times Thursday night. He was warning me that seduction would be next on your agenda, that you would tell me how beautiful I was, that you would get me into bed and manipulate me so I would believe your lies and forget the people who really mattered. I shouldn't have said anything, but he made it sound as if you couldn't possibly want me just for me. So I told him it was too late. I'd already seduced you. I'm sorry." A tear slid down her cheek that he wanted desperately to brush away. "I'm sorry about a lot of things."

She'd reached her car before he managed to speak with the lump in his throat. "Kylie, Charley's my *father.* He's spent more than a third of his life in prison for a crime he didn't commit, and I have a chance to get him out."

"And you don't trust me to not screw that up. After all, I *am* the senator's daughter. I understand."

"I don't believe you would do anything—"

"Please." Finally she swiped away one of the tears. "I'm

sick to death of lies. You don't trust me. Neither does the senator anymore. And you know what's funny about that, Jake? *I'm* the only one who hasn't lied."

With that, she got into her car and started the motor. If it had been him, he would have backed out with a squeal of rubber, would have gunned the engine in a close call with oncoming traffic, would have reached seventy miles per hour before screeching to a stop at the light. She didn't do any of that but drove away as if nothing had happened.

Damn it all to hell.

He sat there a long time, staring blindly at the book on the ground. What could he have done differently to prevent this mess? Stayed hell and gone from her? No way. He'd been attracted to her from the moment he'd seen her in her father's office. He *couldn't* have not fallen for her. Trusted her more? There wasn't enough trust in the world to put his father's future in hands related to Jim Riordan.

That was the problem: not enough trust.

Wearily he got to his feet, picked up the book and put it and the backpack in the passenger seat of the truck. By the time he'd driven a block, a patrol unit was two car lengths behind him. The officer followed him to the drive-in on Markham Avenue where a high school girl on skates delivered his burger and fries to his truck. From there they went to a liquor store, where Jake picked up a bottle of scotch, and then along side streets to the south entrance to the Colby estate.

Kylie's car was visible through the bars of the gate, parked in its usual place near the cottage door. Was she in there crying? Hating him? Wishing she'd never met him?

He couldn't blame her. All he could do was hope that someday…

Behind him, the cop apparently tired of waiting, switched on his lights and climbed out of his vehicle. Jake watched in the rearview mirror as he took a few steps toward the truck, then he eased his foot from the brake to the gas pedal and drove off. With an obscene wave, the cop hastily returned to his car and moments later was on the truck's bumper.

Jake was back at the motel, laptop booted up, a drinking glass from the bathroom half-filled with scotch, when the cell phone rang. He didn't waste time hoping it would be Kylie—didn't look at caller ID at all but flipped it open and said a curt, "Hello."

"Hey, son, it's me."

Closing his eyes, Jake rubbed the ache in his temple with his free hand. "Hey, Dad. What's up?"

"The usual. Eat, sleep, work and stay out of trouble. What's up with you?"

"Eat, sleep, work and get into trouble." Though Charley chuckled, Jake couldn't crack a smile. He was too damn sore inside to be amused by anything.

"You in Oklahoma?"

"Yeah. I've been here a few days." Expectant silence met his words, but Jake couldn't bring himself to rehash everything with him. Not yet. "I'll be going back home in a day or two, but I'll come down to see you first and I'll tell you everything."

"Good." Another silence. Charley had a lot of those these days, when he'd never been hesitant or reticent in the past. "Did you remember much about the town?"

"Not really. The school's about the same. The church has been replaced. The house is still standing."

"Your mother was always afraid that every tornado watch was going to bring the one that would blow it down with us in it," Charley remarked. "All these years, and it's still standing."

You're still standing, too, Jake wanted to say. The house had survived years of neglect and misfortune, and so had Charley. Instead of just surviving, though, hopefully he would soon start to live again.

"Do you think…" Charley's voice trailed off, but Jake didn't need to hear the words.

His fingers gripped the phone tighter, and emotion welled inside him, making his voice husky. "Yeah. We've got a chance, Dad."

The same emotion was in Charley's voice. "That's all I ever wanted."

They talked a few minutes longer before hanging up. Jake stared at the computer and the papers on the desk, picked up the glass of scotch and dumped it down the sink.

No matter how wrong his decision regarding Kylie was for *him,* for Charley it was the right thing. He was going to get his chance.

And someday, when his name had been cleared and he was out of prison, maybe Jake could have a chance, too.

Because Kylie was turning out to be all *he* really wanted.

When Kylie returned from her run on Sunday morning, the senator's SUV was sitting in the driveway and Alberto was loading bags into the cargo area while the senator waited impatiently. Taking a deep drink from the water bottle she carried, she walked toward the truck and both men. Her stomach was knotted, her muscles more tense than a workout could excuse. As she drew closer, she slowed her steps considerably, giving the senator every opportunity to speak.

He didn't—at least not to her. He gave her a look that

could have scalded milk, muttered something to Alberto, then got into the truck and drove toward the gate.

The snub didn't even hurt, Kylie realized as she watched him go. She was totally numb inside, thanks to Jake. She didn't feel a damn thing besides the occasional urge to curl into a ball and cry her heart out.

"Where is he going?"

What Alberto thought of the senator's behavior didn't show on his face. "Oklahoma City. He's having dinner at the governor's mansion tonight."

Ordinarily he invited her to accompany him to such functions. He probably felt he couldn't trust himself to be civil—or trust her to keep her mouth shut. "When will he be back?"

"Sometime tomorrow." Alberto's old gaze softened as he studied her. "Is everything all right, Miss Kylie?"

She smiled. Her perfectly ordered life had fallen into chaos. If she relaxed her control, her heart would break. For all practical purposes, she'd lost her father—the respect, the admiration, the affection. Apparently she'd lost Jake, as well. She felt betrayed, bewildered. She knew she had to make big changes but had no clue what kind of changes or how to start.

"Everything's fine, Alberto," she said with a big phony smile. If life got any finer, she'd give in to the curl-up-and-cry impulse and never stop.

The house was quiet and empty. She showered, ate a bagel for breakfast and pondered what to do with the rest of her day—with the rest of her life. For starters, she sat down at the computer in her small office, typed a letter of resignation, effective immediately, and sealed it in an envelope with the senator's name on it.

That small act eased the tightness in her chest. Finding

a new job would be no problem; she'd rejected offers from various cronies of the senator's over the years. If she found politics no longer to her liking, she could change careers. She was a great fund-raiser, organizer and hostess. She had a degree in marketing. She didn't even *need* a job, thanks to her mother. She could do volunteer work.

Surely she could find something to help ease the emptiness inside her.

Before she could entertain second thoughts—not likely—she left the house, letter in hand, and let herself into the mansion. She saw no sign of Rosalie as she made her way to the second-floor study.

The door was unlocked. She'd been taught since she was a small child that the room was off-limits to her without an invitation. She'd abided by that rule her entire life; her father saw no reason to believe she wouldn't now. He was arrogant. He still believed that when push came to shove, loyalty to him would trump everything else.

He was wrong.

Her fingers trembled when she opened the door. A shiver danced down her spine as she crossed the threshold. The mixed scents of aged wood, leather and the senator's cologne perfumed the air on which tiny motes of dust drifted. She crossed the Persian rug, laid the envelope on the leather desk pad and started to turn away before spotting a photograph on the desk.

The leaded-crystal frame was ornate and heavy and it held a photo of the freshman senator and his family. Kylie was about twelve at the time, and her mother hadn't yet been diagnosed with the cancer that would kill her. The two of them looked adoringly at the senator, while he looked adoringly at the camera. It was eerily similar to their other family pictures.

I loved your mother, he'd said, but not once had the camera ever caught him looking at her adoringly, not even in their wedding portrait that hung in the master bedroom. Usually he just looked satisfied, as if everything was happening exactly the way he wanted.

I loved your mother, but that hadn't stopped him from being unfaithful to her with Jillian Franklin. Kylie couldn't prove it—that look in his eyes when she'd asked the day before wouldn't count as proof to anyone besides her—but she knew it as surely as...

Her gaze slowly shifted to the door tucked between two tall bookcases. It led into a storeroom containing shelves of supplies, liquor for the bar near the fireplace and file cabinets filled with every pertinent record of James and Phyllis Riordan's lives.

Including bank records.

Her mouth went dry, making it hard to swallow. Though it wouldn't answer all her questions, a few answers were better than none. But moving took strength, and she was just about out of that for the time being. She could always look later.

And the senator could always destroy any incriminating information, if he hadn't already done so.

How arrogant was he? Enough to leave confirmation of his blackmail payments in file cabinets in her own house? Enough to believe, as he'd said the day before, *I tell you what to think and you think it?*

Lungs tight, she took the few steps that brought her to the door. Wrapped her fingers around the marble-and-brass knob. Turned. Pushed the door open.

The storeroom was actually two rooms—one for items frequently used and a smaller, dustier space that the senator laughingly called "the archives." That was where twenty-two-year-old records would be. She reached for a second marble-and-brass knob and—

"Kylie?"

With a startled cry, she jerked her hand from the knob and whirled around. Jake stood in the doorway, looking about as miserable as she felt. For an instant, pleasure bubbled inside her, then she remembered and the pain returned. "What are you doing here?"

"I needed to see you."

She understood that need—shared it. But it had been *his* decision not to trust her, to push her away, to deceive her about his identity, to punish her because of her father's actions.

He shifted awkwardly, then dragged his hand through his hair. "I ran into an elderly gentleman outside. He said you were in the house. He said to come on in and give a holler. I did, but you didn't answer."

It was a big house, and she'd been distracted. Since meeting him, she was so easily distracted.

"I—I wanted to talk." He tugged at his hair again, then gestured toward her. "Why were you so startled?"

She must look guilty, standing rigidly, both hands tucked behind her back, as if she had something to hide. Logical, since she did. "I'm not supposed to be in here."

"In a storeroom?"

She freed one hand to wave. "In the study. It's always been the senator's private domain. Even my mother wasn't allowed to come in here without permission."

"He prohibited her from entering a room in her own house?"

It sounded better the way her mother had put it. *Everyone needs their private space, Kylie. Yours is your bedroom.*

Your father's is his study. But even as a child she recalled thinking that *her* space wasn't nearly as private as his.

"What are you looking for?"

She was about to answer when the ache in her chest twinged again. "That's none of your business." It made her feel better to say it, though, of course, if she found anything of interest, she would see to it that he got a copy.

She would use the original to see that the senator got justice.

Folding her arms across her chest, she scowled. "What do you want to talk about?"

Instantly his discomfort returned. He picked up a bottle of port from the shelf beside him, scanned the label, then set it down and did the same with a bottle of sherry. Finally, though, he shoved his hands in his hip pockets and looked at her instead. "Can we do it someplace else?"

"Sure. Call my office tomorrow and make an appointment." Not that she technically had an office anymore, other than the tiny space in her house.

His face flushed. "Kylie, please—"

"Please what? Behave? Mind your manners? Don't make a scene? Remember who you are? Do what I tell you to do? Think what I tell you to think?"

"I don't give a damn about your manners or who you are and I damn sure wouldn't try to tell you what to do or how to think."

Slowly she shook her head. "Not true, Jake. You don't trust me because of who I am."

"If it was just me, I'd trust you with my life, but it's *not* just me and it's not *my* life. It's my father's."

"And a chance to clear his name is too important to risk with James Riordan's daughter." She snorted. "Do you realize how that sounds—a convicted murderer's son telling me I'm not trustworthy because my father used to be a prosecuting attorney?"

His features turned hard and cold, giving her a glimpse of the ten-year-old who'd been beaten for standing up for Charley. "My father is innocent."

"And my father's guilty." Maybe not of murder—please, God!—but of various other crimes. "But I'm not."

"I know." The words were soft, miserable. "But I can't take a chance."

She shifted her gaze away. She wanted to stay angry and hostile, but the hell of it was, she could understand his reasoning. It wasn't fair to her, but if the situation were reversed, would she do anything differently? Would she trust him with her father's life? She couldn't say.

"I'm going to talk to a few more people," Jake went on quietly, "and then I'm going home and I'm going to find the best damn lawyer in the country for Charley. When all this is done, when the witnesses have gone on record and the evidence has been documented…can we try again?"

The small hope inside her flared, then was extinguished by scorn. He was pushing her out of his life after turning her own life upside down, but once it was all over, once there was nothing she could do to cause a problem, he wanted to pick up where they'd left off. He wanted her to just forget that he hadn't trusted her, that he'd caused her more pain and heartache than any man alive, and go back to life as usual.

Some part of her—the part that had indulged in fantasies of a future with him—wanted to say yes. The rational part that understood why he had to put his father first wanted that, too. But her pride said doubtful, and the realistic part of her agreed. His lack of trust in her had shaken her trust in him.

"I don't know, Jake." They were the hardest words she'd said in a long time. "Faith is a critical part of any relationship, and you've shown a total lack of faith in me."

Disappointment swept over his face, turning his brown eyes even darker. "Kylie—"

"Please leave, Jake." She'd been wrong earlier, she realized. *Those* were the hardest words she'd said.

Quivering inside, she hugged herself tightly as he struggled for something to say. He didn't find it, though, and after a long, painful moment he turned and left. His steps echoed on the marble, were muted on the rug, then grew fainter as he walked down the hall. They echoed in her ears long after they'd faded. Then even the echo was gone.

The trembling subsided, and her heart rate slowly returned to a sluggish version of normal. She should leave, too. Should forget Jake. Forget Charley. Forget everything that had happened in the past few days. She had her own life to worry about, her own upheaval to set straight.

But this was no longer about Jake or Charley. She needed to know the truth for her own peace of mind. Turning, she opened the door to the second file room, found the right drawer and began searching through the financial records.

Between them, her parents had had more accounts than anyone needed. The one that ended her search was in her father's name only, an investment account set up to make a single payout every month in the amount of four thousand dollars to an account at First Security Bank. The deposits had begun a few months after Therese Franklin's birth and had continued, though with a change in the receiving account, until the month she'd turned twenty-one.

Weak in the knees, Kylie leaned against the file cabinet. The senator had paid nearly a million dollars over the course of Therese's life. That was how her grandparents had managed to provide so well for her without touching her inheritance. Had they continued Jillian's blackmail? Or had he felt an obligation to support the child who might be his daughter?

Dear God, Therese could be Kylie's half sister. The idea was overwhelming. She'd always wanted a brother or a sister to ease the loneliness of being an only child. Summoning Therese's image to mind, she couldn't identify any resemblance, but that meant nothing. No one in town had seen a resemblance between Jake and his—

Deliberately she forced away the thought of him.

There was only one thing to do: prove—or disprove—that Therese was the Senator's daughter. There was no way he would willingly contribute a DNA sample, but his hairbrush would, and if that wasn't enough, Kylie would, too. If they shared a father, it would show.

If she had a sister, she would never forgive the senator for hiding her all these years.

Chapter 11

After driving aimlessly for a while, Jake found himself on the road that led to his old house. He'd lost his tail at the city limits but picked up another before he reached the turnoff: Coy Roberts, driving his own vehicle. Watching the chief in his rearview mirror, Jake turned onto the dirt road, drove twenty yards, then stopped. Roberts turned, too, and stopped immediately, as if he had no desire to come any closer. But when Jake climbed out of the truck, the chief got out of his car, as well, and approached with a swagger.

"You know, trespassing's a crime here in Oklahoma."

"It's not trespassing when you have the owner's permission." Jake held up the key Therese had given him, then quickly closed it within his fist when Roberts reached for it.

In a nod to his day off, Roberts was out of uniform, wearing indigo-blue jeans with a sharp crease and a white button-down shirt. In a nod to the fact that he was never truly off duty, he also wore a brown leather belt with a pistol holstered on the left.

In the dreams that had haunted Jake the day before, Charley had been holding the knife in his left hand. Strange, considering that he was right-handed and about as far from ambidextrous as a man could get. He'd injured his right hand on the job once when Jake was about eight and had been damn near helpless, unable to do much of anything for himself.

"What are you doing out here?"

Jake smiled. "None of your business." The memory of the same words coming from Kylie that morning gave them an edge that sliced right through him. He shouldn't have gone to see her, but he'd needed a little hope. Instead he'd lost what little he'd had.

"You're wrong, Norris. Everything you do is my business. Anything that has to do with the Franklins, with the Riordans or with Charley Baker is my business. Or should I say 'your daddy'?" His grin held the same smug arrogance the senator was so good at. Was that where he'd learned it?

Jake leaned against the bed of the truck, letting the metal warm his back. "Do you know who really killed them?"

"Baker."

"He had an alibi."

"The alibi's a lie."

"Why would Leonard Scott lie to provide an alibi for someone he hardly knew?"

Roberts shrugged. "People lie all the time. Bartenders. Killers."

"Senators," Jake supplied helpfully, then added, "Deputies who aspire to bigger jobs. How well did *you* know Jillian Franklin, Chief? You obviously weren't a part of her social circle, but then, social status doesn't matter much to some people." Like Kylie. She couldn't have cared less about Jake's lack of privilege. But his lack of faith had meant the world to her.

"I hardly knew Jillian at all."

"And yet you call her by her first name. Seems a little intimate, doesn't it?"

"When you investigate someone's brutal murder, when you spend time with her dead body and learn the details of her life, you tend to get a little intimate." Without a break, Roberts asked, "Where's Kylie?"

Jake made a show of looking around. "Not here."

"You shouldn't go too many places without her. She's the best protection you've got around here."

"Is that a threat, Chief?"

"I don't make threats. I give one warning and then I act. And you've been warned." Roberts raised his left hand, thumb and forefinger extended in a parody of a gun, then winked before walking away.

Jake remained where he was long after Roberts had driven out of sight. The police chief was a lefty, and in Jake's last dream, Charley had wielded the knife in his left hand. Coincidence? Or something he'd read in his research?

He was still standing alongside his truck when the sound of another vehicle broke the day's stillness. It was approaching from the east—a black SUV with heavily tinted windows—and it slowed as it neared the turnoff. The driver stopped, blocking access to the road, and the passenger's window glided down a few inches.

The hair on Jake's neck stood on end as goose bumps raised on his arms. He was an easy target. The nearest house was out of sight down the road, and no one out here would pay attention to a distant gunshot. This guy could drop him where he stood, if that had been Riordan's and Roberts's order. They would win, Charley would lose and Kylie would never know how damned important she was to him.

Without turning his back to the SUV, he eased to the truck door, climbed inside and started the engine. The Fasten Seat Belt warning dinged as he drove up the hill, taking the turn to his old house and putting the hillside and thick woods between him and the SUV. There he turned in a wide circle so he would face incoming traffic, secured his seat belt and took a heavy breath. His hands started to shake so he gripped the steering wheel tighter.

Damn, he'd never been scared on the job before. A little uneasy—he dealt with criminals and lawyers; he expected uneasy. But this was the first time he'd been forced to face how simple it would be for the Franklins' killer to kill him. Their lives had meant nothing to the killer; neither had Charley's, and apparently neither did Jake's.

When five minutes passed and the SUV hadn't crested the hill, he took his foot from the brake and let the truck pick up speed as it rolled down the hill. Back in town, he stopped at Wal-Mart to buy a scanner and was on his way out the door when he bumped into a slight figure.

Therese looked as if she'd come straight from church—a flowery dress that passed her knees, heels, her hair in a braid like the one Kylie often wore. She glanced at the scanner. "Don't you even take Sundays off?"

"Generally not." Especially when he felt tremendous pressure to secure his research. If something happened to him, he wanted his work in the hands of someone who would use it to help Charley.

"Can you use a little help with the scanning? I'd like to talk to you."

"Sure, if you don't mind hanging out at the Tepee."

Her smile was sweet. "I've never actually been there. I'll follow you."

They were at the motel in less than five minutes, where that afternoon's watch dog eyed Therese with an extra dose of suspicion. Jake made room on the desk for the scanner, plugged it into the laptop, then began organizing files in order of importance.

"Why are you scanning all these?" she asked, gesturing to the piles spread across the bed.

He gave her the short version—run off the road, shot at, threatened by the police chief—then faced her. "There's something you should know, Therese—should have known the first time we talked. I'm—"

"Charley Baker's son. Derek told me."

His gaze narrowed on her face—sweet, guileless. "It doesn't bother you?"

She picked up a folder marked Photos, studied the label, then set it down again without opening it. "You let me ride your horse once. Do you remember that?" Her grimace was self-mocking. "*I* hardly remember it. He seemed so huge, and I sat there by myself, so high above the ground, and you walked him around the pasture."

Jake hardly remembered it himself. He'd put her on the pony without permission, but when Jillian had come out of the house, instead of chastising him she'd watched and laughed delightedly.

Therese picked up another folder, this one marked Leonard Scott—Alibi. "Why would it bother me? You aren't responsible for my parents' deaths." She read Mr.

Scott's statement, then murmured, "Apparently neither was your father."

They set up a system—Jake sorted items by priority while Therese fed them into the scanner. Occasionally she paused to read something or to ask a question, but for the most part she worked quietly, efficiently.

They'd barely made a dent in the piles when a knock came at the door. Kylie was the last person he expected to find on his doorstep, but there she stood, a large envelope in hand. Without greeting, she offered it to him.

"What is this?"

"Proof that the senator paid four thousand dollars a month first to Jillian Franklin, then to her parents, for 20 years and nine months."

Jake took the envelope, slid out a thick stack of papers and glanced at a few, then put them back. He wanted to ask why she'd brought them to him, but the question would hurt her and he'd done enough of that already. Besides, he knew why.

She was an honorable person.

The lines of her face were taut with stress, and her eyes were shadowed. Goddess under fire. He'd cost her a lot, as had her father. She deserved better than either of them. But if she ever gave him a chance to make it up to her...

"Why would your father pay nearly a million dollars to my mother and my grandparents?" Therese asked, moving from the desk into Kylie's line of sight.

Kylie paled, then forced a smile. "Therese. I was going to stop by your house on the way home. I wanted to tell you...to ask you..." She glanced at Jake, then at the cop out front, and came into the room, closing the door behind her. She was far too elegant, too beautiful, for the Tepee Motor

Court, but she didn't notice. "How much have you told her about the money?"

He shook his head.

She cleared a space at the head of the bed, sat down, then gestured for Therese to join her. Great. Now Kylie would not only haunt his waking moments but his sleep, too, with her scent on his bed.

"Apparently your mother had a few affairs," she began quietly after Therese took a seat. "We believe the money in her private account came from payments made by the men she slept with to ensure her silence. We also believe that at least one of these men thought he might be your father."

"The senator?" Therese asked numbly. "You think the senator is my father?"

Kylie's features were expressionless, her lips compressed. "I think it's possible. Why else would he pay that kind of money?"

A million dollars over twenty-one years wasn't a tremendous amount to someone who had full access to the Colby fortune, Jake acknowledged, but she was right. Why pay even a dime unless it was possible he was Therese's father? And admitting that meant admitting he'd slept with Jillian, which would have damaged his career and his marriage.

"Then it's possible that you and I—" Therese took a loud, shaky breath "—are s-s-sisters."

Kylie nodded. "I wanted to ask you if you would go to Tulsa with me tomorrow, to give samples of our DNA so we can know for sure."

Therese nodded, too.

What would it mean to them if the results were positive—two women who had no families to speak of, discovering that they were half sisters?

At least Jake wouldn't have destroyed everything in Kylie's life.

"What happened to make you do this?" she asked with a wave toward the scanner.

"I had a little run-in with Chief Roberts and the black SUV." He would bet she'd give a lot to hide the fact that his news worried her, but it was there on her face. It made him feel marginally better.

"This will take forever. If you bring your computer and scanner to the office, we can also use ours and cut the time in half."

Use the senator's office equipment to document his illegal activities. The idea appealed to Jake. So did spending time with Kylie, along with the fact that she would even offer.

He packed up everything, and they caravanned downtown—him, Kylie, Therese and the cop. There they set up in her office, his machines on a worktable, hers on her desk.

After a time, he circled the desk, wanting more than anything to touch her. Instead his fingers knotted on the folder he held. "Why don't you take a break and let me scan these?"

Anger flared in her eyes, along with bitterness. "Something you don't trust me to see?"

With a glance at Therese, concentrating on her task, he lowered his voice. "It's crime-scene photos. The sheriff at the time kept copies of them when he retired. When I started the book, his widow gave them to me."

Kylie's gaze shifted to the folder, and understanding dawned. He'd seen the pictures—could describe the vacant look in Jillian's eyes, the awkward angle of Bert's body, the blood pools, the rage that had created the scene. Hell, he'd seen it for real. He would never forget.

Neither Kylie nor Therese should ever have the need to forget.

She rose from the chair, her fragrance enveloping him as she slipped past. He sat down, feeling her heat on the leather, absorbing her scent. With a watchful eye on Therese, he began scanning the photos, labeling each one in a computer folder. While he did so, Kylie left the office, then returned a few moments later with an empty box. As the machine whirred, she took her degree from the wall, along with a couple of framed pictures. She deposited those in the box, then began gathering items from the bookcases.

"What are you doing?" he asked.

"Packing."

"Why?"

"Because technically I'm no longer employed here. I left my resignation on the senator's desk this morning."

Jake stared at her and was vaguely aware of Therese doing the same. "You quit your job?" he asked stupidly.

"That's generally what a resignation means."

"Why?" he repeated.

She scooped up an armload of books, then turned to face him. "Because I can't work for him anymore, not knowing what I know."

He wished he could feel truly bad that she'd quit her job, but truth was, after surprise, his primary emotion was relief. In his opinion, away from Riordan was the best place for her to be. "What are you going to do?"

"I don't know."

I do. She could go to New Mexico with him. If she wanted to work, there were plenty of opportunities for a woman with her qualifications. If she'd rather stay home, he happened to have a home she could stay in. It needed her. *He* needed her.

Maybe something of what he was thinking showed on his face, because suddenly her cheeks turned pink and she abruptly turned away, dumping the books into the box. Her movements were jerky as she took a few items from the credenza, a few more from the desk drawers.

She didn't touch the photos of her with the senator and other dignitaries. In fact, after she'd finished, it was hard to tell she'd effectively moved out of the space. Twelve years she'd worked for her father, five in this position, and everything fit into one small box.

"I'm sorry," Jake said awkwardly.

Kylie set the box next to the door, then combed her hair back. "You should be," she murmured.

Grimly he went back to work, scanning the last of the crime-scene photos, password-protecting the folder before giving the computer back to her. As soon as she slipped past him, he opened the next file on the stack—the autopsy— and started to hand the pages to her. In midtransfer he stopped, his gaze caught on a line in the report.

"What is it?" she asked.

He read the line again, then backed up and read the entire paragraph before looking at her. "According to the autopsy, the man who killed the Franklins was lefthanded. Charley isn't. The senator isn't."

Remembering his conversation with Roberts earlier-the holster on the left side and the left-handed gesture before Roberts had walked away—he finished grimly. "But Chief Roberts is."

Kylie had no problem believing that Coy Roberts could have murdered two people and framed an innocent man. She'd never liked him—had thought he was an obnoxious, petty little man who reveled in the power of the badge and the gun he wore.

She did have a problem believing her father would risk his career for the likes of Roberts. But if Roberts had been involved with Jillian, he could have known about the senator's affair, as well. Jillian might not have been the only person blackmailing the senator.

Even now, a wave of disbelief washed through her. She'd had such idealistic notions about the man, when she'd never really known him at all. She'd thought he was *good*, had thought they were a team. Sure, his ambition had been the leading force in his life, and he'd always been a bit of a snob, had always had a sense of entitlement. But overall he was an honorable man and he loved her. So she'd thought. But the honor was a sham and the love was conditional.

Everyone's love was conditional, she thought with a grim glance at Jake. Including her own.

It was nearly seven o'clock. when she scanned the last of the documents. After burning a CD, she waited for Jake to verify on his laptop that everything had copied, then deleted the files. Before she left for the night—for the last time—she intended to call Lissa and make sure the files couldn't be retrieved.

And then she was done. With the Baker case. With the senator.

But, please, not with Jake.

"Now what?" Therese asked from the sofa, where she'd curled up a few minutes earlier.

Good question. What would Kylie do now that her life was in shambles?

"I need to use the phone line," Jake replied.

Wordlessly she unplugged the line from her computer and

offered it to him. He hooked up, signed online and began attaching files to an e-mail. Who was he sending the information to? Obviously someone he trusted more than *her.*

Can we try again? he'd asked. When everything was over, when his father was safe from her father, could they pick up where they'd left off? She'd meant it when she said, *I don't know.* After hours of thinking about it, she still didn't know.

She did know that trust had to be earned, not blindly given. That not trusting her was the logical, smart, practical thing for a man in his position to do. That keeping her distance from him was the logical, smart, practical thing for a woman in her position.

But logical, smart and practical had little to do with love, and she did love him. Silly as it seemed, given their brief acquaintance, she wanted to be with him. To spend the rest of her life with him. To have kids with him.

Which meant she had to get over her hurt. This was a unique situation. How many murders could the senator have been involved in covering up? She and Jake could spend the next fifty years together and never run into such a conflict again.

But forgiving was hard when the hurt was still fresh. When every look stabbed a little deeper, when she needed but couldn't allow herself the comfort of his embrace, when she desperately needed but couldn't ask for the soft little words he'd given her outside the Pancake Palace. *It's okay, darlin'. You're all right.* Even though her world was going to hell, there in his arms she *had* been all right, and she wanted that again. When she could forgive. When she could swallow her pride.

With a sound that was half sigh, half sob, she stood up

and found Jake watching her curiously. Before he could ask, she said, "My shoulders are stiff from sitting so long."

He nodded but continued to look at her. She turned away as if the items remaining on the bookcase were of interest. They weren't. Everything she cared about in this room was packed in that single box. Everything except Jake and Therese.

Across the room Therese's stomach growled, and Kylie smiled for the first time in forever. "The pizza should be here soon."

"Good. I'm going to wash up." Rising from the couch, Therese went down the hall to the bathroom, leaving Kylie to pretend she wasn't uncomfortably alone in the room with Jake. Though he stared at the computer, watching the progress of the e-mail, she knew he was aware of it, too.

When footsteps came down the hall, she gratefully looked up, expecting Therese. It wasn't her.

The senator wore a tuxedo better than any man she knew, but tonight he looked disheveled. His tie was askew and his hair was ruffled. Clenched in one hand was a tight roll of manila folders, a handful of the twenty-one files she'd emptied, then stacked neatly on his desk underneath her resignation.

He settled his gaze on Jake. "Isn't this cozy? The murderer's son and my traitor of a daughter, working together in my own damn office to destroy me."

Jake moved, putting himself between the laptop and the door, but he didn't speak.

Kylie rested her hands on the desk to control the tremors rocketing through her, and her fingers brushed something cool, metallic. A tape recorder small enough to hide in her palm, powerful enough to pick up every word of every interview either she or the senator had given in this office. Impulsively she pressed the record button, closed her fingers around it, then circled her desk and leaned against the edge. "I take it you found my resignation."

The senator spared her a glance. "Such a great loss. Replacing you doesn't even register on my list of priorities. However—" he pointed at her with the folders "—you have twelve hours to return my financial records, the originals and all copies thereof, before I have you arrested for trespassing and theft."

A snort came from Jake. "You can't have her arrested. That house belongs to her. She has legal access to every part of it."

"This is Riverview," the senator replied. "I can do whatever I damn well please." He came farther into the room, giving the box with her belongings a scornful look, picking up the file with Charley's alibi from the chair where it topped a stack of folders and treating the page inside to the same scorn. Tossing it down again, not caring when it slid to the floor, he turned to face Jake. "I have an offer for you."

"You don't have anything I want."

The senator's broad smile was smug. "Don't speak too hastily. I talked to your father on my way back from Oklahoma City this evening. I made the offer to him, and he accepted."

The tension radiating from Jake was palpable as he met Kylie's glance. He hated the idea of the senator even speaking to Charley. She didn't blame him. "What kind of offer?"

"You know, there's a case from early in my career as a prosecutor that has always troubled me," the senator said in his best cameras-are-rolling voice. "I have decided it is my duty as a lawmaker and a former district attorney to reopen that case and see that justice is served to all involved."

And he could do it. All it would take was a little pressure on the current district attorney, who planned to run for the senator's seat once he became governor, and on the presiding district court judge, Harold Markham Jr. As he'd said, this was Riverview, where he could do whatever he damn well pleased.

"Justice," Jake repeated. "And how do you define that?"

"Charley Baker is acquitted in the new trial. He walks away a free man."

"But the real murderer isn't charged." She knotted her fists to keep her anger under control. "The people who conspired to send Charley to prison in the first place aren't punished. Those twenty-two years you *stole* from him are gone."

The senator gave her a dismissive look. There was no affection, no hint of respect. In the past few days she had become nothing more than a nuisance, a reminder of a lapse in judgment. "Of course he'll be compensated for those years lost. We agreed that five million dollars seemed a reasonable amount."

"You're just free as can be using my mother's money to pay for your mistakes, aren't you?" Kylie asked snidely. "No wonder she left the bulk of the family fortune to me. You gave her such good reasons not to trust you with it."

"That was her way of getting back at me. Oh, she *forgave* me. She accepted my groveling and said we would pretend it never happened, but she never forgot. If I spoke to another woman, if I even looked at another woman, she made my life hell. Every month those statements came, showing that payment, and every month she made me suffer. Leaving everything to you, making me dependent on the whims of a *child*, was her final insult."

The senator pushed back his sleeve to check the time.

"Come on, Norris. I'm a busy man. Are you going to accept or not? Keep in mind before you decide that the deal is all or nothing. You don't drop this book, Charley doesn't get his freedom or his money."

Jake was torn. Kylie knew that freeing Charley, clearing his name, meant everything to him. But selling out to do it, letting the guilty parties continue to live unpunished ...

The sudden cessation of movement in the dimly lit hallway caught her attention—a flash of flowers, a glint of light. Therese, returned from the bathroom, had stopped abruptly upon hearing the senator's voice and now retreated out of sight. Kylie was sorry the younger woman had to hear any part of this conversation, sorry she had to see for herself the kind of man who might have fathered her. But she would have found out soon enough.

Kylie moved a few steps closer to Jake, her arms folded across her middle, the recorder's microphone aimed at the senator. "Can you guarantee the outcome of this reopened case?"

"I guaranteed a conviction twenty-two years ago. I can guarantee he'll walk this time."

"Will you put it in writing?"

He scowled. "You can't possibly be that naive, Kylie."

That was okay. She had it on tape.

"You knew he was innocent, didn't you?" Jake asked quietly.

The senator chose his words with care. "I had my doubts about his guilt."

"You knew who really killed the Franklins."

He made a show of straightening his cuffs, then adjusting his tie. "I had my suspicions. Truthfully I didn't want to know."

"One of your friends killed two more of your friends," she protested, "and you didn't want to know which one?"

"I live with these people. I go to church with them, play golf with them, sit down to dinner with them. No, I didn't want to know."

Even after everything, he still managed to surprise her. How could he bear to look at his friends and know that one of them was a killer, that *he* had helped him get away with murder?

"They're good people," the senator went on. "One of them made a mistake. It was a one-time thing—a crime of passion. It's not as if we're talking about a career criminal here. It never happened again. It never will happen again. Riverview is a better place because of these men. They have families, friends, people who rely on them. Why upset all that because of one twenty-two-year-old mistake?"

"You *all* made mistakes!" she said heatedly. "They're called felonies! You don't get to just say, 'Oh, I screwed up,' and walk away from this!"

"That's exactly what I intend to do, Kylie. Just like I intend to walk away from you."

No. This time she was doing the walking. He'd given her a twelve-hour ultimatum to return his papers; she would give him a thirty-day ultimatum to get those papers and everything else he owned out of her house, her office building and her life.

The relief that accompanied that spur-of-the-moment decision was comforting.

"Clock's ticking, Norris," the senator said. "Take the offer and you can have her, too. I have no further use for her."

The barb didn't even twinge. Relieved by that, too, she gazed at Jake. Her lungs tightened at the anger that smol-

dered in his eyes—anger for her, offense taken on her behalf. His mouth thinned, and a muscle in his jaw twitched.
"You just don't get it, do you, Riordan? People aren't yours
to control. You can't play God with their lives and get
away with it. You can't sacrifice them for the good of your
reputation or for your ambition."

"Of course I can. I'm Senator James Riordan, soon to
be Governor Riordan."

There was that sense of entitlement. When she'd
thought he was a good man, it had been an acceptable
flaw. Now that she knew the truth, it made her sick to
witness it.

"Kylie's your *daughter.* That should mean something to
you. You should love and appreciate her and you should be
grateful every damn day to have her. Just once you should
put her ahead of your career. Just once you should act like
her *father.*" Jake's gaze shifted to her and his voice softened.
"And when you screw up, you should hope like hell that
she'll understand and forgive you and love you anyway."

She understood. The more she saw of her father, the more
she agreed with Jake's decision to remove her from his investigation. She would have done the same in his place.

Easing to stand next to him, she slipped her hand into
his, then turned her attention to the senator. "You're wrong,
sir. You can't play God…and you're not going to be governor." Opening her other hand, she displayed the tape recorder for him to see. "We have enough evidence to clear
Charley without your help. We have enough evidence to
get *you* investigated—to prove that you knowingly presented a false case against Charley, that you, Markham,
Jenkins and Roberts are guilty of criminal collusion and
that one of you is guilty of murder. Our money's on Coy

Roberts, but who knows what the authorities will find when we notify them?"

The senator's face paled, and he swayed unsteadily. "You can't— It'll destroy me, Kylie. It'll destroy everything your mother and I worked for—everything you and I worked for!"

Stubbornly she shook her head. She wouldn't let him blame her or anyone else. For once he had to be held accountable. "You destroyed it, sir, when you chose to have an affair. When you chose to prosecute an innocent man for murder. When you lied and twisted the law to protect yourself and your friends."

"You can't do this to me! I'm your father!"

"And I can't change that. Believe me, if I could, I would."

Drawing himself up to his full height, the senator shook his finger at her. "I forbid you—"

"What was the last thing you forbade me to do, sir?" Without giving him a chance, she answered. "To see Jake. And look how that turned out. I not only saw him, I fell in love with him, and one of these days I'm going to marry him. Don't think you have the right to tell me what I can and cannot do. You forfeited any say in my life the first time you lied to me."

Jake's fingers tightened around hers, and she looked up to see him watching her intently. If he was happy to hear her say she loved him, it didn't show, not with the worry there. But it was in his voice when he murmured, "Name the date. I'll be there."

"You'll be sorry," the senator threatened wildly. "I'll ruin both of you!"

"Make that your life's goal," Kylie said. "It will give you something to occupy your time while you're in prison." Releasing Jake's hand, she went to her desk, picked up the phone and pressed nine on the auto dial. The number was the home number of state Attorney General Frank Buchanan, an old friend on the Colby side. He liked the senator and considered him a friend—but he considered *her* family.

"Uncle Frank," she said when he answered, and the senator crumpled into a chair in front of her. "I've got something to tell you."

Epilogue

The sound of voices outside drew Jake's attention to the courtyard, where Kylie was talking with the construction crew. Their English was better than her Spanish, but they were less willing to use it, so she'd resorted to gestures. He watched her animated movements, then smiled when her laughter rang out, clear and happy. The men might not always understand what she wanted, but they made her laugh. That was worth a hundred times what he was paying them.

Leaving the foreman with a pat on the arm, she crossed the terra-cotta tile to join Charley on a wrought-iron glider near the fountain. He made her laugh, too, and she made him feel welcome in their home.

She made Jake feel welcome in her life.

After saving his file, he left the computer and walked through their new old house. It was in the mountains outside Albuquerque, nearly a hundred years old and in bad need of renovation. He'd been in favor of tearing it down and building new, but she'd seen the potential in it. He'd bought it and she was making it a home.

It had been an eventful year since they'd met. Charley's conviction had been overturned. The senator, along with his partners in crime, had been indicted. Always looking out for himself, Riordan had made a deal with the state; Markham and Jenkins had soon followed suit, and all three had testified against Coy Roberts. Though their sentences were light—five to eight years each—compared to Roberts's life sentence, they had all paid with more than freedom. The scandal alone was almost punishment enough.

Almost.

As for the book, he'd sent it off to his agent the week before. She'd been happy to get it. He'd been happy to finish it. She had finally deleted the massive files he'd sent that Sunday night for backup, and he'd packed everything away in boxes in his storeroom. Case closed.

He let himself out the French doors and touched his father lightly on the shoulder as he passed. Charley gave him a distant smile—it was going to take a long time to bring him all the way home—then Jake scooped up Kylie, slid in beneath her and settled her onto his lap. "What are you two doing out here?"

"Planning," Charley said at the same time she replied, "Nothing."

"Hmm. You want a minute to figure out the right answer?"

They exchanged looks, then Charley said, "Nothing," at the same time she said, "Planning."

It hardly seemed worth trying to pin them down. It was a warm afternoon, the sky was bluer than it had any right to be, the clouds fatter and whiter. The horses were nickering in the corral, his work was done for the day and he had Kylie in his arms. Life was good.

But she was grinning, and Charley was looking more like his old self with a faint memory of a gleam in his eye—too good an enticement to ignore. "What kind of nothing are you planning?" Jake asked, setting the glider in motion.

They exchanged looks again, then Charley said, "A wedding kind of nothing."

Jake looked at him blankly. "You been sneaking out at night to meet that pretty redhead you sit beside in church?"

After twenty-two years in prison, Charley still managed to blush. "No," he denied, then added, "Well, not that often."

"Then what—" Jake shifted his attention to Kylie, resting her head against his shoulder as if there was no place else she'd rather be. Even with her eyes closed, she knew he was looking at her and responded with a sweet smile before her lashes fluttered open.

"I'm naming a date," she said quietly.

One of these days I'm going to marry him, she'd told Riordan the last time they'd spoken. *Name the date*, Jake had replied. *I'll be there.*

Since then, she'd refused to set a date. She loved him, but she'd needed time, and he had understood. Those five days last October had led to huge changes in both their lives. He could give her all the time in the world as long as she spent it with him.

It took him several tries to get the question out, but he managed. "When?"

"How about Saturday? Right here by the fountain. Eleven o'clock."

He stared at her. "Can you put a wedding together that quick?"

"My groom is already here. My father-in-law is here, and my mother- and stepfather-in-law are only an hour away. My sister has her airline reservations. She'll be here Friday afternoon." She shrugged. "Those are the people I love. What more do I need?"

"Nothing at all, darlin'." He held her closer, resting his chin against her hair. If they hadn't met, her eventual wedding would have been a major event for a thousand or two of Oklahoma's political, financial and business elite. It would have taken longer to plan than they'd even known each other and would have cost more than this house where they would spend the next sixty years of their lives.

And it wouldn't have mattered, because any man other than him would have been the wrong man. Their being together was fate. Destiny.

Which, he'd figured out, was just another name for love.

"Will you be there?" she asked, her voice soft and sure. She knew the answer, but he gave it anyway.

"Absolutely."

With a soft, satisfied sigh, she relaxed against him. "I love you."

She knew his next words, too—knew what he thought, what he wanted, how he felt. Knew him because she was a part of him. Destiny. But he said them anyway. "I love you, too, Kylie."

Life was damned good.

* * * * *

Happily ever after is just the beginning...

Turn the page for a sneak preview of
A HEARTBEAT AWAY
by
Eleanor Jones

Harlequin Everlasting—
Every great love has a story to tell. ™
A brand-new series from Harlequin Books

Special? A prickle ran down my neck and my heart started to beat in my ears. Was today really special?

"Tuck in," he ordered.

I turned my attention to the feast that he had spread out on the ground. Thick, home-cooked-ham sandwiches, sausage rolls fresh from the oven and a huge variety of mouth-watering scones and pastries. Hunger pangs took over, and I closed my eyes and bit into soft homemade bread.

When we were finally finished, I lay back against the bluebells with a groan, clutching my stomach.

Daniel laughed. "Your eyes are bigger than your stomach," he told me.

I leaned across to deliver a punch to his arm, but he rolled away, and when my fist met fresh air I collapsed in a fit of giggles before relaxing on my back and staring up into the flawless blue sky. We lay like that for quite a while,

Daniel and I, side by side in companionable silence, until he stretched out his hand in an arc that encompassed the whole area.

"Don't you think that this is the most beautiful place in the entire world?"

His voice held a passion that echoed my own feelings, and I rose onto my elbow and picked a buttercup to hide the emotion that clogged my throat.

"Roll over onto your back," I urged, prodding him with my forefinger. He obliged with a broad grin, and I reached across to place the yellow flower beneath his chin.

"Now, let us see if you like butter."

When a yellow light shone on the tanned skin below his jaw, I laughed.

"There…you do."

For an instant our eyes met, and I had the strangest sense that I was drowning in those honey-brown depths. The scent of bluebells engulfed me. A roaring filled my ears, and then, unexpectedly, in one smooth movement Daniel rolled me onto my back and plucked a buttercup of his own.

"And do *you* like butter, Lucy McTavish?" he asked. When he placed the flower against my skin, time stood still.

His long lean body was suspended over mine, pinning me against the grass. Daniel…dear, comfortable, familiar Daniel was suddenly bringing out in me the strangest sensations.

"Do you, Lucy McTavish?" he asked again, his voice low and vibrant.

My eyes flickered toward his, the whisper of a sigh escaped my lips and although a strange lethargy had crept into my limbs, I somehow felt as if all my nerve endings were on fire. He felt it, too—I could see it in his warm brown eyes. And when he lowered his face to mine, it seemed to me the most natural thing in the world.

None of the kisses I had ever experienced could have even begun to prepare me for the feel of Daniel's lips on mine. My entire body floated on a tide of ecstasy that shut out everything but his soft, warm mouth, and I knew that this was what I had been waiting for the whole of my life.

"Oh, Lucy." He pulled away to look into my eyes. "Why haven't we done this before?"

Holding his gaze, I gently touched his cheek, then I curled my fingers through the short thick hair at the base of his skull, overwhelmed by the longing to drown again in the sensations that flooded our bodies. And when his long tanned fingers crept across my tingling skin, I knew I could deny him nothing.

* * * * *

Be sure to look for
A HEARTBEAT AWAY,
available February 27, 2007.

And look, too, for
THE DEPTH OF LOVE
by Margot Early,
the story of a couple who must learn that
love comes in many guises—and in the end
it's the only thing that counts.

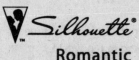

Silhouette®

Romantic
SUSPENSE

Excitement, danger and passion guaranteed!

Same great authors and riveting editorial
you've come to know and love
from Silhouette Intimate Moments.

New York Times
bestselling author
Beverly Barton
is back with the
latest installment
in her popular
miniseries,
The Protectors.
HIS ONLY
OBSESSION
is available
next month from
Silhouette®
Romantic Suspense

Look for it wherever you buy books!

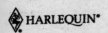

HARLEQUIN®

EVERLASTING LOVE™

Every great love has a story to tell™

Save $1.00 off

the purchase of any Harlequin Everlasting Love novel

Coupon valid from January 1, 2007 until April 30, 2007.

Valid at retail outlets in the U.S. only.
Limit one coupon per customer.

5 65373 00076 2   (8100) 0 11302

HEUSCPN0407

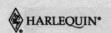

EVERLASTING LOVE™

Every great love has a story to tell™

Fall from Grace

Kristi Gold

Save $1.⁰⁰ off

the purchase of
any Harlequin
Everlasting Love novel

Coupon valid from January 1, 2007
until April 30, 2007.

Valid at retail outlets in Canada only.
Limit one coupon per customer.

52607370

HECDNCPN0407

Hearts racing
Blood pumping
Pulses accelerating

Falling in love can be a blur…especially at

180 mph!

So if you crave the thrill of the chase—on and off the track—you'll love

SPEED DATING
by Nancy Warren!

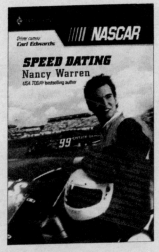

Hearts racing
Blood pumping
Pulses accelerating

**Falling in love can be
a blur…especially at**
180 mph!

**So if you crave the thrill
of the chase—on and off
the track—you'll love**

SPEED DATING
by Nancy Warren!

HARLEQUIN

Deep cover:
Carl Edwards

//// **NASCAR**

SPEED DATING
Nancy Warren
USA TODAY bestselling author

99

REQUEST YOUR
FREE BOOKS!

2 FREE NOVELS PLUS 2 FREE GIFTS!

Silhouette® Romantic

SUSPENSE

Sparked by Danger, Fueled by Passion!

SRS07

Silhouette®

Romantic

SUSPENSE

COMING NEXT MONTH

#1455 HIS ONLY OBSESSION—Beverly Barton
The Protectors
After rescuing the alluring Dr. Gwen Arnell, Dundee agent Will Pierce
realizes that they are both searching for the same man. Together
they set sail, island-hopping in their quest to find their target and a
mysterious youth serum…while battling an attraction neither can deny.

#1456 MISSION: M.D.—Linda Turner
Turning Points
Rachel Martin is dying to seduce the gorgeous doctor who lives next
door, but a stalker wants to stop her. Will Rachel be able to keep her
distance despite the growing desire she feels for her neighbor?

#1457 SHADOW SURRENDER—Linda Conrad
Night Guardians
Special Agent Teal Benaly finds dangers hidden at every turn as she
sets out to investigate a strange murder on the Navajo reservation. But
nothing holds the potential danger she finds in the arms of the dark
stranger sent to protect her.

#1458 ONE HOT TARGET—Diane Pershing
When an innocent woman dies, police believe that Carmen Coyle
might have been the potential target. With the help of her lawyer-
friend JR Ellis, Carmen tries to track down possible leads—and resist
the temptation to explore a more personal relationship with JR.

SRSCNM0207